Pernicious
True Evil

-Angelika Koch

ISBN: 9781712657478 (Paperback)

I dedicate this book to anyone who feels alone in their life.

PROLOGUE

Standing in a field of wilting flowers, Zephyra gazed upon the only person she ever truly loved. Her heart felt unbearably heavy. It seemed that at any moment she would feel the bones in her chest snap and her heart would fall onto the ground below. Though the sun shone brightly in the sky, the day could not become any darker.

Zephyra pulled at her fingers while her eyes moved back and forth in search of the right words to say. Her cheeks felt hot against the crisp air that pinched at her skin. Thoughts spun in her mind as she tried to reach out for the sentence to begin this dreaded conversation but found that every time she did, the words would slip away with her breath.

This was a day that would change everything. Zephyra knew the fate of her loved one rested upon a decision so difficult that not even those with the most courage would feel strong.

"Is everything okay?" Lamia asked while looking innocently at her friend.

Zephyra ground her teeth upon one another, feeling the hard bones crunch from the pressure. She needed to pull herself together.

"Cadoc knows." Zephyra tried to trap the tears within her dampening lids. "He just sent Sidero and Prosperine to come find you."

"What?" Lamia's lips formed a hard line. Her eyes widened at the edges. "Are you sure?"

"Yes."

"No this can't be," she choked, barely able to get the words out of her mouth. "I can't... I can't go back there."

Zephyra felt her chin quiver. Pulling herself together seemed almost impossible. She bit her bottom lip and pushed through the emotional maelstrom happening within her until she was able to feel numb and hold onto the only morsel of sanity she had left.

"He has his men searching for you right now."

A moment of tense silence felt like a lifetime of anguish as the two friends stared at each other. Zephyra wanted nothing more than to embrace her friend and cry upon her shoulder, but her tears had to be contained in order to build the courage necessary to do the unspeakable.

"What am I going to do?" Lamia whispered. Her shoulders sank.

Zephyra took a shuddering breath into her tight lungs. Wrapping her fingers around one another, she attempted to control her shaking muscles and squeezed them tightly until she felt pain. She needed a distraction, any distraction.

"There is a way out of this," Zephyra's voice shook as she spoke.

A spark lit in Lamia's eyes, which felt like it had destroyed the only thing that was keeping Zephyra together. She knew this would be the last time she would see her loved one feel hope of any kind and the information she was about to tell her would darken that light for the rest of her life.

"What is it?" Lamia bit the edge of her lip.

Zephyra broke. The strength she tried so hard to hold on to shattered under the crushing weight of what was to come. She tried to compose herself but couldn't. The muscles in her legs could no longer hold her and she collapsed onto her friend, sobbing uncontrollably.

"I have a spell I can cast to send your soul to the one place that Aduro would never expect you to be. As long as you are there, he will never find you." Zephyra hung on tightly to her friend. Memories of their childhood together flashed in her mind.

"I don't understand why you would be sad about this. This is great news! Can you cast the spell? Please! Before it's too late."

"There is a catch." Zephyra looked up to the heavens at the darkening clouds forming in the distance.

"Well, what is it?"

"I need your heart."

"Wh-What?"

"To cast the spell and send your soul somewhere safe, I need your heart. Your soul will be safe, and I will put you in another body, but your heart must remain with me."

Lamia looked down at the ground, her eyes searching back and forth as if the blades of grass would somehow have the answer for whatever was going on in her head. It was clear to Zephyra that no matter how much Lamia tried to make sense of this, she couldn't.

She knew Lamia felt trapped, but she had no other choice. If Lamia was recaptured, Vojin would go after her. It wouldn't just mean a small punishment for him, he would be tortured for the rest of his life. Lamia's fate would be sealed. She would be tortured next to him, and he would be able to do nothing more than helplessly watch.

Lamia took in a deep breath. "Tell Vojin I love him. If you are not able to do this in person, then please tell him through his dreams. Whatever you do, never tell him you were the one who ended my life. He will kill you without regard to the consequences."

Her heart ached so deeply within her she felt as though it might stop on its own. "You will live through his dreams and tell him yourself that you love him. I will make sure of that."

Zephyra looked around herself. This was the field in which Vojin had told Lamia that he loved her. She remembered it like it was yesterday, though she knew it was so long ago. Lamia had come to Zephyra with a spark in her eyes she had never seen before. When she told her friend about what happened, Zephyra was so happy for her, she almost cried.

Now every memory she will ever have of her friend will be tainted with the reminder that she had to kill her to save her.

"Do not bury me. Leave my body out in the open. He needs to see that I am dead, so he won't go searching for me." Lamia paused. "Will it hurt?"

"A little," Zephyra nodded. "But I will kill you as quickly as I can… Forgive me for what I am about to do."

"There is nothing to forgive. We don't have another choice. Hold me," she whispered as she leaned her head into Zephyra's chest.

The Princess wrapped her arms around her friend and kissed her on the head one last time. She felt the power of her gift boiling within her; her fingers glowing red with heat. It was time. Taking one more breath she tried to calm down her soul, which was deafeningly screaming "no."

"I love you," she whispered before she thrust her hand into Lamia's chest and ripped out her heart with one swift motion.

CHAPTER 1

Sitting on the wooden swing, beneath the canopy of the sycamore tree, Astra stared blankly into the dry field speckled with floral weeds. The scent of manure filled her nostrils from a nearby muck pile that had become so large, it looked like a small hill. Not even the honeysuckle bushes that were suffocating the fence were able to even slightly mask a smell that strong.

Ominously thick clouds rolled on top of one another while thunder rolled from the distant tree covered mountains, warning all who lingered underneath, that it was about to unleash its fury upon the land. A sticky spring breeze whipped a few strands of hair over her face while in the distance a lone dog howled sorrowfully to its masters, begging for them to let him back in. Humidity strangled the air, causing misery to all those who remained outside, while the crickets that once chirped merrily only an hour before, now rested in a state of silence.

The dark and deep pressure which had built in her chest as soon as she'd seen her mother's corpse, refused to subside. How long was this sensation supposed to last? It had been months already, and she had tried everything to get through this—therapy, horseback riding, journaling, and pills—nothing worked.

People say a broken heart hurts. She never knew what they meant until now. Her heart ached, sometimes so much she could hardly breathe. The feeling of being numb seemed like an unattainable paradise. She longed for a morsel of relief but that morsel of relief, God refused to give to her. Instead, he sat in his kingdom watching her with amusement, while he held her mother's soul captive; the soul he'd ripped away from her.

People say 'time heals' but she had begun to believe the statement was a lie created from the mouths of those who were replete with nescience. When she closed her eyes she could see her mother's cold dead gaze staring back at her.

Thunder once again rumbled over the land as a gust of wind raked its fingers through the trembling leaves. The wind made its way towards a blooming cherry tree and ripped the buds from the branches, scattering them over the ground. It was comforting to know the flowers that once felt safe on the tree would now be rotting on the dirt. It was proof to Astra that nothing beautiful would ever last.

Rubbing her weary eyes, she yawned. It had been a while since she'd had a good night's sleep. Hell, she could hardly find the will to eat. Every night she stayed awake, staring blankly at her empty wall until she passed out, only to wake up screaming from the nightmares that tormented her. In order to even function she pushed these stygian emotions deeper, popping the pills she was told to take, hoping they would somehow ease her from this hell she was trapped in.

What made matters worse was at night, after she turned out the lights, she would see shadows moving around her room. Were they real? Or her imagination? Was she going mad? Every night since the accident she felt as though she was being watched by an evil presence.

Now that her life had changed so drastically, she detested being around anyone. She couldn't stand their pitying glances or how they whispered behind her back as if she didn't know what they are saying. Her destruction was their entertainment, a lunch time topic spoken about by people she once called her friends. While some used her as an excuse to make themselves seem more 'Godly,' praying loudly for her as they raised their hands up to the heavens in honor of their own form of self-glory, other's felt sorry for her and treated her as if she was nothing more than a crippled puppy.

The mere words, "Do you want to talk?" made her want to scream and break whatever object was nearest to her. No, she didn't want to talk. She had talked so much that there was nothing left to say that she hadn't said before. It didn't alleviate her pain; instead it had the opposite effect, reminding her of what happened, as if she didn't have enough memories to taunt her.

Everything that surrounded her had become a painful memory of the one she had lost; every song on the radio, every flower she passed by, every scent she smelled—even the phantom ones. Sometimes she felt as if she was slowly losing her sanity. She would hold herself at night, wishing for her mother's arms to be wrapped around her and not her own. She would whisper to the air, "I love you," hoping and praying she would hear her mother respond, but a reminder of the hollow depth that remained in her soul was all that greeted her lingering words.

Thunder rumbled over her head as an explosion of rain soaked her skin and clothing. No matter how much water drenched her flesh, the tar of her sin clung onto her soul, refusing to be cleansed. Closing her eyes, she listened to the clattering sound of the wind knocking around the tree branches above her head. The sycamore tree groaned under its own weight as it rocked back and forth with every gust. Her toes grazed across the mud as a large branch split from the trunk. It barely missed her head as it tumbled onto the ground and cracked in half upon impact. She didn't flinch.

Looking up to the blackened sky she screamed to the heavens, "You fucking missed!"

God laughed in the form of a growling thunder, vibrating the surrounding air. He was taunting her, she knew it. He was letting her know he could have shown her mercy but instead was forcing her weary heart to keep beating.

The sound of the screen door creaked open as Aunt Lilly stepped onto the porch. Lilly had reminded her of this storm only an hour before and made her promise she would come inside with the first sound of thunder. Her aunt had gained a fear of thunderstorms after a bolt of lightning killed a herd of her cows, just a few years before. She came out the next morning to the cows laying on their side with their legs stretched out.

"Girl, I am about to tan your hide if you don't get yourself out of this weather," Lilly called out in her thick southern accent. She glared at her with a tense jaw and pursed lips as raindrops soaked her skin. "Have ya lost yer marbles?"

The woman frantically waved for her niece to come inside with wide eyes that seemed to bulge out of her head. A gust of wind whipped her floral dress around her chunky body. Lilly glanced towards the field and knitted her brow.

"Come on!" she encouraged. "Yer gonna catch a cold if you stay out here."

The thought of going inside that home made her stomach twist. This awful place was nothing more than a reminder of everything she had lost. Littering the eggshell walls were photos of her mother smiling happily; something she could never do again now that she was rotting six feet in the ground. No matter how much Astra pleaded with her father to take these images down, he responded only with silence and a glare so unbearable that she felt as though her very existence was an abomination.

She pushed herself off the wooden swing and felt her toes sink into the sticky mud. It coated her skin like slimy pudding. God the storm felt good. She couldn't help but stretch her arms out and enjoy it for just a moment longer.

Though she didn't want to go inside, she knew she had little choice. Her aunt was angry enough as it was, but empty promises were sometimes needed in order to maintain sanity. She dragged her feet as she walked towards the old Victorian house.

"What are ya thinkin'?" Lilly's voice softened as Astra made her way through the garden. "Ya can't go around puttin' yourself in danger just cuz yer feelin' blue. Now get inside and clean up. You look like you just got into a pig wrestling match. Yer father and I are gonna have to have a long talk about you." Lilly once again looked up at the storm as thunder growled so loudly it rattled the windows. "Hope my cows are doin' okay," she muttered under her breath.

Astra quietly walked inside and lowered her head so she wouldn't have to look at the photographs littering the walls. This building which used to be filled with so much love, was now void of all happiness. It had become a glorified coffin for the living, filled with memories of the dead, and as much sorrow as one would find in a cemetery.

As she walked down the narrow hallway, she turned and saw her father, standing in the kitchen, wearing a tattered shirt that should have been washed days ago. His eyes were locked on his phone which was illuminating his spectacles in the dim light of the room. His expression was unreadable; his emotions remaining hidden beneath the scraggly brown beard he had not groomed for months.

"Hey Dad," she blurted out, hoping he would acknowledge her existence. For a moment, he paused. He raised his bloodshot eyes just over the phone before looking back down and continuing to scroll. "I got you a sweet tea with extra sugar to cheer you up. It's in the fridge."

Without even making eye contact, her father picked up a half empty bottle of whiskey he had bought a few hours earlier, then turned his back to her and left the kitchen to make his way into the living room.

Astra's heart felt like a sinking ship in her chest. Her eyes burned as she stared at the empty kitchen. Dad hadn't spoken to her since the accident—not even a single word. Every time she tried to speak to him, he would either walk away or ignore her as if she didn't exist. She was as welcome as a termite from the man who used to tell her he loved her more than life itself.

There was no point in standing in an empty kitchen and torturing herself with questions, so she walked into her bedroom and slowly sank down on the rocking chair. She could hear the echo of the discussion happening between her aunt and her father through the air vent.

"Derick, ya can't just go around ignorin' her like that. She's goin' through just as tough a time as you are, if not worse. Frankly, I think she's becomin' too skinny. I don't think she has eaten a good meal in months and unlike you, I've been keepin' an eye on that girl. Have ya seen how she looks? She looks awful! Lord, Derick don't you see? She already feels terrible. You ignorin' her like yer doin', is destroyin' her. She needs her daddy."

Her father paused for a moment before responding with a voice so cold, it sent shivers down her spine, "I know. It's just hard."

"She's still yer daughter. Ya gotta get over this. Man up. Ya need to be there for her."

"I know this sounds awful but…"

"But what?" Lilly asked.

"I sometimes feel like it would have been easier if she was gone too. I love her but I can't stand even being around her. She reminds me too much of Marina. It's just too hard."

When Astra heard those wretched words, she felt like someone had punched her in the gut. The muscles in her chest ached as she gasped to catch her breath. How could he say that? Did he no longer love her? She made a mistake, an awful mistake that cost her mother's life, but never did she think her father would lose his love for her. She didn't want to hear anymore, but she couldn't seem to stop listening.

"Derick with God as my witness, if I ever hear you say that around Astra, I will slap those lips right off yer face. How could ya even think that way? She's yer daughter," Lilly responded, her voice elevating some.

"I know… And I know the accident wasn't her fault, but for some reason I blame her."

Astra closed her eyes and bit her lip until she felt her teeth break through her skin and the bitter silk of blood touch her tongue. Grabbing onto the nearest frame containing the happy smiles of her family, she smashed it against the dresser. It felt good to watch the shards fall onto the floor because it reminded

14

her that she wasn't the only thing that was broken. She yelled at the top of her lungs, which almost seemed to match the deafening screams of her tormented soul.

On the floor was a large shard of glass about the size of her palm and as sharp as a knife. She grabbed it, walked over to her bed, pulled down her pants, and pressed the sharp glass onto top of her thigh. For a moment her skin resisted the glass before it finally gave in, splitting open and causing a small stream of crimson to trail down her leg. Finally, a moment of peace. She breathed in deeply as the physical pain dulled the emotional agony that created chaos within her. Yes, she was aware that she wasn't supposed to do this anymore, but she needed to find relief and this was the only thing that seemed to bring her any.

Her attention lurched to the corner where she saw one of the shadows that seemed to follow her everywhere. Was it her imagination playing tricks? For a moment, she could have sworn it smiled, taking pleasure in the misery it was witnessing.

The shadow moved across the room before disappearing into thin air as if it never existed. Yes, it must have been her imagination. Shadows don't move on their own and ghosts don't exist.

A dull throb in her leg called her attention. The small trail of blood had made its way onto the sheet she sat upon. Damn it. It was stained. She couldn't even do this without ruining something.

Why couldn't she just disappear into the ether? It's not like anyone would miss her. Her existence would become nothing more than an unpleasant memory.

She felt trapped inside the one person she didn't even want to be around. The one person she could not escape. Even crossing paths with a mirror felt like she was looking into the face of her worst enemy.

"I can't do this anymore. I can't go on like this," she gasped as she grabbed the rose gold case that wrapped around her cell phone. Searching through her contacts, she scrolled through the list until she found her uncle's name.

How would he answer? she wondered as her finger lingered above the cobalt call symbol. Taking a deep breath, she pushed her thumb down, watching the screen turn from white to black as the sound of ringing echoed through the speaker.

"Hello?" the familiar scratchy voice of her uncle said after picking up the phone.

"Hey, I gotta talk to you." She bit her lip.

"It's been a while."

"Yeah, it's been quite some time."

"Sorry I didn't come down to Tennessee. I couldn't get away from work—it's been busy up here. How have you been handling things?"

"Not good." She could barely find her voice since her thoughts were deafened by her screaming mind. She wanted to beg. She wanted to plead and tell him everything. But she couldn't. What would his response be to the question trapped behind her lips? The possibilities were endless, and she knew this conversation could easily go both ways.

"Do you want to talk about it? I know things have been tough for you."

"I have to ask you something."

"You have my full attention. What is it?"

Astra took in a shuddering breath. "I can't do this anymore," her voice cracked. Why does a simple question become so difficult to ask when the heart is involved? "I need to get away—I mean far away—and I know you have places in New York that you rent out. I saved up money. It's not much but I can pay for a deposit and the first month in advance. Do you have any places available?"

"Sweetie. You're so young. It's a big jump and far from home. New York is a different kind of animal. They eat and spit out sweet girls like you here." Astra felt as if someone had lit matches underneath her eyelids. She could feel the blood pumping through her fingertips and every word that her uncle spoke deepened the nausea brewing inside her. "Besides, what's your dad think of this? Shouldn't this be a time where you both are there for each other?"

For several moments a tense silence lingered on the phone. Her teeth chattered as her emotions seeped through her like poison. "Dad doesn't want me here. He wants me out. He says it's too hard to even look at me." Her voice trailed off as she attempted to gather herself, pressing the phone closer to her face. "I need a place to go and I don't have anywhere else. Please help me."

Her uncle sighed heavily. "I have a studio open right now in downtown Manhattan. If you want it, it's yours. I'll cut you a deal so you can afford it." Astra released a long breath, feeling her fingers loosen. This is what she needed. "Are you sure about this?"

"Yeah," she replied. "I really am"

CHAPTER 2

New York

Astra's heart pounded as she stood in front of the rust stained door that led to her new apartment. What was that smell? Her nose curled as she chewed on her lip. It smelled strongly of cat urine mixed with vomit, which was permeating from the carpet that was poorly secured to the sides of the hall. To make matters worse, the dimly lit hall had a flickering florescent light at the end of it. Flickering lights were always irritating to be around.

The lock slid back on the inside of the door, ending with a faint 'click' that could barely be heard. She held her breath. This was the first time she had seen what this apartment looked like. Although her uncle gave her a vague description of its appearance while she was on the phone with him at the airport, she still wasn't sure what she was walking into.

Slowly she pushed open the heavy door. Between the cracks on the walls and the suspicious black stain on the ceiling, she felt like she was entering a prison cell. It was a single room with a small bed, a dresser, and a few decorative vases that didn't look like they belonged. In the corner of the room was a warped mirror; an obvious attempt to make the tiny room look bigger. The walls were painted a strange shade of pink and in some areas, large pieces of paint were peeling back as if even the color was too repulsed to remain in place.

Her ears picked up the sound of a leaking sink, and she could have sworn she heard a faint scratching sound coming out of the walls. Did she have a mouse problem? She imagined coming home to a tiny flea covered animal scampering across the floor, while leaving poop in its path. There was something about those hairless tails that made her squirm. Rodent tails looked like a deformed worm coming out of a mangy body.

She stepped further inside and noticed a few small roaches making their way out of the bathroom. Unlike the roaches she had come across down south, these had no fear of humans. They boldly climbed up the wall and into a crack, as if they owned the place and she was the one intruding in their home.

A deep yawn stretched across her face. She couldn't wait to take a nap. Her body felt heavy and the bed, though it was in need of new sheets, still looked better than the airplane seat she tried to take a nap on only hours before.

Her flight should have been only two hours but the layover in Atlanta was long and gruelling. Thankfully it saved her a few hundred dollars, but she was still not sure if the inconvenience was worth it. Though it was her first time flying, she decided it would probably be her last. Something about sitting in a flying tube, hoping it didn't decide to malfunction on the way, didn't sit right with her.

She rolled her heavy suitcase behind her as she walked over to the bed and laid down. The bed was clearly old and had only a thin layer of padding to shield her from the springs. Every movement she made ended with an odd squeaking noise, which was a far different experience from the memory foam she was used to sleeping on.

"Hello roommates," she muttered as another roach crawled up a wall. Would she ever get used to seeing those awful bugs? "Are you going to pay rent or just mooch?"

There were certainly things that she would need to take care of. Yes, she now lived in a roach infested apartment that might still have lead paint from the 1950s, but it was now her home, and she decided she would make the best out of it.

* * *

The sound of porcelain shattering jolted her from her sleep. What was that? She searched the darkness as she lay in her bed with covers pulled up to her chin. There it was, a figure in the darkness as black as night and as tall as the ceiling. It stood in front of the window watching her, before finally moving across the room, allowing the light from the city to filter through.

The vase. It was smashed on the ground in front of the dresser close to where she first saw the dark figure. It slowly moved across the room before bending over and crawling into the mirror, disappearing inside.

"I am not crazy. It's only my imagination," she reassured herself. Her fingers twisted around the sheets until her hands hurt. No, it was not her imagination. Someone had to have shattered that vase and that "someone" was watching her sleep.

She couldn't allow herself to think this way. If she did, it would mean she was going insane. Shadows don't break things and shadows don't step into mirrors. Or at least that is what she told herself.

Astra needed a distraction; something to take her mind away from the chaos that seemed to linger within her and around her. Leaning over, she reached into her purse and pulled out her phone, quickly unlocking it with the touch of her finger.

The screen flashed on, stinging her eyes with its harsh glare. She paused as she gazed at her green inbox containing a tiny red circle. A message? Who would text her at eleven at night? Touching the inbox her heart lurched as she saw the name "Dad" flash on the screen with the word "hey."

Her fingertip tapped on the box and she scanned the words he had written to her. It was the first thing he had said to her since the accident and she couldn't believe what she was reading.

"Hey… We need to talk. I just landed. I'm at the airport. Can we meet at a diner somewhere? I'd understand if you don't want to, but I had to come find you. I can't lose you too."

Was this real? Did he really come to New York to find her?

A smile crossed her face as she wiped a tear that had formed at the edge of her eye.

"Yes. I am up. What diner to you want to meet at?"

The screen glared into her eyes. She bit the edge of her lip as she waited for a response that couldn't come soon enough.

"There is a diner off 8th Ave. It's open all night. Meet me in an hour?"

She couldn't type the word "yes" fast enough before ripping the sheets off of her and walking over to the light switch.

What would she wear? Unzipping the suitcase, she pulled out a pair of black pants with large pockets at the sides and a white t-shirt that fit snuggly around her. To help keep out the crisp spring air, she threw on a lavender colored jacket and a thin teal scarf. From her makeup bag, she pulled out a mirror and rubbed concealer to cover the dark circles under her eyes. She finished her look with waterproof mascara and coral eyeshadow.

"Astra," a voice whispered behind her.

She froze in place and shut her eyes as tightly as she could. It was her imagination. There was no voice. It was probably someone outside in the hallway who said something that sounded like her name or perhaps it was from exhaustion that she thought she heard something she didn't. She needed to convince herself of this, but she knew it was all a lie.

"Astra," it whispered again.

Her head snapped from corner to corner of her dimly lit apartment. It didn't look like anything was around her, yet she felt like she was being watched.

"Just my imagination," she said out loud as an icy rush tumbled down her spine.

* * *

Getting out of the apartment couldn't happen fast enough. Every sound, every sight, and every step seemed to come with a form of terror of its own. Even the walls of the elevator seemed to be unusually close as it slowly rattled down to the entrance lobby of the apartment complex. She needed to remember this was a happy time, not one where she needed to think about what just happened.

The streets were filled with bright lights, honking cars, and pedestrians making their way to their next destination. Hovering over the tips of the skyscrapers were clouds that looked pregnant with rain. The cold wind snatched her hair, raking its fingers through the streets, slapping around anything loose and light that came into its path. Spring was far warmer in the south than it was here in New York. It was April for god's sake. Why was it still so cold up here?

She walked a few blocks before hearing a woman call her name, which caused her to stop in her tracks. Did she really just hear her name? Was there someone watching her? She was seemingly invisible to the New Yorkers who rushed to and fro but for some reason she felt as if a pair of eyes were burrowing into her soul. A cold sweat formed on her tense palms. Was this another moment of insanity?

No. There was something out here. She knew it. She could feel it.

"This is ridiculous," Astra muttered under her breath. There was no logical reason for her to feel this way. She needed to get over it. She couldn't show up to the diner in this mental state. The last thing she needed was for her father to question whether or not him coming was the right decision.

The sensation of a needle scraping across her neck made her want to scream. She bit down on her tongue to prevent any noise coming from her lips. Swinging around, she looked for the one who had touched her, but no one was close enough. Though the street was busy, the people who passed her by seemed to like their space and kept enough distance between each other.

She needed to maintain her sanity, but it felt like the more she tried to hold on to it, the faster it slipped away from her. Her heart felt like a mallet slamming against a gong. Someone was watching her. She could feel it. Slowly her head turned until she gazed down a shadowy alley.

There it was, a figure standing in the middle of the dark pathway, at least ten feet tall with six spider-like arms coming out of its skeleton body. Slowly, this creature raised its hand and pointed directly at her. Its white eyes opened and with a smile crossing its face, the beast revealed a row of sharp teeth.

"Astra," she heard the whisper of a woman drifting through the wind—the same whisper she'd heard throughout her life. It was that thing. This was whom she had been hearing the whole time. It wasn't a ghost. It wasn't a shadow. It was a creature so frightening that it looked like it was pulled out of hell.

Her legs shook as she swung around and ran. Diving between excited tourists taking photos of bright colorful signs, she raced towards her apartment. All around her, vendors selling clothing, trinkets, art prints, and food, yelled out their specials while in front of her, a screaming and laughing drunk bachelorette party made their way down the road, eyeing the next bar as if the contents inside was equivalent to the gold in El Dorado. Astra pushed by them, almost running into a topless woman with an American flag painted over her breasts.

"Watch out!" The woman yelled as she stumbled over the sidewalk and continued to run.

Her heart smashed inside of her chest as her mind raced faster than her feet could ever go. What was that creature she just saw? What did it want with her and why was she the only one who seemed to be able to see it? She had no answers. Her mind screamed for her to find safety within the walls of her apartment. She wanted to lock every door and every window, wrap herself up in a blanket with a knife in her hand, and pray to whatever god was out there not to take her to hell. Was this the devil there to collect her soul? She was sure of it. Never in her life had she seen anything so evil.

Astra raced down the sidewalks and dodged an overflowing trashcan, barely missing a rat that scampered from the refuse. She jumped over a sleeping homeless man, holding up a sign made of cardboard, and when she ran across the crosswalk, she came a hairsbreadth away from being hit by a yellow cab who was taking a turn. Before the cab driver even had a chance to yell out of the window, she had already disappeared into the sea of people who seemed not to even notice her state of sheer terror.

She ran until her lungs screamed for a moment of rest, but she refused to give her body this release. In her panic, she took a few wrong turns but finally found herself back at the apartment complex and slid into the elevator. Rapidly she pushed the button before watching the doors shut tight. The box traveled upward, beeping with every floor it passed. Looking down at her hands, she wanted to scream and cry but found herself so overwhelmed she couldn't do either.

She grabbed her phone and searched for her father's name. The phone rang once before he picked it up.

"Hello?"

"Daddy help me," she gasped. "Please! I'm scared."

"Honey where are you? What's going on? Do I need to call the police?"

If this was all in her head, then why did it feel so real? Why did she feel like she was running away from something inescapable? Was she truly losing her mind or was her life becoming a living nightmare?

All she wanted was to be safe in her father's arms. She needed him more than she'd ever needed him before.

"Please Daddy, I think she's going to hurt me. She's been following me."

"Who? Baby you're cutting out." His voice remained in control, but she heard the panic beginning to form. "I can hardly hear you. Who is trying to hurt you?"

Suddenly, the surrounding air rapidly dropped in temperature and the smell of a rotting corpse pierced the inside of her nose. Opening her mouth, she could see her breath leave her lips like a small puff of fog. She wasn't sure if she was shaking from the cold or from the sheer terror that gripped her soul.

"She's here."

"Where baby? Where are you? I'm going to call the police, but I need to know where you are!"

24

Her chest tightened like a large fist wrapped around her ribcage. Every muscle in her body tensed up as hot, sulfuric-smelling breath gently grazed the back of her neck. Swinging her head around, she searched the empty elevator. Where was this beast? She knew it was there but couldn't see it.

"My apartment… I don't want to die Daddy. I don't want to die."

Her heart slammed with such ferocity she wondered if it would break every rib it came into contact with. She needed to get out. She needed to get out now.

"Baby find a place to hide an—"

The sound of beeping echoed in her ear. The phone call dropped. No signal.

She wanted to scream but her throat couldn't utter a sound. She felt like an animal trapped in a cage, waiting for a brutal slaughtering. With flickering lights above her head, she twisted her neck to look behind herself. Though Astra could not see anyone around her, she knew the beast was there. She could feel her eyes ripping into her soul.

Finally, the steel trap opened its doors, revealing an empty hallway. Without warning, her body was thrown out of the elevator and slammed into the wall in front of her.

"NO! HELP ME! SOMEBODY HELP ME!"

She tried to get away, but whatever force had a hold of her was not about to let go. This was not her imagination. This was her hell.

All around her head, the walls cracked as the building groaned. She was released slightly before once again getting slammed into the wall. Her head exploded with a loud ringing that screamed between her ears. She opened her eyes. No. This couldn't be true. This had to be a nightmare.

Crawling out of the elevator as if it was crawling out of the pits of hell, a new beast approached. It had broad shoulders, a muscular frame, and walked with jagged movements on its hands and feet, each paw ending in three razorblade claws. Small moving tentacles protruded from its jackal shaped ears, twitching to every sound on top of its black skull.

Her chest sank as its midnight eyes pierced through her soul, examining every inch of her. This monster allowed its jaw to hang loosely, revealing thousands of jagged teeth, moving around as though it was a separate organism. Its snake-like tongue flicked back and forth, dripping with clotted blood.

"Astra," he hissed in a deep masculine voice. "We've been watching you."

Every inch of her body trembled as a smile curled on the creature's lips. The beast inhaled deeply. His eyes rolled to the back of his head, showing a small amount of white at the edges.

He climbed over her body, and as he did so his claws sank into the wall she was pinned against. The sound of tapping averted her attention to the elevator. Behind the new beast was the creature she saw in the alley. This monster was clicking her nails against the walls.

The nearest beast shoved a claw inside of her mouth and pried her jaw so wide open, it felt as if he was trying to break it off. She could feel his razor blade beginning to slice through her tongue as the metallic taste of blood filled her mouth. He placed his lips over hers and exhaled, forcing a thick smoke to pour into her lungs, before he pulled his claw out of her jaw.

"See you on the other side," he chuckled as she coughed, her vision and mind fading into darkness.

CHAPTER 3

Astra wasn't sure where she was, but she had a hard time opening her eyes. It took all of the strength within her to finally open them, allowing light to pierce the inside of her corneas. It felt like a thousand tiny needles were jabbing into her brain all at once, but she refused to give herself relief, forcing her eyes to remain open, glued on the softly lit skies above. It looked like it was morning or maybe it was evening, but either way, the sun was not fully up in the sky. It was warm here—too warm for the spring, causing sweat to drip down her forehead.

Her body was against the base of a cliff inside of a deep canyon. The sandstone walls looked like God himself had painted the rocks in vibrant shades of red, orange, white, and tan. Her legs were stretched out in front of her, slightly spread apart as her back leaned upon the smooth walls that seemed to reach to the sky.

She was sitting at a dead end with one path in front of her that split into two paths just a hundred yards away. Though she was in a wider area, she could tell that some areas of the paths in front of her became narrower. Thick, swirling, purple-grey clouds loomed ominously over her head while a burst of lightning cracked in the distance and flooded everything around her in white light. She could smell the electricity in the humid air. The storm's anger screamed from the heavens and threw its fist down onto the ground.

Her muscles felt like ground meat, with every infinitesimal movement causing her body to beg her to stay still. A loud ringing screamed in her ears, overpowering all the noises around her. The ground appeared to be moving the same way that maggots writhed inside of a corpse. With thick humidity lingering in the air, her lungs weighed heavily in her chest, while her hair stuck uncomfortably to her head.

What happened to her? The muscles in her throat tightened. She tried to remember but her mind was trapped in an eternal fog, with every thought slipping away into the milky atmosphere.

Slowly, her lips parted. She attempted to take in a deep breath, but her lungs felt like a balloon refusing to fully inflate. A sharp pain radiated from the wound inside of her jaw. How did she get that and why was it so hard to breathe?

She lifted her arm as if it was made of cracking porcelain and shut her eyes as she ran her bleeding hand down her side. Her eyelids tensed as her fingers dipped into a gash on her thigh. The warm, soft fat left her fingertips sticky with blood.

She needed to call someone. She needed to get help. Her fingers slipped in the pockets of her jacket and her pants. Where was her phone? She looked around her. Nothing. It was gone.

Her mind raced as reality shattered the fragility of her mind. Every fiber inside her screamed she needed to hide but she couldn't grasp why. She wasn't sure how she became injured or how she got there but what worried her more was the feeling she was being watched, which came over her like waves of the ocean, drowning her mind with horrible delusions of who was near.

A low growl of thunder in the distance gave a warning that a storm was approaching. There was nothing worse than being lost somewhere in the middle of bad weather.

"I need to get up… get up… please get up…" These words were repeated like a mantra, as a pathetic attempt to encourage herself to move somewhere safe.

Her jaw tensed underneath her lips. She hoped that when she opened her eyes, she would be home in her bed. But as her eyelids split, the dark pits of her cornea forced her once again to see she was in an unfamiliar land.

How did she get here? Was someone cruel enough to kidnap her and leave her stranded in the middle of nowhere? Who or what hurt her?

"This can't be real," she whispered as she looked down the paths and inhaled the musky air into her lungs. Her fingers dug into the warm ground. "This has to be a nightmare."

She examined the wound on her hip before taking off her jacket and wrapping it around her waist. The gash could have easily used a few stitches, and it needed to be cleaned. Her split skin looked like open lips coated in blood. Would this lead to an infection?

She touched the cut tenderly, watching blood seep out. Pulling off her scarf, she wrapped it around the wound on her leg to at least keep as much dirt out of it as she could.

There was an odd scent that reminded her of decay. It lingered in the air and punched the inside of her curling nose. Her head snapped back and forth. She expected to see something rotting near to her, but there was nothing in sight, only churning dirt. Why was the dirt moving like this and where was that smell coming from? Was she near the food of a dangerous predator? Would it come back to finish its meal only to find its next victim waiting to be crushed within its muscular jaws?

Images of eternal possibilities flashed inside her mind. Her sanity begged for mercy, only to once again receive another reel of images playing mercilessly; taunting her soul.

The ground shook and a large rock the size of her head tumbled from the heavens and crashed only fifteen feet away from her. Upon impact, it split into three pieces. That could have been her skull. She imagined how it would have looked, cracked open like an egg as blood seeped onto the ground below it. Would she have remained alive for a few seconds as shattered pieces of her bone surrounded her, or would she have died with the stone's impact? No, this was not just thunder that she was hearing. The land she was on was angry and waking from its slumber.

She touched her chest and felt her precious heart attempt to burst through, as if it could also run and hide. Just as her heart

29

was trapped within her body, she was trapped within these cliff walls. Where should she go? What should she do?

If she called for help, she could attract the wrong attention. She trusted neither man nor beast. Both were unpredictable and dangerous.

The squirming ground drew her attention. Black and brown speckled dirt reached onto her shoes as though it was trying to crawl on top of her, before tumbling back down onto the ground below. With every burst of lightning, the mud became more active and seemed to emit a foul aroma. *What kind of hell is this?*

Thinking back to the classes she had taken in school, she tried to remember if they ever covered anything like this. No. She had never heard of moving dirt unless there were bugs involved and it didn't look like that was the case. *How is this even possible?*

Her eyes absorbed the terrain around her. Slithering up the sides of the cliffs, clear roots pulsated with dark red liquid connected to something that appeared to be a thorned plant. These plants alone were a sight she had never seen before. Like long tentacles extending out of a thick white base, they moved their arm-like vines slowly from side to side as though they were in search of something. Thick, white, crimson tipped thorns seemed to grip onto anything they touched.

She gazed at the red roots before studying the branches of the plant. Questions pounded her mind. What was it in search of? How was it able to move on its own? Why did the thorns look like the ends had been painted by the blood of its victims?

Her eyes traced the side of the cliff wall, following the roots of this flora. The ends of the roots were clear, while the closer to the bulk of the plant they were, the more filled with a bright red substance they seemed to become. Was it blood that she was looking at? Was it a sort of sap or naturally occurring liquid?

Her heart sank. Her eyes begged for the sight she looked at to be nothing more than a lie told by her anxiety ridden mind. Clinging to the side of a cliff, one of the smaller bushes had wrapped its branches around what appeared to be a massive bat, but she wasn't sure since she could only see the tip of one of its wings. The plant tightened its grip even further and as it did so, more of the roots filled with liquid. Like a spider to its prey, these living plants drained their victims of their life source, slowly drinking away at a substance more precious than gold.

Her eyes scanned the looming walls of the canyon. Though she knew they were not moving, it felt as if they were closing in on her. She was a prisoner to this land with no way to defend herself. A wild beast was not the only danger in this area. She suspected getting too close to one of those plants could lead to an excruciating death. What if one of them captured her the way it captured the last animal? The thought of this sent an icy shiver down her spine. This must be how bugs felt when they flew into a spider's web.

Where was she? She doubted she was still New York. It was far too hot for that and the terrain didn't fit with everything she knew about the state. Perhaps she was in Arizona? No. She had never heard of any plants that moved like that in the States. Maybe she was somewhere in Australia or China? She had heard those countries had many natural wonders as well as strange plants that were unheard of to most of those who lived in the United States.

She had never been in an area so far from civilization before and had minimal training on survival skills. Though her father would go hunting and fishing, she always refused to join him, telling him that she thought it took too much time. The only survival skills she had was basic knowledge, like how to build a small fire using kindle, wood, and newspaper, and what plants were edible in the smoky mountains.

"What did he teach me?" she muttered. "The rule of three."

Her teeth ground together as another burst of lightning caused the canyon to explode in white light. The clouds growled with rage, challenging the shaking world below it to a fight. Small rocks fell from the cliff side like hail. The sharp pebbles bounced off her skin, leaving tiny cuts and bruises. This was not a safe area.

She needed shelter but there was none; only the open walls of the canyon mockingly standing around her as another roll of thunder slammed against the clouds. She needed water but she was surrounded by dusty walls and dirt ground.

Her soul curled. She felt as if a thousand invisible eyes were watching her, admiring her weakness and laughing at her confusion. Gripping her head with her palms, she tried to think back to the last thing she could remember before she woke up here, but her memories cowered in the shadows of her subconscious.

A drop of sweat crawled down her face, leaving a small trail of moisture on her skin. She massaged her temples, hoping she could coax the memories out of their hiding. But they refused to come.

Another roll of thunder howled from the heavens and a streak of lightning cracked across the blackening sky. The ground around her rumbled, throwing another massive stone from the cliff above. It shattered upon impact, its sharp pieces flying through the air like bullets.

Her body begged to stay, but she had to move. She had no choice. Mother nature was angry and wanted the world to experience her wrath.

Her body felt as if it was weighed down by rocks. There was a deep pressure between her shoulder blades from a pulled muscle which throbbed as a constant reminder. Her muscles begged her not to move, aching all the way to her bones but she knew what she needed to do. She pushed her body off the ground and stumbled down the rock-strewn path. Wincing, she felt her feet complain from carrying the burdening weight. Why did her body have to hurt so much?

There was a lump in her throat that she just couldn't swallow while her tongue felt like it was resting on raw meat. Even the smallest noise made her twitch and her heart flutter. She wasn't sure what was worse, her imagination or the potential reality of who or what was out here. What kind of animals would live in a place like this? Were there dangerous men who roamed these narrow paths? She imagined a rock falling from the cliff and pinning her to the ground and then wondered what it would feel like to slowly starve to death. She took a slow breath in and wished that her head would stop spinning like an out of control merry-go-round.

With every step, Astra felt more lost. Instead of feeling like she was going towards a destination, she felt like she was wandering deeper into nothingness. With the exception of rubble, the paths were empty and devoid of life. There were no bugs or animals, and with the exception of the brewing storm, not even noise. On the odd occasion she would come across one of those awful plants, but they were never close enough to reach her.

Where would this unmarked trail lead her to? Would it lead her to a person who could help or towards someone or something capable of doing unimaginable things? How could she tell the difference between who could and couldn't be trusted?

By the smoothness of the rocks on the lower section of the canyon, it was clear that at one point, water had softened the edges. Though there was no sign of the precious liquid anywhere, she had hoped that she would come across a water source. The best circumstance would be that she could get out of this wretched place and find a river. Where there is water, there are eventually people. Though she knew there were people on Earth that were evil, she had to take the risk and find someone that could help her get back home.

She looked at the top of the canyon. Its sharp edges looked like razor blades cutting into the sky. What part of the world was she in? How long had she been unconscious for? It must have been a significant amount of time. What happened to her during her journey? She shuddered. Whatever journey she took was not a pleasant one and that was clear by the gash on her leg.

What happened? She needed to think. She remembered her father texting her and her stepping out of her apartment. But then what? Why wouldn't her mind allow her to see the last moments before she became unconscious? She searched her mind but only found darkness. It was as if someone had scooped the memory out and placed it in another body.

A deep tension pushed behind her eyes, throbbing with such vigor she was surprised her cranium didn't crack open to relieve the pressure. Damn this migraine. Maybe when the pain subsided her memories would return but until then she was left a victim to her imagination.

A strong wind pulled at her sweat-drenched hair, slapping it across her face like a whip. Rapidly, she blinked away the blur from her eyes to get a better look at what laid before her on this barren trail. It was twice as wide as the trail she had been walking down for quite some time with walls that seemed more jagged than smooth. The sky appeared to be a lot darker than it was when she first woke up. Was it because the storm clouds were thickening or was it from the sun setting? She assumed both.

Where would she rest? Her body was about to give out at any moment. There was not a shelter in sight—not a cave, a hole, or a rock covering. There was nothing more than a path surrounded by steep walls.

She spat on the ground. Damn this place and damn whoever did this to her. She screamed at the top of her lungs until her voice cracked and throat ached. To give up seemed like the easiest thing to do but she couldn't. Not yet at least. With curled fingers she walked as fast as she could, hoping she could find some sort of shelter in a place that didn't seem to have any.

The clouds raised their fists in a fit of rage and growled as they rammed into each other, building up in the sky as if it was a competition for who could reach the highest. It was a heavenly war where none would win, but the tears of those who lost would pour from the sky until there was nothing left with the exception of the memory shown on a muddy ground.

When her feet cried out they could go no more, she caught sight of a deep hole in the ground with a thick jutting rock that protruded from the cliff above it. It was a wider area of the path that opened up almost in the shape of an egg. The hole in the ground looked almost unnatural and out of place, since this was the only hole that she had come across so far. It was as if someone had dug it out just underneath the rock above. Was this the shelter she was searching for? Had fate finally shown her mercy?

She stopped in her tracks. What if something else had found this shelter and made it their home? Would a hungry mountain lion live there? What if it was lurking in the shadows waiting for its next victim to approach? Her mind traveled to a rhumba of rattlesnakes, coiling and slithering over one another as they flashed their sharp fangs at anyone who came near. One bite from one of those would kill her within two days. She couldn't imagine how painful it would be to experience a bite that lead to a slow, grueling death.

An explosion of light illuminated everything around her and within an instant, the ground rumbled with such strength her teeth chattered beneath the folds of her lips. She wearily looked at the jutting rock wondering what the chances were of it breaking, but the sound of approaching rain interrupted her thoughts. There was no time to think of the endless possibilities and live in the 'what if.'

Astra limped over to the dark hole. Her stomach tensed until she peered inside. Nothing. There were no snakes or scorpions crawling about. Though it was large enough for a mountain lion, there was nothing inside with the exception of a yellow, foul smelling algae with a distinct scent that reminded her of old rotten eggs. Her nose curled and her pounding migraine begged her not to add something else that would antagonize it. She had no choice. She needed to take the risk.

Hesitantly, she crawled into the musky safe haven and laid down on her side, curling up in the fetal position. Would the scent that permeated within this place make her migraine worse? She rested her head on the soft ground and hoped that would not be the case. The putrid smell trapped in this shelter was so strong she felt like she could taste it.

Thunder rattled the ground beneath her as the sound of pouring rain exploded over the top of the rock. The harsh winds howled like an angry beast through the canyon. Shivering, she could feel the temperature rapidly dropping as a mist from the rain billowed onto her face. It was good she made it to the shelter in time but there was still the risk some other animal might look for one. What would she do if something came into the shelter with her still inside?

Cupping her fingers, Astra reached out of the shelter and allowed the rain to fill her hands. She drank this liquid until she felt as though her stomach would burst. There was no telling when the next opportunity to get water would come. If only there was something around to help her gather this precious liquid for her future travels, her chances of survival would increase. But there was nothing.

She winced as she touched the cloth that wrapped tightly around the gash on her thigh. The muscle that lingered beneath her wound throbbed like someone had taken a meat mallet to it. Turning her body ever so slightly, she groaned as her muscles begged her to stop moving. Her body couldn't come to an agreement on what was a comfortable position since each one involved certain muscles to bear her crushing weight.

She needed sleep. Her body longed for it as her sanity beseeched her to escape into an unconscious state. She needed a few hours of relief from the uncertainty that had become her life. But though she yearned for sweet release, Astra's mind screamed for her to stay awake. Falling asleep would mean letting down her guard. Even a moment of weakness could lead to danger or an anguishing death. This inner battle inside her, with her mind against the will of her body, went on for what seemed like hours. Exhaustion pulsated through every ounce of her inner being until finally her mind could no longer fight against the need of her body.

CHAPTER 4

An icy wind howling over stone snapped her back into a conscious state. How long had she been sleeping? She curled up in a ball and massaged her throbbing temples before pulling her jacket off her hips and pushing her arms through the sleeves. At least it provided some warmth but not nearly enough to feel somewhat comfortable.

Light trickled through the canyon, illuminating the hole she took shelter in. It was daytime, so she must have slept through the night. Though the smell was still strong, the cold temperature at least helped to tone down some of it.

There was a thick layer of ice surrounding the perimeter of the hole she'd slept in. How did this happen? How could a thunderstorm turn into an ice storm? She wrapped her arms around her shivering body as a poor attempt to warm herself. It didn't work, not even to an infinitesimal degree.

Was she imagining this? Was this real? She pinched her arm, hoping somehow it would lead to her waking up. But the sharp sting on her skin was an unfortunate reminder she was already awake, and this was the reality she was forced to remain in.

Hesitantly, she pushed her body off the ground and peeked out of the shelter. She couldn't believe she was in the same area she was in before the storm came. The rain which soaked the land last night had turned into an ocean of dense ice, blanketing the ground and cliff walls. Hanging from the surrounding canyon, large icicles clung onto the rocks with icy fingers pointing towards the ground.

How did this happen? How was it so warm and muggy just the day before and now it felt more like an arctic tundra?

She broke off a piece of an icicle hanging near to her and placed it in her mouth. The ice numbed her tongue but quickly turned into water and slipped down her throat. She needed to continue to hydrate herself for as long as she could; a human can only last three days without water.

Astra's eyes trailed across the land that surrounded her. Where was she going to go? Where was the nearest town or city where she could find help? She knew she would need to go to the police but what would she tell them? She couldn't remember what had happened or how she ended up here.

Her stomach growled angrily and reminded her that it had been a while since she had eaten. The thought of having a juicy hamburger with fries and a drink seemed like heaven. She didn't know how long it had been since she had her last meal and she didn't care to know how much longer it would be until her next one. Hopefully it was soon.

Pulling herself out of the shelter became a challenge. The ice was as slippery as it could be and each time she tried to push herself out, she would slide back in. This game with nature seemed to last far too long but finally Astra won and found herself standing just outside of the hole.

Where should she go now? Which direction was the right one? There was one path that she stood on—one way leading back to where she had come from and the other leading into the unknown. Getting to higher ground to scout the area for a river was out of the question since the walls around her were too steep to climb. She needed to find civilization before she froze to death or worse, was attacked by a feral animal, so taking the risk and going deeper into the unknown was exactly what was needed.

The walls that surrounded her were no longer as vibrant as they were before. Now they were muted from the frozen liquid that clung onto the sides. Every step she took was a slippery fight to maintain balance and one that she was losing at.

Her knees cracked into the ground, forcing a splitting pain to radiate through her legs. Damn it. That was going to leave a bruise. She didn't get up until the echoing sensation of aggravation faded from her legs.

With fingers straining against the walls, she pushed herself back up and continued down the path. How long was it going to be like this? If she could have pulled the sun right out from the cloudy skies, she would have.

The ground rumbled and as it did so, one of the thick icicles snapped off the side and shattered the ice it landed on, only a few feet away from her. The shards of ice looked like broken glass, opening up the ground below.

She stopped in her place. Her hands shook with such fervor that she knew even if she had wanted to hold them still, she wouldn't have been able to. Would she be impaled by one of these giant spikes of ice? She didn't want to move. She didn't even want to breathe in fear that this might be her last breath.

A fierce wind shoved its way through the narrow paths of the canyon, snapping her out of the trance. The wind howled like a ghost, ripping its icy fingers through her hair. She felt like she could hardly breathe without her lungs screaming for mercy, and every bitter-cold breath she took caused her chest to ache and burn.

"Where do I go?" Her words barely left her lips. "I don't even know where I am."

Astra scanned the walls of the canyon, feeling every muscle in her body tense as her teeth uncontrollably chattered. Damn this wind. The temperature alone was bad enough, the wind made it unbearable. She felt like the tin man in need of oil, her muscles hardening with every gust.

Tiny clear ice crystals clung onto her hair while her clothing provided little warmth to her shivering pink skin. When the wind was not blowing, the land around her became so quiet that the only sound she could hear was her own breath. Looking at the path in front of her, she nodded her head. She couldn't just stay here and wait to die. She had to find help.

Small rays of light burst through the thick swirling clouds, bringing patches of flickering sun to this desolate maze. With one foot in front of the other, she struggled to not slip on the thick ice below but found herself once again on the ground.

As the morning faded into the early afternoon, the clouds broke apart revealing a bright sun illuminating the blue atmosphere. Stretching across the heavens, just opposite of the sun were two thick lines. They seemed to go from one side of the planet to the other, as if the planet was nestled around rings. Her heart lurched. She stopped in her tracks and rubbed her eyes. No. No this can't be. It must be a hallucination from exhaustion.

She looked down at the ground. The ice had melted enough for her to see the mud squirm. How did Earth suddenly have rings and how did this mud move on its own? There was only one explanation she could think of. Her heart crawled into her throat. No. Please don't let this be real. She wasn't on Earth. She had been abducted.

Where was she? Where the hell was she?

This was bad. Not the kind of bad where she could recover from, but the kind of bad where she had no idea what her next move was and the one thing that seemed inevitable in her life was the panic attack which was about to ensue. She needed a shot whiskey… or five. Though she didn't even drink, right now alcohol sounded better to her than she ever thought it would.

Feeling her legs grow weak, she gripped onto the wall of the canyon before she slowly sank down onto her knees. She gasped for a breath of air but felt like she was breathing out of a straw. Curling up in a ball, her chest heaved as it struggled to take in oxygen.

What was she going to do? How is this even possible? What could have possibly happened that led her to be on another planet?

She searched her mind but could not remember anything. Why was her memory refusing to cooperate? The way to get to back home might be trapped in her subconscious but she didn't know because she couldn't seem to remember anything of value. Her fingers scratched against her scalp. She screamed at the top of her lungs before pounding her head with her fists, hoping she would knock the memory back to the surface of her mind.

Astra felt like she was trapped in the quicksand of inquisition and the more she struggled to find out about what happened to her, the deeper she was consumed by its crushing weight. The image of her father burst in her mind. He would spend the rest of his life searching for a body that would never be recovered. He would spend the rest of his life wondering what happened to his daughter and would jump to the worst possible conclusions. She would become his nightmare. She would become his guilt and the thoughts that would torture his mind would become his destruction.

She opened her mouth to let out another scream, but not a sound came. Her voice was trapped within her, strangled by the breath struggling to leave her lips. Every muscle in her body felt as if it had turned to stone, applying a crushing weight to her bones as if her body was working against itself to break her.

Her mind tingled as a pressure clutched its fist around the rear of her eyes. She leaned her back against the wall of the canyon, raking her fingers through the tangled mess which had become her hair. Her mind was a tornado of a thousand thoughts, passing by so quickly that it had become difficult to make out one thought from the next.

* * *

For a few hours Astra remained on the ground in a state of shock before she stood up and aimlessly wandered. What was she walking towards? She wasn't sure. She didn't want to have the burden of thinking, because to allow her mind to flow meant to allow an ocean of emotions to drown her.

The single path opened up to a labyrinth of different paths, winding and crossing through the canyon. Some of the paths led to dead ends while others led to new paths. Some were so narrow that she could hardly fit between the sides, while others were so spacious that it would have taken her a few minutes to walk from

41

one side to the other. The areas that were more spacious seemed to house more of the plants that stretched out their thorny vines in her direction any time she came within a few feet of them. Though most of the time she was good at avoiding the plants, there were several times that she would feel the sharp reminder of the dangers of this land when the branch of one of the plants would lash out and the tip would catch her skin. Though this was painful, luck was on her side. Each time the plants would try to capture her, she always managed to stay just out of reach. Every cut they left was a reminder to keep her distance.

She could feel the air around her as it heated rapidly and once again took off her jacket. At first the warm sunlight felt good against her shivering skin, but soon she discovered the frustration of trudging through the heavy slush the melting ice had created. With thick mud sticking to the bottom of her shoes and crawling over the top, each step felt as if she was being held back by a rubber band.

She ground her teeth together as she once again hit another dead end. Why were there so many paths that led nowhere?

The harsh rays of light beat down on her skin, burning her arms to a crisp red, while waves of heat slithered into the air. The once moist ground became dry and cracked. Droplets of sweat coated her forehead and soaked her back while the inside of her mouth felt like sticky sandpaper.

She scanned her surroundings with squinted eyes. Everything looked the same. All around her, smooth and sweeping walls were layered with different shades of reds and oranges, reminding her of layers inside of a cake. The paths she walked down were narrow and winding, with one boulder or plant looking like the other ten.

The sun cast shadows across the path as it made its way over the cloudless sky. The shadows deepened, giving moments of cool shade and protection from the harsh rays. She groaned as she hit yet another dead end and turned around to retrace her steps.

THUMP. Something heavy landed in the dirt behind her. She froze in place. What was that? The sound of a low growl crawled through the air, piercing her ears.

She curled her fingers into her palms and stared at the empty path in front of her. Astra longed to break into a run but needed to know what or who was behind her. She felt eyes burrowing through her, pulling at her soul. Swinging around, a lead weight dropped onto her stomach. No. Not this. Her screaming mind gazed into the raven eyes of a monster.

A smile cracked across his square face showing thousands of jagged teeth that seemed to move on its own. Chunky blood seeped from his mouth and dripped down his sharp jaw, staining the ground below him. His pointed ears twitched with every breath Astra took. It was as if he could hear even the smallest of sounds. Could he hear her heartbeat too?

He was about the height of a large mastiff and stood on all fours. He had three sharp claws impaled in the ground that were each several inches long. He had black leathery skin without fur of any kind and thick veins that weaved their way over his bulging muscles.

It was in that moment that everything came rushing back. This was one of the monsters who had taken her. The one who had crawled over her while pinning her against the wall. She did the only thing she could think of doing, run.

Her legs moved as fast as she could. She turned a corner and slipped on the dusty path before she jumped over a small jutting rock. Quickly she turned another sharp corner, attempting to navigate through this maze. Sliding between a crack in the cliff wall, she found another path that was narrow and covered in pieces of pale broken bones; remnants of creatures that had long since passed.

She swung her head around, facing an empty path and felt a morsel of relief but this relief was short-lived. The creature ripped around the corner and glared at her with glowing eyes full of determination.

She turned another corner, then another again, before finding herself at the end of the path, leading to a cave beside one of the plants that seemed to have a life of its own. She gazed into the black cave. The hole was as tall and wide as a three-story house. Though there was a chance that there was something else living in there, there was the reality that someone was chasing after her. She had no other choice but to take that chance.

Astra raced towards the cave when suddenly, she heard a growl echo from the darkness. She slid to a stop. Shit. There was another monster. Now she was trapped between two beasts. She swung her head towards the gap she ran through, her eyes falling upon the predator who was chasing her. He was blocking the only escape, while the other one was blocking her only hiding place. Backing up against the wall, her chest heaved. Where was she supposed to go?

The monster who had been hunting her approached with a smile etching over his face. With every step, his broad muscles flexed as his bladed claws sank into the dirt. He walked with the sort of confidence that an undefeated warrior would have.

"My wife and I have been searching for you. You slipped right out of my fingers. But we finally found you running like a rat trying to find her way through a maze. Don't you see? You won't escape from here."

"Why me? Why did you take me?" she spat out.

The beast cocked his head to the side. "Your species is a virus and you are the antibody fated to save both worlds. You are the change we need."

"What are you talking about?" She felt tears stinging her eyes as her back scraped against the wall.

"How are you so blind to the truth? Your destructive and narcissistic species is an abomination of existence," the beast's icy cold voice echoed as he spoke with a chilling calmness that made it seem like he could snap at any moment and bring down the entire canyon. "Your kind brings nothing but death and torment to all of those around you because of the insatiable lust for power ingrained within you. Humans are a disease that can only be cured through a cleansing of life. You deserve to be eaten alive, but I can't do that now, can I? No. You're a very special girl. Everyone of your kind deserves to be tortured and eradicated and you're going to help make that possible. You are coming with me."

"I don't want to come with you." She glanced towards the black cave. The other creature was just out of sight. "Just leave me. Please," she gasped. "Please don't hurt me."

"Oh," his voice cracked and his onyx eyes glistened. "Pain will be the least of your worries. By the time we are done with you, you will beg for death, but I promise, we won't give you that peace. We want you to suffer the way you made my people suffer."

"Don't take another step towards her," a deep raspy voice growled from the darkness.

The monster stopped in his tracks. His jackal ears twitched with the sound of the voice. Snapping his head towards the darkness, a large clot of blood dripped from his lips as the tentacles in his ears rapidly moved around.

"Who do you think you are to threaten me? Do you know who I am?" the beast growled as he spat another glob of blood onto the ground.

"I know who you are, Sidero, and I do not fear you. Where is your wife, Prosperine?"

A creature the color of a storm cloud and twice the size of a grizzly bear stepped out of the cave. His hollow eyes looked almost soulless as he glared at Sidero, baring razor blade teeth almost seven inches in length that could easily peel muscle off bone. This monster was made of pure muscle and had a massive head with a mouth big enough to easily fit two human heads inside. He had slits for nostrils and a hole on each side of his thick skull. Dripping from his pale gums, a yellow substance fell onto the ground, blackening anything it touched.

Sidero's eyes lit up as he glanced towards the top of the canyon, "Vojin," he hissed. "I should have recognized that voice. Do I need to remind you we still believe in the same cause? You have already done enough damage. I'll show you mercy, because of the time you came to my aid. But you know better than to cross me. If you dare try to help this monster, it will be considered treason and I will have no other choice but to execute you."

As the last words left his lips, the beast snapped his head towards her. With extended claws and an open jaw, Sidero lunged. Her stomach lurched to her throat. She braced for the impact but just as he was about to collide with her, Vojin slammed against him, knocking him out of the way.

Roaring, Sidero slid to a halt and swung around, his black eyes turning blood red.

"How dare you."

The stranger cracked his neck as he glanced towards Astra.

"Did he hurt you?" he growled looking down at the bloody scarf wrapped around her leg. "Did he do that to you?"

"I don't know," she whispered, touching her aching wound. "I woke up with it."

Sidero's eyes burned into the monster in front of him.

"You care about this evil?" he snapped. "After what her kind did to us, to our planet and to her own? After everything you have seen them be capable of?" Shaking in rage, he could barely speak as more blood slipped from between his teeth. "You traitor."

Both of the monsters lunged at each other, tearing away their enemy's flesh upon impact. Dodging every bite, Sidero hooked his claws into Vojin's flesh, ripping open his skin.

As if God himself was holding her prisoner, she stood paralyzed. Her mind screamed for her to run but her legs wouldn't let her. *Who was winning?*

Every inch of her body shook as the bigger monster sank his claws into Sidero's back and flung his head towards him in an attempt to bite. Before his teeth could make impact, Sidero hooked his claws into the beast's face and rammed his head into the side of the cliff wall, breaking open the skin on his skull.

Sidero pounded his claws into the monster's throat, shredding the skin till the top layer looked more like spaghetti squash.

Right as Sidero threw his head towards the beast's neck, with teeth ready to tear, Vojin bit down on his arm.

"NNOOOOOOO!" The sound of a woman's scream echoed through the canyon.

Astra looked up towards a jutting rock just fifty feet above them. There, standing on the rock, was the other monster that had taken her. She stood on two legs with her scorpion tail resting beside her. Her fingers from all six of her hands were cupped over her mouth and the expression she wore on her face made it obvious that she did not expect Vojin's actions.

Prosperine lowered her hands. "Why? You were our friend. Why would you betray us like this?"

Her knees crumbled to the ground as her eyes remained glued onto her loved one. Reaching her quivering fingers out towards Sidero, the image of her body began to flicker. She was a hologram. She must have been watching the fight as it happened from a different location.

Sidero suddenly stopped, his eyes widened as he stumbled back. The wound on his arm sizzled and bubbled, splitting open his skin even wider.

"I told you not to touch her," he growled as he took a step away from Sidero and towards Astra. "You don't touch what's mine."

"My beautiful love." Prosperine covered her face with her hands as she let out a gut-wrenching sob. In the moment Astra heard this noise, she felt a taste of Prosperine's pain, radiating through her core. "You will regret this," she whispered, holding onto her chest before disappearing into the wind.

Sidero screamed as his skin bubbled up. The boils grew larger until they burst open, releasing what looked like hot steam. He collapsed on the ground with his eyes bursting from his skull, leaving trails of red streaming down his face. Coughing up blood and chunks of his meaty insides, Sidero gasped for a burbling breath of air, before his head sank to the ground.

The monster walked over to his fresh kill. He tore open Sidero's chest with his teeth before thrusting his claw into the corpse and ripping out the heart. Lifting it to his mouth, he tore into it, snorting and munching as he chewed and swallowed its flesh. Once he had done so, the skin around his wounds weaved itself together, forming a fresh layer and leaving no trace that he was ever hurt.

Vojin turned towards Astra and approached. Every step he took left a trail of bloody footprints in his path. Was he going to kill her the way he just killed that beast?

"Please! Stay away from me!"

Her head snapped to the cave. It was only a few feet away but there was no telling how deep it was or if it led to a dead end. Even if it was deep enough for her to temporarily hide from him, he was surely able to navigate through the darkness better than she ever would. In order to return back to the path she was on in the first place, she would have to go through him and by how quickly he was able to move, she knew she could never outrun him.

Vojin was massive and seemingly more so, the closer he got. His presence was suffocating. Having leathery charcoal skin and a square muscular body, he seemed to have strength beyond any creature on Earth. The beast in front of her made gargoyles look as tender as a pup and he walked like a victorious warrior after battle.

He opened his mouth, revealing a row of teeth, still dripping in the blood of his fresh kill. Some of these teeth were the length of her hand while others were longer and serrated on the inside. Vojin licked his lips with a snake-like tongue and shook his body, splattering residual blood on the sides of the smooth canyon.

He cocked his head to the side and glared at her with deep set eyes. She felt like he was visually devouring her.

"I am not going to hurt you," he said with a slow nod as he took a step back. Vojin's eyes rolled into the back of his head as his bones cracked and melted together. The beast stood on two legs, his spine shortening, as short dark hair grew on the top of his head. Within seconds she was no longer standing in front of a monster, but instead a man with piercing dark eyes and a grayish complexion. "I'm here to help you."

Her mind had become a maelstrom, twisting and turning till every thought felt like an unrecognizable blur. Who was this man? What was he? Her mind screamed not to trust the monster in front of her.

With a sharp rock, he made a small incision on his arm and dipped his fingers into the blood. He approached her and kneeled down beside her, his muscles flexing naturally with every movement.

"Give me your leg," he gently said with a nod.

She looked down at the crusty cloth wrapped around her thigh. What did he want with her?

"What are you going to do?"

"You need my blood. You're hurt and your wound is infected. I can smell it. You don't want sepsis to set in," he said, pointing to her leg.

"I also don't want a bloodborne disease," she said as she covered her leg with her hand and winced as her fingers caressed the top of the scarf.

Vojin sighed and took a step back, "There are no bloodborne diseases on this planet." He narrowed his eyes and hid a smile. "I only want to help you. I promise I won't do anything that causes you harm. The blood here is different from what you are used to. Will you trust me to help you with your wound?"

Trust him? He just tore apart a predator in the form of something horrific, only to turn into a human. The monster he ripped apart claimed they both were fighting for the same cause. Did he turn on his own friend? If he was fighting for the same cause, did that mean that he also saw her as a virus? Vojin seemed to be a man who had no sense of loyalty. He could turn in an instant and do the same to her as he did to that beast. Did she now owe him her life? Was that why he claimed that she was his?

"I don't know you and yet you expect me to trust you?" her voice quivered. "You-you're a monster. I saw you kill that thing in front of me. You both knew each other!"

Her heart raced inside of her as she stared down at the corpse, imagining her future fate. Speaking about it made it feel like it was happening all over again.

"That person you just called "a thing" was the right hand of Cadoc, so we should show some respect when we speak of him, even though he has passed away. Trust me when I say that his intentions were likely less than favorable toward you. Sidero had a reputation and he was the kind of person you do not want to cross. You're afraid and that is perfectly understandable. You have reasons to be afraid," he said as he sat down in front of her, morphing back into his original monstrous form. "But please know that any enemy of yours is now an enemy of mine."

Vojin looked down at the ground. He grabbed a rock the length of her hand and effortlessly carved into the stone with his claws as if it was made of butter. Gently and quickly he scooped away at the object until it formed the shape of a handle. Once he was finished, he set the handle down in front of him.

This massive beast opened his mouth. Reaching inside, he grabbed one of his sharpest teeth and took a breath in. Blood seeped from the monster's lips as he rocked the tooth back and forth.

What was he doing? She wanted to tell him to stop, but her words were trapped in her throat. Finally, with a loud, CRACK, he pulled the long tooth from his gum.

The beast clenched his eyes as he reached deep inside his mouth and into his body. He gasped. Astra cringed. Hot bile crawled up her throat as his hand bulged though his hollow chest.

She wanted to turn away, but her eyes were locked in place like a prisoner shackled to the view before her. She could see the skin moving underneath his chest and with a burst of blood, he pulled out a long, thick yellow vein. Grabbing the handle he'd created from the rock, he pounded the tooth into one end before reinforcing the object by wrapping the vein around the bone. He then weaved it through the hollow tooth before dropping it down on the ground.

"Now you have a knife to help keep you safe out here," he said in a weak voice. He wiped the blood off his chin with the back of his paw. "If you squeeze the vein, a highly toxic poison will come out of it and cover the tooth. If you use the poison too much, you will run out and vein will dry out. The weapon will still be useful. I am immune to my own poison but if I were to ever attack you, punch the tooth as hard as you can into my temple. It will kill me. Keep this in mind with all of your attackers. Whatever you do, don't touch the poison or your fate will look similar to Sidero's."

She looked at the remains of her attacker. The bubbling pool of flesh and organs made the beast unrecognizable compared to how he once was. By now, the poison had begun to liquify his bones, leaving no solid form behind.

Standing on his hind legs, Vjoin's bones once again made crunching and cracking sounds as he formed back into a man. Leaning over, he reached down and picked up the weapon, tossing it at her feet. The knife was several inches long with an orange stone handle. Though one side was smooth, the other was slightly serrated with small holes around the base and between the serrated edges. The vein was wrapped three times around the weapon and the poison sloshed within it.

"Do you trust me now enough to at least help you?"

Astra gazed at him in his human form, trying to determine whether or not she could trust him. He was naked, standing in front of her with no weapon in hand. His once serrated teeth had formed into flat surfaces and his claws had become short nails nestled at the tips of long fingers. He was muscular, with a strong jaw and striking features that reminded her of someone out of a magazine. Though he could change at any moment, she knew if he was close, she would have enough time to plunge the dagger

51

deep into his temple. It took at least thirty seconds for him to return to his monstrous state and it would only take a moment for her to end his life with the weapon he had made from his tooth.

She picked up the knife and held it close. Though she had never had to use a weapon before, she knew this was the kind of place where she would have no other choice but to learn. Nodding, she glanced down and flinched as he came closer.

Vojin kneeled down and gently unwrapped the knot which had been holding the cloth tightly against her leg. A radiating pain emanated through her leg as he pulled the scarf off and placed it back around her neck. The wound was wet with pus and surrounded by swelling skin.

She flinched as he wiped the blood over her wound. Almost instantly, the puss melted away and her skin weaved itself together, leaving no evidence the wound was ever there.

"How did you do that?"

"The blood here, it heals. With wounds that are not as deep, you can get away with just applying it topically. But if you have something deeper, you might want to make sure that you drink some of it," he said as his lips moved smoothly across his white teeth before forming a perfect smile. "Larger creatures need to eat the heart. You're small though," he chuckled. "You can get away with just a little taste."

"That sounds really vampiric."

Vojin laughed and shook his head. "There is a difference between mankind's stories depicting the undead and the reality of those who are very much alive and just in need of some healing."

She swallowed the rock that had formed in the back of her throat. Slowly her eyes crawled up the body of the chiselled man who stood in front of her. How did he look so much like a human now but was monstrous before?

"So how do you really look like?" she stared at the shape shifter.

"What do you mean?"

Her eyes lowered as she took a slow breath in. "I've seen you take two different forms. Which one are you? Are you a man or you know… the other."

"You have seen my original form. I can change into whatever form I wish, but the way I was born is my strongest."

"So, if you are weaker as a man, why are you one right now?"

"Because you looked like you were about to pee on yourself and this form is less intimidating. Trust me when I tell you that this is not the form that I would want to be in on this planet. I mean look at me, I have paper thin skin right now and my teeth are flat and weak. What am I going to do with these short nails? Slap someone to death with my nubs?"

"People kill people all the time."

"True, but if you put an unarmed human against even a weakling here, the chances the human would survive would be slim."

"But what are my chances now that you made me a weapon?"

"Higher than they were before you had it," Vojin cackled.

She gazed at her surroundings. The cliffs that stood around her seemed ominously high which made her feel so much smaller than she already felt. Scattered throughout the walls, random rocks stuck out like shelves.

"Where am I?" she asked, hiding behind her hair and wishing she could disappear. "How dangerous is this place?"

"You're on Pannotia and it is safer if you are not a human."

"Well I am a human so that really doesn't bring me any comfort now, does it? Where is that anyway? I've never heard of that place."

"Let's just say we are far enough away from your planet, that you don't know we exist, yet close enough that we can watch you."

"What?" She shook her head with confusion. "Why am I even here? What do they want with me?"

"They want to use you to help create a more sustainable Earth by eliminating mankind. For some reason, Cadoc is convinced that you are the key to opening a gate, which is why they brought you here. Prosperine and Sidero were going to bring you to him."

"What gate? What are you talking about?"

"It is a gate that can only be opened with the key. Once it is opened, it will allow Cadoc's army to eliminate mankind." He smiled, "How did you get here, Astra? Do you remember anything?"

How did he know her name? She stared into his eyes, almost afraid to ask. He knew her. She didn't know him, but he knew her.

"I never told you my name," her voice cracked.

"You didn't need to."

"Are you responsible for this? Is that why you are asking me if I remember anything?" She held the weapon tighter.

"Breathe," he said with twinkling eyes. "You need to just take a breath and calm down."

"I am trying. I'm trying to calm down, but I don't think I can."

"Don't worry about the small things like how I know your name. That isn't important. Am I responsible for you being here? I wouldn't say I was. Cadoc was the one who wanted you here and his followers did nothing more than obey his command. The only thing you need to worry about right now is staying alive."

She nodded her head. "You're right. I'm sorry. I'm just scared."

"No shit. You don't know this place and your presence isn't the most welcomed one," Vojin smiled. "It's okay to be scared but remember this, if you want to stay alive on this planet, you cannot trust anyone."

"Even you?"

"Not even me," he replied. "I need you to promise me that you will stay on your guard at all times. I need you to promise me that you will never give up and keep fighting for your survival."

"Why do you care? Why are you helping me?"

"Do I need a reason to help someone in need?"

"Yeah, you do," she replied, crossing her arms.

Vojin playfully smacked her on the arm, "See? That's the kind of distrust I was talking about! You are going to do just fine here."

"Um, that hurt."

"Just helping you toughen up little lady," he said as he made his way into the cave.

"Where are you going?"

"It's getting dark and we need to sleep before we get started tomorrow."

"Get started where?" she asked as she followed him.

"We need to get you to a safer area."

CHAPTER 5

Astra sat in the light of a snapping fire, enjoying the stinging warmth as it pinched her skin. She leaned against a large stalagmite and stretched out her limbs. In front of her, Vojin placed more wood upon the flames—wood that he had collected from a thorn bush only an hour before.

The fire on this planet burned a little bit differently than it did on Earth. It seemed to produce very little smoke and though the tops of the flames were orange, the bottom of them glowed a shade of pale pink.

It was already dark in Pannotia and even darker in the cave to which they had walked deep enough into so that the light from the fire would not be seen from the outside by any curious eyes that passed by.

As soon as the sun had set, the land seemed to come alive. Every few minutes a distant howl or scream would echo through the canyon, bouncing off the walls and making it hard to tell which direction it was coming from or exactly how far away they were.

Where was Prosperine? She seemed so betrayed after she watched Sidero die. Would she come back here in the dead of night and kill them while they slept?

What did Sidero mean when he called her a virus? What was he intending to do with her? How was he planning on using her to open this gate and what would he do if he found out that she wasn't the key? She knew whatever it was, it was bad.

"Did you enjoy the food?" Vojin's voice snapped her from her thoughts.

She looked down at the remnants of plants she had just eaten. Her stomach was filled and her thirst quenched.

She nodded. "I am pretty sure that was about the best damn meal I have ever eaten. Thank you for gathering those for me. Where did you get them anyway? It seems so barren out here."

"It's only barren if you don't know where to look."

"Can I ask you something?"

"You can ask me whatever you want. It doesn't mean I will answer it but feel free to ask anyway."

"What did you mean when you said to that monster, not to touch what is yours? Am I your prisoner now?"

He rolled his twinkling eyes as he crossed his arms. "You do realize that we are not the monster? You are."

"That's ridiculous. I'm not a monster."

"To most of the species on Earth, you absolutely are."

"Well we are not on Earth so why would your kind see mine as a monster?"

"That is a long story. Your species is viewed as being one of the most evil in existence by even people on Pannotia. You are our biggest enemy."

"How did we become your enemy? We aren't even from the same planet."

"That is a story I will explain when it isn't this late at night," Vojin yawned. He morphed his body back into his original form. "Come here. You are safer if you remain close to me."

Her cheeks burned and eyes watered. Why did he change back? What was he planning?

"Why did you change form?" she asked as she touched the knife at her side.

Vojin rolled his eyes and shrugged. "Because you are not going to want to wait for me to change out of my human form if someone sneaks up on us at night. During the day, I can see any attacks coming. At night, I need to be prepared for the worst. If you stay close to me, I can protect you easier."

"Why are you protecting me?"

"Because you remind me of someone I used to know."

"Who?"

Vojin's eyes lowered. "Someone I lost long ago but if it's okay with you, I don't want to get into that."

"I understand, but how do I know you are not going to attack me? How do I know you are not just saying this to get me to put my guard down?"

"If I wanted to attack you, I would have already done it," Vojin replied as he rolled his massive body over on his side.

"How do you change form? Am I able to do that too now that I'm here? Is there a technology or something?"

"No, there is no technology to help," he chuckled. "I can shapeshift into whatever form I choose because of evolutionary traits. It's the perk of being a Besnik."

"A Besnik?"

"It's my species. Human's call us demons but we are actually called Besniks."

"You're a demon? If you are a demon and you live here," she could barely get out the last words, "Is this hell?"

"Hey," Vojin said with a gentle voice as his eyes softened. "Calm those thoughts. I am not a demon. Human's call us that because they slap a label onto anything they don't understand. This place is far too beautiful to have such a horrible name tied to it."

"But you're called a demon and I was always taught that demons live in hell and are evil. Are you telling me what I was taught was wrong?"

Vojin nodded his head. "Your religion has tarnished your mind. Just because you were taught something, doesn't make it true. You have to question the information that you are fed. Especially stories that have been told by power hungry men with political agendas, who use religion as a way to control the masses through fear."

"Does this mean there is no heaven or hell? Is there no God? Was everything I believed in, a lie?"

"There is eternal paradise and there is a place of punishment, but it is far different from the stories your species have come up with to explain the unexplainable and yes, there

58

are higher beings. The place of punishment is a place of justice. The only evil that resides in that place comes in the form of those who are punished. Paradise, from what I have been told, is a place where those that are truly good reside. There are a few judges who determine who will go to which place."

"Are there demons who live there?"

"You could say that, but they are not evil. They are nothing more than justice seekers, making sure that no crime goes unpunished."

Shadows danced across the walls. The dark outlines created ominous shapes, far bigger than the objects that stood in the way of the light. Though the hot fire reached its flames up to the ceiling of the cave, she felt cold.

"This all makes no sense to me. You are telling me that you are called a demon, but you are not a demon and that is just something that religions have come up with. Then you tell me that there are demons, but they are not bad. So, what part did religion come up with if demons exist?"

Vojin smiled, "Come here, lay down and I will tell you what you want to know. Consider it a bedtime story."

She squinted her eyes and crossed her arms. "What am I, five now?"

"No, but you're going to be sleepy like a five-year-old by midday if you don't start resting soon."

She sighed and walked over to the beast. Curling up in a ball, she leaned against his stomach and put her cheek on his chest. His warm heat throbbed against her face, bringing her a strange sort of comfort.

"Okay, now explain," she said with a yawn.

"There are certain species here that watch humans through a different plane of existence. It is parallel to your own. When religion first began on your planet, mankind thought that these creatures who came in the form of shadows, were demons. They were not. They were watchers.

"Religion was formed to explain the unexplainable and to control others through fear. It had very little to do with being a good person and more to do with creating a nation of individuals who would do what their leaders commanded. They wanted them to think the way their leaders wanted them to think, using the crutch of a religion to enforce these views and laws. No matter how heinous the commands would become, people felt justified to do the unjustifiable just because they believed their 'god' told them to do it."

$$* * *$$

Astra woke to a soft nudge on her shoulder. She curled her nose as the aroma of something sweet caressed her senses. The cave was dimly lit by a small crack found on the top of the ceiling, close to her head. Her legs felt warm now that they were close to the smouldering ashes of what was once a fire. She looked into the dark eyes of the one who'd saved her. He was squatting in front of her with a round, prickly fruit in his hand.

Astra rubbed her eyes, trying to get them adjusted to the dim light of the cave. All around her, stalagmites and stalactites clung onto the surfaces. Each formation slowly fed the other with small droplets of mineral rich water. There were some that had become thick columns, while others looked more like tiny spikes clinging onto the walls.

"I know you're used to eating breakfast, so when you were sleeping, I dug this up."

"How did you know that I eat breakfast?" she wearily asked before she took the food from his fingers. Her stomach grumbled.

"Because I have studied your kind."

Shrugging her shoulders, she smiled, "Learn anything interesting?"

"Only that you are a weird species."

She chuckled, "How so?"

"Well your species likes to decorate beaches, forests, and virtually anything that is naturally beautiful, with trash. You enjoy sitting in front of a box containing flashing lights for hours, watching other people's lives, instead of going out and living your own life. You eat virtually anything that is edible, even at the cost of your own health. Every year you make a list of goals on the first of the year but never seem to follow through with those goals, and in your culture, you ask people how they are doing but most of the time, don't even mean it. It's just a weird way of saying hello and if anyone answers the question honestly, things get awkward."

"First of all, there is nothing more relaxing than to watch other people's fake lives unleash their drama onto other people on the television. Second of all, my new year's goal this year was to lose five pounds and exercise more often and I am pretty sure that by the end of this "vacation," I will have met both of those goals. For the rest of the stuff you mentioned, I have no excuses for those. We are kind of weird."

"See? That's what I mean. You are a strange species," he chuckled.

She sank her teeth into the surface of the fruit, enjoying the sweet and tangy taste that burst into her mouth. It was by far the best fruit she'd ever had.

Pulling off some of the juicy flesh, she handed it to Vojin. "I don't want you to be hungry."

"Thank you," he smiled. "But I rarely ever need to eat. You on the other hand, require regular feedings."

"Well you are missing out. This fruit tastes like the love child of a strawberry and a kiwi."

"What?"

"Only the two best fruits on my planet."

Wiping the juices from her jaw, she slurped up the remaining fruit before setting down the seed. Vojin immediately picked up the seed, dug a small hole in the ground and buried it.

"What did you do that for?"

"Why waste a seed? The next person who spends the night in this cave might be hungry. I want to make sure that they are fed too." She smiled as she looked at the man in front of her.

"What's that smile for?" he asked with a twinkle in his eyes.

"No reason," she shrugged, hiding behind her hair as she looked down at the ground where the seed was buried.

* * *

Vojin and Astra walked for hours through the maze of the canyon. The air was hot but not as hot as it was yesterday. She wiped the sweat off her brow as she looked up at blue heavens cut in half by the thick lines in the sky.

"Are those rings?"

Vojin glanced up. "Yes, they are."

She thought of her father. What was he doing? Was he okay? She couldn't imagine that he was, and the thought of how distraught he must be, made a pain shoot through her stomach.

"Vojin," she said as she nibbled on her lip and looked at him.

Vojin turned his head and raised his brow. "What is it? Are you okay?"

Astra's heart sank even lower as she thought about her father. Did he think she was murdered? She imagined him finding a way to contact her uncle and rushing to her apartment, only to find an empty room. Would he feel guilty? Would he blame himself for her death the way she blamed herself for her mother's death? It was hard enough for him to lose someone he loved so dearly but now his daughter too? She needed to get back home. She needed to let him know she was still alive.

"I think my father thinks I was murdered," she said, touching her chest as she tried to find the right words to say.

"I am sorry to hear that. I know from experience how hard it is to go through life knowing that you lost a loved one. This must be very painful for him."

"I'm sure it is. But he doesn't have to live with that pain if there is a way back for me. Is there a way I can get back home?"

"Yes, but I have to figure out a safe way to get you back. Right now, it's too dangerous for you out here. That is why we need to get you to a safer area first. I'll leave you with my friend.

He is the one person I trust the most on this planet. I know he'll care for you like you were his child and will protect you, even at the cost of his life. That's where we are heading."

"Wait, you're leaving me with a stranger?" Her jaw clenched so tightly, she thought her teeth would crack.

"I am bringing you to my friend who I trust. You have nothing to fear, I promise."

"You told me not even to trust you and now you're telling me that I'm about to be given up. How do I know you aren't going to give me to the people who kidnapped me in the first place?" Her fingers shook as she thought back to Prosperine. Though Sidero was dead, she wasn't sure how many others were searching for her and planning on bringing her to Cadoc.

"If I wanted to give you back to the people who took you in the first place, why would I kill one of them? I would have just let him take you. That would have been easier for me."

She nodded her head. "I'm sorry, I'm just on edge."

"And I want you to stay that way. You can't trust anyone, not even if they look like you. I want you to live. I want to help you get back home."

"So how am I going to get back home? What do you need to figure out?"

"There is a door on the other side of the world. It's a pretty long journey and a dangerous one too. I need to figure out how to get you there alive and undetected, but that's the easy part. The difficult part comes with getting you through the door undetected and finding an opening that will allow you to cross over from our planet onto yours."

"Has anyone ever found an opening?"

"A few have, which is why you have stories like Medusa. The stories of myths claiming monsters once were or are roaming the lands, are just lost people trying to find their way back home."

She chuckled and raised her brow. "So, you are telling me that a woman with snakes on her head was a real thing?"

"She didn't have snakes on her head, but I can see why people would have thought that since her hair looked similar to it. The story behind her was made up but she was not," Vojin sighed. "She was actually a sweetheart. Unfortunately, she was murdered by your people."

"According to the legend, she turned people into stone. That doesn't sound like a sweetie to me," she shrugged.

"The legend was not entirely wrong, but the real story was twisted to make her look like a villain when she was actually the victim."

"How so?"

"She was just studying mankind and she accidentally fell through an opening which quickly closed up behind her as soon as she fell through. I was there, but on the other side. I tried to help her get out by finding another one. Openings are very rare and difficult to determine when and where they will happen." Vojin looked off into the distance. "I couldn't get to her in time."

"What was she like?" she wondered. "What happened to her?"

"She was a peaceful person, a good mother, and loyal to those she loved. Despite the distain that so many have for mankind, she was not one of them. Medusa believed that mankind had good in them, despite their evil tendencies. She felt as though they were misunderstood.

"When she fell through the opening, she fell into a busy market square. She tried to calm the people down around her, but they started screaming that she was a creature of hell. When they became aggressive, she became afraid and ran.

"She was hunted down like a wild animal and her last defence was to turn some of her attackers temporally into stone. But there were too many of them and they ripped her apart using animals as weapons. When they were done with her body, they cut off her head and gave it to the king. He preserved it in cedar oil to display as a bragging right."

"Why did they kill her if she wasn't harming anyone?"

"Because humans on Earth would kill anything that they are not comfortable looking at or being around, no matter the innocence," Vojin replied. "Even their own kind."

*** * ***

Astra gazed upon the walls of the canyon as they climbed up a mountain slope. The red rocked walls had given way to green vines, bushes and trees. It had taken a few weeks before they finally got to this lush area. All around her, ancient trees with thin curling bark and a dense canopy loomed over her head, protecting her from the sun's harsh rays. Below her, an emerald ribbon of water curled through the gorge, drinking from the white waterfall tumbling from the heavens.

During the day, they traveled through the twisting paths of the canyon. As soon as the night fell upon the land, they would find a place to sleep for the night. Sometimes it was behind a large rock, while other times it would be in a cave.

For the most part, they didn't cross any other dangerous creatures. When they did, they would hide behind a boulder until it passed, before continuing down their path.

Astra's legs ached from traveling up and down the steep terrain. Her swollen feet begged for a full day's rest but Vojin wouldn't allow it.

"You'll be there soon enough and then you can rest for a few weeks. My friend will take good care of you." He smiled and shook his head.

There were times he took pity on her and would morph back to his original form when he saw her begin to limp. He would wipe his healing blood over her blistered feet and allow her to climb on his back for an hour or two while he walked, just to give her a moment's rest.

"Am I too heavy? If I am, I understand. My feet are fine now that you healed them. I'm a bit tired but I can walk."

"No, you're not too heavy and you need to rest a bit before you continue by foot," he nodded.

Astra rocked back and forth as Vojin climbed up the mountain. Closing her eyes, she felt a cool breeze gently push her hair behind her shoulder. To get a moment's rest felt like heaven to her aching muscles.

Gazing up at the canopy, she saw small creatures with a hooked face and bulbous eyes, jumping from limb to limb, watching them from above. They chattered to each other in a strange tongue, nodding their heads before hiding behind clusters of golden leaves.

"Are these creatures dangerous," she asked as one of them pushed another off their branch.

"No. They are talkative but never dangerous. In fact, they have no idea what kind of a creature you are. They are not the most intelligent beings and though they have been exposed to the war, they still don't understand it."

"What war?"

Vojin abruptly stopped and twisted his head to the side, glaring at the sky with hollow shark eyes. She gazed down at the beast she sat upon. Vojin's neck cracked. His lips raised above his serrated teeth. For a moment he looked like a statue carved by the hands of Lucifer.

"Get off of me," he growled.

Quickly, she slid from the side of his back. "Did I do something wrong? Should I not have asked about the war? I'm sorry if I offended you or—"

"Shut up," he snarled as he turned to face her. "Do not say another word. Do you hear me?"

She nodded her head. Was this it? Was this the moment he turned on her? With shaking fingers, she slid her hand into her pocket and felt the handle of the weapon.

Astra wasn't sure if she was ready to use this and to use it against someone she thought was her ally. It felt unnatural. Would she hit him in his temple in time? She knew he was able to move with blinding speed and now that he was already in his natural form, there would be little chance she would move quickly enough to even make a paper cut upon his flesh.

"Get your hand out of your pocket and leave the weapon there until you absolutely need it," the beast took a step towards her.

She took a step back, raising her hands in the air to show that she was unarmed. "Please. Please don't hurt me."

"When I tell you to run, I want you to run. Run as fast as you can up this mountain and to the other side. Do not look back, no matter what you hear." As Vojin spoke, droplets of poison flew from his lips, blackening the leaves of the plants in front of him. "I will find you. Stay hidden. Stay safe and follow the brightest star in the sky. It will get you to where you need to be."

"Hello Vojin," Prosperine said in a bone chilling voice behind Astra.

"Run." As the words left Vojin's lips, the beast jumped over her head, colliding with the monster behind her.

Her heart lurched in her throat as the mixed sound of roaring and screaming exploded in the air. As she rushed up the mountain she heard the cracking of a tree as the monsters slammed into its bark. With a thunder, the tree came tumbling down, its canopy scratching the back of her legs. That was close, too close.

"Don't look back," she repeated to herself like a mantra while begging her aching body to move faster. Ducking under another branch, she took a fast turn, jumping over the roots of a tree as she continued to run up the mountain.

Astra couldn't move fast enough. She could see the peak of the mountain beckoning her to come to it, reaching its arms out like a mother to her child.

Her legs flew across fallen logs. She ducked underneath low hanging branches, before she jumped over several large rocks. Her screaming mind silenced her lips, only allowing the sharp wind of her gasping breath to rush in and out of her.

She pushed herself onto a rock and climbed the large stones as fast as she could. The sun attempted to light her path, brightening itself as a cloud moved away from its yolk body.

Crossing over the peak, she weaved between trees and stumbled over stones before making her way down a thin path. Though the sounds of the beasts fighting grew fainter, she felt as though they were just as loud as when they had first begun.

She felt the sting of the bark as she scraped by a tree and the ache of her lungs as they sucked in another mouthful of air. Her head swung behind her. There was nothing but forest and it was in that moment she regretted not listening to Vojin's warning, to not look back.

Her body twisted, then her foot slipped out from underneath her. It was in that moment that time seemed to slow down. She felt her body fall backwards and the sensation of the wind ripping through her hair. She felt the way the air rushed between her fingers as she grabbed onto nothingness and the way her muscles stretched around her bulging eyes. For a moment, she could have sworn her heart stopped beating, until the wind was punched from her lungs by the rocks her body bounced off of.

She tried to scream but not a sound came from her lips. She tried to grab onto the ground to slow herself down but felt her nails instantly bend back, ripping from her tender nail bed. She was falling down the mountain and could hardly slow herself down.

"OH GOD, OH GOD!" her mind shrieked repeatedly.

Finally, with a firm THUD, her body skidded to a stop. A puff of dust circled around her while coating her body with its residue. She lay on her back, trying to catch a breath of air, which proved to be difficult to do as her lungs no longer wanted to fully inflate.

"Astra… Astra," the sound of her mother's voice whispered through the wind forcing her eyes to flutter open, but she was greeted by only the sight of the sun shining through the brown branches of a tree.

She lay on the dirt ground which was scattered with sticks and rocks. They poked into her soft flesh. The leaves of the tree danced in the wind as it pushed the thin branches back and forth. As it did so, tiny beams of light opened and shut, leaving an abstract design on the ground.

Her temples throbbed. Every muscle in her body felt like it had been forced through a grinder. Slow and shallow, her breath slipped from her nostrils while her fingers and eyelids were the only things she could move.

"Hey over here!"

Faintly she heard a male voice fading in and out with the breeze. She wanted nothing more than to turn her head so she could see who this person was, but she found that her muscles refused to cooperate. Now more than ever, even doing the simple task of opening her eyes had become a challenge.

"Alek! Get over here! I found her, and she's really hurt!" the voice called out in a slightly scratchy tone.

She looked up and saw the blurry outline of what she could have sworn was a man. Was this another Besnik who had changed form?

"What's wrong with her? Did they attack her?" Another voice responded with urgency. "Should I grab the herbs?"

"Grab everything," he desperately replied as he bent down and tended to her wounds.

Even though he was close to her, he sounded as if he was miles away. From the little bit that she could see, she could tell he was tall with a muscular build and pale skin. For some reason his eyes looked unnaturally large and dark but she couldn't quite tell if that was just her blurred vision fooling her.

She closed her eyes and felt the sensation of warm blood trickling from her nostril and down her lip as the vibration of another pair of footsteps approached. *Who were these people and what did they want with her?*

"Oh God, oh God," she faintly heard the voice of another man seep into her ears.

"Alek, this doesn't look good, look at this… When I pull apart her eyelids, the whites of her eyes are red," he said with distress, before her consciousness faded into the darkness.

CHAPTER 6

When Astra woke up, the first thing she saw was a single wispy cloud, making its way across the sky. Where was she? She could see she was being dragged on a mat by a man with long dark hair, who was accompanied by another man with shorter hair. Her fingers grazed across the threads. It wasn't soft at all. It was itchy and coarse, made out of what appeared to be woven grass.

Who were these two men and what did they want with her? They didn't seem to notice she had woken up since they were walking in front of her.

The one who was dragging her seemed to be less muscular and was a bit shorter than the one walking beside him. He had an old leather bracelet strapped to his wrist that reminded her of something she would see at a gift shop. She wasn't sure if she was seeing right but she could swear the man dragging her was unnaturally pale, while the other one, from what she could see, appeared to be normal.

Astra was surrounded by emerald grass that stood on top of rolling hills. Though there weren't many clouds above her head, she could see on the mountainous horizon, there was a thunderstorm brewing. With the exception of grass, the land was void of a diverse amount of plant life. There were no trees, bushes, or flowers anywhere.

What was that smell? It reminded her of stale meat and body odor. Was that her or was that coming from the mat?

The hot sun beat its unforgiving rays down on her face while her body rocked back and forth on a coarse, unstable surface. Thoughts circled around in her mind as she felt a droplet of salty sweat roll down her cheek.

She felt like a prisoner trapped in her own body. She couldn't move and could hardly breathe. Her head had become a snare drum that pounded on and on, while her body felt like a voodoo doll subjected to thousands of needles.

Every breath she took released an explosion of pain, making her want to breathe as little as possible. Sometimes the only relief she could get from this pain was by holding her breath until her body screamed for the release.

The air around her felt different. It even smelled different. Although the sun was strong, it was nowhere nearly as strong as it once was.

Her ears twitched at the muffled sound of running water that gradually became louder. She looked over and saw a small creek just a short walk away. As she moved her tongue around her jaw, her body screamed for some of this substance. The sound of the liquid splashing against the rocks tormented her. It called out her name, causing the need for this precious liquid to become amplified.

Her mind raced as she tried to figure out how she could get some of this element inside of her. She longed for it so much that she could almost taste it. Mustering every ounce of strength she had, she opened her mouth ever so slightly and made a small squeaking noise from the back of her scratchy throat. She winced as the movement of her mouth caused her lips to split open.

How long had she been out for? She felt a cool breeze raise goosebumps over her skin as she closed her eyes for a moment. Concentrating with every ounce of strength she had within her, she tried to move her arms and legs but could only feel her toes and fingers twitch. A wave of exhaustion washed over her muscles and mind, weighing them down like bricks. She wanted nothing more than to allow her body to slip back into sleep, but she couldn't let that happen. She needed water.

Astra felt her body slow to a stop and then came the sound of shuffling, first leaving her side and then approaching. How was she going to get their attention? She wanted to scream, "I'm awake!" She wanted to flail her arms and beg for them to bring her water. She longed to feel it slip down her throat and loosen her tight stomach.

Opening her lips, she attempted another sound but this time she mouthed the word, "water."

"Hey, look at who is finally coming to," a man's voice softly cooed as he sat down beside her. "You are a fighter."

She forced her heavy eyelids open, turned her head, and looked at the person who was squatting beside her. He looked human but she wasn't sure if he was or was not. She couldn't assume on a planet like this. He had a square jaw, almond eyes, and thick dark eyebrows that rested above his hooded eyelids. When he smiled, he showed a set of sparkling white teeth with a small gap just to the left of his front tooth. He had thick lips with a cupid's bow and had a look that reminded her of a surfer boy.

"Alek, I told you she was!" The other man's perky voice exclaimed from the other side of her. She wanted to turn her head and see who this was, but she was just too tired. "Just so you know, I'm going to be your favorite."

"Whatever." He cracked a smile and rolled his eyes. "Ignore him. He's delusional."

A strong hand scooped her head, gently lifting her skull. Once the hard rim of a cup was placed to her mouth, she felt water slosh onto her face. Opening her lips, she allowed this river of liquid to gush inside, choking her with pure euphoria. She lowered her jaw as wide as she was able, to allow more of this delicious fluid to flood her body. As the water soaked her mouth and tongue, her stomach swelled and loosened. She wanted to drink until her stomach could fit no more. Once again, she opened her mouth to give an indication of what was needed.

Immediately another burst of liquid flooded inside and coated her lips with a soft seal. This time it wasn't water but something far thicker and grittier. This nutrient rich liquid tasted like a strange mixture of herbs and raw eggs. What was this? Why were they giving it to her?

Every ounce she swallowed made her feel stronger. Her headache subsided and a tingling sensation began at her toes and ended around her forehead. Whatever they were giving her helped her aching body to feel numb.

Alek looked up and dropped the cup. The smile on his face faded. Slowly, he laid her head back down.

"Get your weapon," he mouthed to the man on the other side of her as he pulled a knife made of sharp stone with a handle wrapped in leather from his pocket.

"Take her and run," she heard the voice from behind her say. "I'll buy you some time."

"No, we can fight this thing together," he replied with a flip of the knife.

"It's too risky and she's in no condition to fight if it gets to her. Take her. Now."

Astra turned her head. The other man stood with his back to her. He had a weapon in hand while he faced a beast who was about fifty feet away and approaching quickly.

Why did this beast look so much like a smaller version of Sidero? It was about half the size of him and had his black eyes, his hanging jaw filled with sharp teeth, and his pointed ears filled with tiny twitching tentacles. Bloodied foam dripped from its lips as it let out a low growl.

"No one else has to get hurt." The beast had a soft feminine voice, almost childlike as she stopped just a few feet away from the other man. "Just give her to me."

"What do you want with her?" the man whose back was facing Astra asked.

"She belongs to my mother."

Astra's heart sank. Was Vojin dead? Did this mean he lost the fight? She didn't want to believe it.

Alek carefully lifted Astra into his arms. Her body ached with every movement, now that the drink's numbing effects were quickly fading away.

"No, she doesn't." The man further away from her said.

"If you let him take her, I'll kill you both." The beast's eyes narrowed. "Let's not make this into something that it doesn't need to be. Besides, I can see you're one of us. You're clearly not like the other two, so use a little bit of sense. Is your life worth sacrificing over something as awful as theirs?"

"Yes," he said flatly. The beast lunged.

Alek tightened his grip around Astra, swung around, and broke into a run. He moved with a speed she had never thought possible in a human.

She could hear the sound of a man yelling like a warrior accompanied by the roar of a beast. She could feel the wind rushing through her hair and how her body bounced around with every step he took.

The grip he had on her was almost painful. One of his hands was in the form of a fist, still holding onto his weapon. She was nestled in his arms with her head on his tattered black t-shirt that was wet with sweat. He smelled like dirt and musk and he ran like a marine.

"ALEK! SHE'S HEADING YOUR WAY!" she heard the cry of the man faintly in the distance.

Alek slid to a stop. He put her down on the scratchy green grass. "You're gonna be okay. We are gonna get you out o—"

He didn't even see the beast coming. She slammed into him like a train, knocking him off his feet, and pinning him down by his shoulders. They were only a few feet away from Astra. He held the beast back by her shoulders as she snapped her sharp teeth towards his face. She didn't even notice the blade pressed to her neck.

Her eyes were as red as blood. Yes, this must have been Sidero's child and Astra was the reason why her father was killed.

Alek wrapped his fingers around her throat with his left hand and with the right one, he attempted to stab the creature. But no matter how many times he tried, the knife wouldn't break her skin.

Blood streamed down Alek's arms from the wounds that hung open on his flesh. He pushed his knees under the beast and with a flick of his legs, he catapulted the monster over his head and jumped onto his feet.

Twisting around, he collided with the beast. His knife flashed in the light of the sun as he once again tried to stab her while barely missing her gnashing teeth. His weapon was useless.

The sound of a howl redirected Astra's attention. Running on two legs another beast approached. He had unusually large black eyes and pale skin covered in small purple veins. He looked like a hybrid of a human and a monster. She could see by the way he opened his mouth that he had sharp incisors and held an expression that reminded her of a rabid canine. He had a slice across his neck that was bleeding a mixture of black and red blood, which stained the dirty white shirt he was wearing. His hair was dark brown, almost black and was pushed across his sweaty forehead. He had black nails that looked almost like claws and not an ounce of fat on his muscular body. He looked angry and he looked like he was ready to attack.

Crack! It was the last sound she heard. The sound of something hard slamming into the side of her temple, knocking her out.

CHAPTER 7

A sharp stream of light pierced Astra's eyes. She lay on the ground with nothing more than blue skies lingering above her head and an itchy mat below her body. She could feel the moisture in the air and could almost taste the smell of flowers from a fuzzy bush covered in small pink floral buds that stood directly beside her.

She was at the edge of a hill covered land, choking with emerald grass and speckled with tiny pink flowers. The dirt no longer moved on its own and stood still under the roots of the plants. Nearby, she could see a thick curving river slicing the land in half, flowing into the mountain range beyond and giving life to everything around it. In the far distance, on the other side of the river, she saw a land almost desolate of life except for a few barren trees surrounded by boulders of all sizes. It was a strange contrast to the lush area she found herself in. The rolling hills seemed to be cut by the river and the other side was strangely flat.

Surrounding her was a disturbing amount of life. Between a variety of colorful insects and moving clouds of what appeared to be flocks of some sort of a bird-like animal, there were species unknown to her all around. Though she knew she should be afraid, for some reason they didn't even seem to notice her presence.

She slowly twitched her fingers, then toes, before she finally could move her arms which seemed like a close to impossible task at first. It was strange to use her muscles after her body had refused to allow her to. Her body felt like it had been beaten with a two-by-four and any of her skin not covered in cloth was itchy and uncomfortable. Though she had not thoroughly examined herself, she was sure she was covered in bruises and knots and she could feel a nasty bump on the side of her head. She knew she could move, but she was so sore she wasn't sure if she even wanted to or if she would rather just lay there.

Then the thought hit her like a train. Where were the men who were protecting her? Did they die fighting those monsters? Was she captured by her enemy?

Lifting her hand, she wiped her mouth. Dried blood. Why was there blood on her lips?

She shook as she struggled to push herself up. Damn her weak muscles.

Only ten feet away from her, a plump creature the size of a cat approached. It had long floppy ears and large blue eyes. It curiously sniffed the air with its tiny yellow nose. Covered in brills of some sort, it waddled towards her before cocking its head to the side. it appeared as though it was trying to figure out exactly what she was, but then quickly became distracted by a bug and chased after it, stretching its claws out and snapping hungrily.

Why did her skin itch so much? She looked down and realized that she was still on the mat. Although it was scratchy, it was well made, with an intricate decorative pattern woven in the center. Did this mean they were still alive? Did they somehow defeat the demon?

She turned and saw two men quietly whispering to each other by a tree not too far from where she sat. Her chest raised. Alek nodded his head and pointed in her direction. The other man turned. Her heart stopped. He was no human. He was the demon she saw approaching before she was knocked unconscious.

She pushed herself back and bit her lip. Peering through his long black eyelashes were golden, red, and blue speckled eyes, nestled in a bed of darkness. Every time he blinked, two separate eyelids folded over each of his eyes, moisturizing them with a shiny film. The off color of his skin made him look almost dead with cheeks that sunk into his face. Though most of his teeth were flat, he had two very distinct incisors that were twice as long as the other teeth and sharp enough to tear skin. He wasn't as tall or muscular as Alek but he looked ten times scarier.

"I'm so sorry! I didn't even know you had woken up yet! I'm Sagan. What's your name?" he asked in a friendly tone, holding his hand out to shake hers. She glanced at the bracelet. He was the one who was dragging her.

"WH-WHAT ARE YOU?" she cried out, her voice cracking as she spoke, "What do you want with me?!"

"No-no-no don't be scared." Sagan raised his hands and backed away slowly, "We're nice! I promise... Alek, can you please come here?" he pleaded, "I could use a little help."

"Told you, you wouldn't be the favorite!" Alek jeered as he approached behind Sagan. Alek, a handsome man with a chiselled jaw, looked as if he'd stepped off the runway. He squatted down in the grass beside her. She remembered him. He was the one who was protecting her, but why? Why would he protect a stranger? What did he want with her?

"He might be annoying and ugly but I promise those are the only things you need to worry about," he said with a chuckle and a confident shrug as he flashed a brilliant smile filled with perfectly aligned teeth.

"Keep in mind this information is coming from a man who tends to be grumpier than a cat without food," Sagan retorted.

Chuckling, Alek held out his hand and shook hers. "My name's Alek. It's nice to meet you."

"I'm Astra." She touched the back of her head tenderly and winced as her fingers traced over a nasty scab.

"Astra, what a beautiful name. It's fitting for a beautiful woman like you."

She cringed. This was not the time for pickup lines or charming words from a stranger.

"What happened? How am I even alive right now?" she wondered.

Alek paused. His lips formed into a hard line and his dark brows furrowed, "You must have fallen down the mountain. You're lucky that we were in the right place at the right time. You were hurt pretty badly but I was able to reverse some of the damage with different herbs that grow here but the major healing came this morning when we fed you a heart.

I also may have accidentally kicked you in the head when I was fighting. Sorry about that. In my defence, I was a bit preoccupied with trying not to die."

"Well trying not to die is understandable so I'll give you a pass on the knockout. I don't remember eating anything. Whose heart did you feed me?"

Alek shrugged his broad shoulders. "Well, that's because of an herb I gave you. It causes some temporary memory loss, but you needed it for the inflammation."

"Don't worry, you didn't do anything but sleep!" Sagan chimed in. "The first time I had that herb, I woke up naked in a hole, wearing a bra made out of grass. I asked Alek if he was playing dress up with me, but he denied it."

"I still do. Trust me when I say no one wants to see you naked."

"The only reason why you don't want to see me naked is because you would want me. Your sexuality would suddenly go into question and you would cross the rainbow border into the land of glitter and joy," Sagan retorted.

"Not to interrupt your time of reflection and realization but whose heart did you feed me? You didn't answer this before. Is there a reason?" she asked.

Alek tensed his jaw. "That's a little bit of an intense topic but yeah, I'll go into it. We had an incident happen when we were taking you back. There was a creature who wanted to take you back to its mother. We fed you her heart after Sagan killed her. Do you know anything about that? Why is someone after you?"

Astra looked down at the ground for a moment. She didn't know them well enough to tell them what she knew.

"I don't know. I don't even know how I got here. I just woke up here."

"You're lying," Alek snapped.

"How would you know?" She folded her arms. "Do you know how you got here?"

"I know exactly how I got here. Just like I know that you are lying through your teeth."

"Alek, stop." Sagan glared at his friend.

"How long was I unconscious for after the fall?" she asked, desperately wanting to change the subject.

"I'm… not sure," Sagan hesitantly responded. "A few weeks… maybe? I don't know. The hours on this planet are different than the ones back on Earth so it's really hard to tell. That's where Alek and I are from."

She narrowed her eyes. "You're not from Earth. Alek looks like he could be, but you don't."

"I am pretty sure I know where I am from. I was born in Detroit the last time I checked."

"People from Michigan don't look like you."

Sagan raised his brow. "Have you ever been to Michigan?"

"No."

"Exactly. Where are you from?"

"I was in Manhattan but I'm from Tennessee… a small town outside of Maryville right next to the mountains," she responded meekly.

"YES!" Sagan cried out with delight, jumping in the air and firmly clapping his hands together. "FREAKING told you she was human! What did I tell you?! Yep, a HUMAN! Apparently, they were right!"

"As I said before, you only have to worry about the annoyance level he can take things to and having to look at his face," Alek said as he raised his perfectly formed eyebrow.

"My face has grown on me. It makes for a great conversation starter… I love breaking the ice and sparking interest," Sagan replied, his double eyelids slipping over his eyes.

"Well, your face hasn't grown on anyone else there, buddy. You about made her shit herself with how ugly you are," Alek replied with a deadpan expression as he looked at his friend, refusing to blink.

"Don't be jealous that she had more of a reaction to seeing me than your bland ass. Normal looking people are boring and don't cause reactions. I bring life and excitement."

"Are there more people here?" she asked, trying to redirect the conversation.

"Not that we know of. It's just us for now," Alek replied.

"I thought I was the only human until you guys came."

Alek's stoic expression softened. "I thought we were the only ones too. It was just us for years, but you proved that wrong when you showed up. I know you lied to us when you told us you didn't know. So, I am going to ask you again and pretend like it never happened, how did you get here and how long have you been on this planet?" Both men leaned forward as they waited for her answer, their eyes widening.

She looked down at the ground, nervously pulling at a blade of grass as she thought back to what happened. No matter how nice these men were to her, she needed to heed Vojin's warning. There must have been a reason why he told her the things he had.

"It's a long story and I would rather not go into it."

"Seriously? What will you tell us?" Alek mused as he rubbed the small sable hairs on his chin.

"I'm not sure," she replied.

An awkward silence flooded the air as her eyes boomeranged between the men. Alek crossed his arms over his chest. Beside him, Sagan cocked his head to the side and narrowed his eyes a bit.

"Why are you looking at me like that?" She questioned as she felt her jaw tense. *Did she say something wrong?*

"I'm sorry," Alek replied suspiciously, raising his eyebrow ever so slightly, "I just don't get why telling us how you got here is such a big deal. What are you hiding that makes it so difficult for you to tell the truth?"

Sagan cocked his head to the side. "She doesn't know us and therefore doesn't trust us, but I sense there is something more. You feel threatened by us. Why?"

She remained silent. How did he know this? How was he able to read her so well?

"You're on a strange planet with people who you don't know. You're scared, I get that. But you have to let go of your fear and trust us if you want to survive out here. This place isn't safe, but we have survived. Had Sagan and I not trusted each other, we wouldn't be here right now."

"Did you guys know each other before you came here?"

"Sagan has been my best friend since elementary school. He's a brother to me."

She raised her brows. "That's why you trust each other. I don't know you. I am not trying to be rude, I just need to be cautious."

Alek's narrow eyes pierced through her. "You're not being rude, but you can't keep secrets if you are going to be around us. In order to survive, we need complete transparency with everyone involved and we need to know exactly who we are around."

"Eh, Alek I see where you are coming from on this," Sagan interjected, "but I respectfully disagree."

"Why would you disagree?" Alek shot Sagan a nasty glare as the muscles around his thick jaw tensed.

"Because the possibilities of what kind of people we are is left to her imagination until she gets to know us better. I think what she needs is for us to answer her questions. Not the other way around. The least we can do is show her the respect she deserves by earning her trust, and through that, we will get the transparency you want."

"I don't know Sagan. I don't like having someone around who keeps things from us."

"What exactly do you think she'll do? She has noodle arms."

"Hey, not cool." She looked down at her arms that lacked in both definition and strength.

"It doesn't matter. We have already protected her against one creature who was determined to bring her back to its mother. How many more do you think there will be?"

Sagan turned to Alek, "We don't know and I am pretty positive that we have a very angry momma who is still looking for her. But we are the only humans out here, so it is best that we protect our own kind. What happened to her, could have happened to us too." Turning back to Astra, he raked his hair over his ear and sighed. "So, let's start out on the right foot. What questions do you have for us?"

She looked at both of the men who sat in front of her. She wondered what Vojin would think of these men. Would he advise her to keep her distance?

She thought back to her friend. He was the only one she trusted on this planet, even though he told her not to trust him. He made her feel safe and was trying to help her get back home. These men didn't even know there was a way back home.

Her heart sank as she thought about her last moments with Vojin. He promised he would find her, but was he even alive?

Alek turned his palms to the sky. "I'm an open book. We both are and I promise you that we will be honest."

"What did Sagan mean when he said, "They were right,'" Astra wondered.

"When Sagan was out hunting, he overheard an argument between two creatures. Apparently, one was physically there and the smaller one looked like it was a hologram. They seemed angry that they had lost you but had an idea where they could find you. While they were arguing, they mentioned the possibility that you were in the canyon. As soon as that was said, the hologram disappeared. So, we were on our way over there when we found you after you tumbled down the mountain like a poorly inflated ball."

"How did you understand what they were saying?" she asked Sagan.

He shrugged. "Being "different" has allowed me the ability to understand most of the languages spoken here."

"How did you get this way?" she asked.

"Charming and adorable? Well I was born adorable and my charm developed over time."

Alek raised his brow and crossed his arms. "Adorable to whose standards?"

"Um, everyone. Especially you. Don't think I don't see how you look at me, Alek." He covered his chest with his hands and whispered sharply, "I am not an object."

"Just ignore him when he starts to annoy you and talks bullshit. I do it all the time," Alek said with a toothy smile. "Okay, let me reword this. You claim that you're human but only your friend looks human and we all know you don't look like anything found on Earth. Did you always look like this or did something happen to you?"

"Something happened to him," Alek interjected. "He used to look normal up until some time last year when he was out hunting. He thought he had killed the creature he was hunting but it turned out that it was still alive—barely. It bit him right before it died and did something that caused the change to happen. The bite almost killed Sagan but as he was dying, he managed to cut the heart out of the creature and eat it. Somehow, when this beast bit him, it changed his DNA structure, so unfortunately my best friend got a makeover. Don't get me wrong, he's always been ugly to human standards but now he took it to the next level."

"Wouldn't the change make him a liability? How are you sure that it didn't change him to become unpredictable and dangerous?"

Sagan chuckled. "I am dangerous but not to you."

"What do you mean by that?"

"Alek and I are far better equipped to deal with this world than you are. We are stronger and faster than the average human."

"So, you are saying that if you wanted to kill me, you could do it."

"Yes," Alek interjected. "We both could with very little effort and no repercussions but that doesn't mean we will. We didn't come searching for you to kill you. We came to protect you."

"Why?" she wearily asked. "What are your intentions with me?"

"We don't have impure intentions, if that is what you're getting at. You're not exactly Sagan's type and I don't like an unwilling participant. If you haven't noticed, there aren't many of our kind around. So, we got to stick together and be there for each other, even if we start out as strangers."

"How did you get here?" she asked Alek.

"That's a long story but to sum it up, there was a rip or something that appeared in the woods and we fell in."

"It's getting late. Alek, can you get us some dinner and meet us at home?" Sagan stood up and brushed the crumbling dirt off of his pant legs.

"Yeah no problem," he replied quickly. "What do you feel like eating? Should we go with vegetables or meat? You're family now, Astra. You get a vote in this too."

"Meat!" she responded as she thought about how good it would feel to sink her teeth into a juicy hamburger.

"I second that!" Sagan patted his stomach as he looked down at his core.

"Well, looks like something is gonna die tonight," he said with a narrow smile as he took out a long knife.

Her heart dropped as she thought back to Vojin. She imagined him being hunted down by this man, before having his throat slit, the flesh lying open like a silent scream. "Wait, what? Stop."

"Is there a problem?"

"I just… You're going to kill something. What are you going to kill?"

Sagan chuckled. "He's going to kill whatever is an easy target."

85

"Okay, I need more details. I'm not so sure I am okay with this."

Alek narrowed his eyes and scoffed. "A second ago you told me that you wanted to eat meat. You do realize all meat requires that at some point something dies, right?"

"I know but—"

"You're going to need to suck it up and get used this kind of stuff. How did you not put two and two together? Didn't you grow up in Tennessee? Don't they snap chicken necks out there before dinner?"

She took a deep breath in, trying to cool down her burning cheeks.

"I didn't grow up on a farm, so no, my family never snapped chicken necks before dinner. My mom would go to the grocery store and pick up the meat but we never saw a face tied to it so there was never the thought that at one point it was living and breathing. It just feels different knowing that your decision requires the death of another living being."

"Have you ever had a problem eating a steak in the past?" Alek snorted.

"Well, no. It's not like I saw the cow. I just ate what was put in front of me."

"Did you know it was a cow at one point?"

"Well yes but I didn't think of—"

"Then don't pretend like you suddenly have a moral conscience just because someone states the obvious facts that you already knew."

Alek turned and walked into the field shaking his head and mumbling to himself, leaving her wanting nothing more than to crawl under a rock and disappear. She cringed. She hadn't even known this man for a day and he was already rubbing her wrong. As she watched him walk further away, she could feel the tension lift and breathed out a slow breath.

Sagan turned to her and smiled. "Am I the favorite yet?"

"If there was an award in this, you would win it."

"He's just hungry but I'm glad to know that I am a winner. That was like watching a slow train wreck happening and my lord it was awkward. Were you uncomfortable? Because I was."

"God yes. Is he always like that?"

"He has moments where he is the sweetest guy you will ever meet, while other moments you just want to slap the inner bitch out of him. As far as killing is concerned, I do see where you are coming from. It's one thing to buy a package of flesh from the grocery store, but a whole other thing when you see its beady little eyes staring up at you. Alek has a way of saying things that tend to have a bit of a shock factor involved. It's like he lacks a much-needed filter."

"No kidding."

Sagan sighed and smiled at her. "I know things are a bit fresh and rugged but the rough life gets easier with time."

"Really?"

"Yeah, you get used to things you never thought you would. The first time I gutted an animal, I vomited."

"Oh God."

"Don't worry, I aimed for Alek since he was the one who made me do it."

"Do the animals suffer?"

"Not too much. We make the kills as quick and painless as possible and try to hunt in a way that they don't see it coming. He's probably going to go after something similar to rabbit or deer. I mean… they don't look like rabbit or deer, but they behave similar to them and they taste a bit gamey."

She looked at the mountains in the distance as she rubbed her arms, feeling tiny bumps form as a crisp breeze caressed her skin with its icy breath. Quickly she pulled loose her jacket from her hips and pulled it over her shoulders. Much better. The jacket was just light enough to cut the edge off the cold.

"He doesn't kill anything larger than a deer, right? Like a besnik?"

"What's a besnik?"

"It's this really big animal here that I have kind of grown fond of."

"That's weird that you are going around naming animals like Adam in the bible, but no. He only kills what he can carry and if this "besnik" species is larger than a deer, you have nothing to worry about."

In the distance, her ears picked up the sound of a faint roar that ended in a sharp yelp. Her heart lurched. *Where was Vojin?*

Her imagination took her to the darkest places, reminding her that his body might be nothing more than a rotting corpse. Did he suffer? Was Prosperine still alive? Was she searching for her? She then remembered Prosperine's child. How many children did she have? Were they all hunting her?

She looked down at her thin arms and realized that Vojin was right when he said that humans would easily be defeated by even a weakling here. By the lack of definition found in her arms, it was clear that she had a long way to go until she would even have a fighting chance on this planet. She needed to become stronger, but would she ever be strong enough to fight a monster like that? She hoped the men would be able to protect her, but would they even be willing to? She doubted anyone was as selfless as Vojin. He sacrificed everything for her, and she never even had the chance to repay him for his kindness. Did he ever know how grateful she was for him?

Trapped in a whirling sea of emotions, she felt like she was fighting to stay on the surface of the water, only to be pushed back down. She was filled with the reality of possibilities. A part of her wished she could look into the future and see a glimpse of her fate but the other part of her didn't want to know. What if it was bad? Was living in ignorance a blessing?

"Okay, you and I will go to the campsite. I need to build a fire before it gets dark outside. It gets cold here at night during this time of the year. Do you know how to build one from scratch?" Sagan asked, snapping her out of her trance.

"Um... yeah. I know how to build one, but I never cared much for making them."

"Eh, it's all good. I don't mind getting sooty. I've always been a fan of building things."

"I built a tree house one time," she said as she pushed herself up and allowed her cramping legs to stretch properly. Astra hadn't stood in so long that she felt weak, but despite every muscle in her body shaking, she was happy she could stand.

"Are you okay?" Sagan asked with concern. She felt as if she was going to collapse. "Do you need help walking?"

"No," she faintly smiled. "I'm an independent woman. I don't need a man's help."

Sagan's inky eyes sparkled in the dimming light. "We must be soul sisters! I can't stand it when men think I am a damsel in destress. I'm like, 'boy, give a lady some room!'"

"See, I knew you would understand. Just give me a few minutes to get used to this."

"Take your time. You haven't stood in a while, and I know how I get when I haven't been able to stand for a few days. I can't imagine how rough it is on you right now," Sagan replied as he reassuringly placed his hand on her back.

"Please don't touch me," she said, taking a step back while looking at the beast in front of her. "I don't want to be touched."

"I'm sorry." He raised his hands in the air, showing her his palms. "I wasn't trying to disrespect you. I have always been a physically affectionate person, but I will try my best not to be that way around you."

"I'm not big on the whole hug and pat on the back kind of a thing," her voice trailed off.

"It's fine," his lips tensed. "Just let me know if you need any help. Even the most independent people can sometimes use a hand," Sagan responded distantly with a shrug. "Are you ready?"

She took a deep breath in and hobbled towards him. "Yeah, let's go."

The sun's last rays peeked over the horizon, stretching its fevered yellow and crimson colors towards the approaching night sky. Though the walk had begun in silence, as the evening began to settle into night, the air became a cacophony of screaming insects, piercing her ears with their high pitched shrill. The insects seemed to be coming from black leaved bushes the size of her fist scattered through the emerald land. Though the bushes were small, the sound that came out of them was quite loud.

"See there?" Sagan asked after a small walk, as he pointed to a dark cave just fifty feet from a large and winding river. "That's our home. I know it doesn't look like much, but we have been living in this spot for about a year now. It's grown on us and it's homey if you have the right mindset."

"And what mindset is that?"

"A positive one," Sagan replied as he looked at her out of the side of his eye.

Astra's heart lurched in her throat as she saw something massive move inside of the cave. Should she warn Sagan that they were not alone? Was he aware? She wasn't sure what it was, but she could make out a faint outline in the shadows and it looked massive. Her lips parted to say something, but she couldn't move or speak. Fear had grabbed her and shackled her in place. An icy chill ran down her spine as the small hairs on her arms stood at attention.

The horrific creature stepped out of the dark cave. It raised its head high in the air and looked directly at her.

It had muscles that bulged from its coarse white fur and eyes that were nestled at the sides of his head. There were four eyes, two in each socket and they were such a bright shade of orange that they looked almost like they glowed in the dimming light. The beast had no tail with rounded hindquarters that flexed with every movement. It had massive paws ending in thick clear claws that sank into the ground. It was at least 1000 pounds of pure muscle with clear horns on the top of its head that split into several points and were filled with veins.

The monster cocked its head ever so slightly. Clear saliva dripped out of its lips and dangled from its jaw like shoe strings. The creature stared at her before approaching. As it lifted its lips, the lips split in half and folded over its snout, revealing a row of razor-sharp teeth.

She turned to Sagan who smiled from ear to ear as if he was seeing an old friend. *Who was this monster and why didn't he seem afraid?*

"Be nice Elde," he said sternly. "We like this one."

It nodded its head in response but let out a low growl.

Elde? He knew this monster was in this cave yet didn't warn her. What other unpleasant surprises did he have in store for her and what did he mean by "be nice?"

Her head spun as it came closer. She wanted to turn and run but she was paralyzed by the mere sight of it. Five feet. Four. Three. Two. The monster was now so close she could smell its steaming breath as it came within an inch of her face. What was it about to do? The seconds scratched forward, feeling like hours that refused to pass.

Sagan smiled a toothy smile. "This is going well! He seems to like you!"

She refused to respond. The beast gave her a firm nudge with his head, causing her to stumble back and fall onto the ground. Once again, the creature moved forward, looking larger than before, now that she was looking up at him from the ground.

Slowly his lips lowered, once again concealing the weapons that grew out of his jaw. Elde kneeled on the ground, lowering himself to her level before rolling on his side and making a strange groaning sound.

"I know you're not a hugger but he wants you to know that he won't hurt you and I think he wants you to pet him." Pet him? He just growled at her. She wasn't sure she even wanted to be near this creature, let alone touch him. "I think the petting is more for you than for him. I noticed that anytime I am upset, he rolls to his side for me to pet him and it makes me feel better."

She took a quivering breath in. "What are you talking about?"

"Elde is like a coconut. He looks hard on the outside but he is pretty soft within," Sagan chuckled as he sat down and stroked the beast. Elde licked and smacked his lips as he ground his teeth together.

Hesitantly, she reached out her trembling fingers, grazing across his dusty coarse fur. The creature leaned his head on her shoulder, allowing her to scratch his pointy ears. Sagan was right. It did help. Elde grunted and closed his eyes, relaxing before he stood back up.

"I guess he is kind of sweet," she said unconvincingly, before standing. "Has he ever turned on you?"

"Nope. Elde is our "guard dog." He came out of nowhere when we were being attacked by this massive creature. If he hadn't stepped in, Alek and I would be dead right now. This animal is loyal as hell.

"After Elde killed the animal, he followed us home and hasn't left since. I admit we thought at first that he was just fighting over us for a meal, but when he didn't eat us, we figured out what had happened." He ran his fingers through Elde's fur one last time before walking towards the entrance of the cave.

Sagan gathered dried wood and grass into his arms from a small pile that lay just outside of the entrance. The pile was beside some drying fish meat that was hung from a rope. "This is our wood pile. It's pretty much our life support. I hate being cold."

"Would you rather be hot or cold? Because personally I hate being hot," Astra asked.

"Put it this way, my version of hell is a place where it is cold all the time. I don't mind the heat. Waking up sweaty is like waking up covered in a blanket of liquid comfort."

"How the hell is sweating a comforting feeling?"

"Because the best things in life happen when you are sweating. Hiking up a path to a beautiful waterfall, laying on a beach on a summer day, summer vacations, and best of all, a wild night of sex."

"So, I take it you won't be vacationing in Antarctica if you ever get back to Earth?"

"Who even goes there? I can tell you right now that if I ever get back home, the only places I'll be vacationing at are warm tropical resorts."

Her face sank. She examined the person in front of her as they both entered the cave. His arms were thick like the wood that was about to be lit. Crawling up his muscles were tunnels of blue veins bulging just beneath the surface of his pale skin. He looked as if he had been built from the side of a mountain, chiseled from the largest of rocks and though he was smaller than Alek, he still could snap her neck in half without even breaking a sweat.

What would he even do if he got back to Earth? She thought back to the story Vojin told her about Medusa. No matter how sweet he was, the public would perceive him as a threat because they perceived anything they were not familiar with as one. No matter how much he felt like he was still a human, the truth was that he wasn't. He was a hybrid and she wasn't sure if it was even reversible. If he did make it back to Earth, she wouldn't put it past the people in leadership positions to turn him into a scientific experiment. They would poke and prod him like an animal and use him for research until there was nothing left of him.

Her eyes met Sagan's. Though he was trying to smile, the muscles that dropped in his face told a different story. He looked away and cleared his throat. Did he know what she was thinking? By the way he was working on building up the wood, he looked more like he was trying to distract himself than peacefully create a fire.

After striking two rocks together and creating cherries, he blew into the tinder until it caught flame. He slowly tended to this until it became a warm, crackling fire.

The fire lit up the cave enough for her to make out the details of what they called home. It was shockingly organized. To the right were leather bags that were lined up against the wall and in front of those bags was what appeared to be a bed made of fur pelts. Towards the front of the cave was a stone chair and a small stone table with a half-made object that she assumed would eventually be a knife. Beside the weapon were small strips of leather and a few other stones of various shapes and sizes. On the other side of the cave was a massive rock that separated a small section. She could make out what appeared to be another bed, but one that was more private. Beside that bed was a small vine with glowing white flowers.

"Food," a deep voice barked from behind her, causing her heart to lurch in her chest from the unexpected entrance.

Astra swung her head around and saw Alek holding a large dead animal in his arms. Blood from the corpse dripped down his skin and trickled onto his pants, soaking it with a hue of red against the dirty green. The beast must have weighed at least a hundred pounds or more, but Alek seemed to hold it up without even straining. She swallowed hard as she looked at the corpse whose clumpy carbon colored tongue lolled out of its mouth. If she ever got on his bad side, or any of them for that matter, they could kill her with no fear of legal repercussion. They were in a world where the laws obeyed by man did not exist and she was left to trust the moral conscience of two strangers.

Alek dropped the meat next to Sagan. He glowed with pride at his large catch. "You asked for meat."

Sagan rolled his eyes. "Don't get too cocky now. You and I both know that this was just a lucky catch."

"Not luck, skill."

"Is that what we are calling it these days?"

Alek ignored Sagan and grabbed the corpse before moving it towards himself with one firm pull. He then took out his knife and began at the ankles of the animal, cutting around them before sliding his weapon across the inside of the legs. Wrapping his fingers around the tail, he trailed his knife across the underside of the vertebrae before slicing his weapon over the center of the stomach.

The knife peeled the flesh, revealing its meaty insides. Though she wanted to look away, she couldn't take her eyes off him. The way he skinned this animal was as though he had done it a thousand times before. He didn't appear disturbed in any way, shape, or form.

How did he feel when he took this animal's life? Did he enjoy it? His eyes seemed cold to her, almost devoid of a soul.

Once all the skin was removed, Alek waved Sagan over and handed him the pelt. Immediately, Sagan took it and threw it over string that hung like a clothing wire across the entrance of the cave.

Alek turned to Astra and pointed to her with his knife. "We still need to remove the membrane, fat, and meat off it before we put it out to dry. There is a solution that Sagan will put on it made of brain along with a few other ingredients that keeps the pelt soft but does the job we need it to. Tomorrow it will be put in the sun where we will break and dry it. It gets cold out sometimes and it is always nice to have a warm pelt to cover up in. You need to learn these things if you are going to survive out here."

"You mean like during the winter or a sudden change in temperature?" She raised her eyebrow ever so slightly.

"No and yes," Sagan chimed in. "Though there are what we think could be classified as seasons, the weather is unpredictable. Temperatures around here can rise and drop overnight to extreme points. Normally after there is a large storm, we see a drop in temperature. Sometimes it's as quickly as overnight, while other times it is within a few days."

She looked at what was left of the corpse in front of her. The beast lay on its side, its glassy, cloudy eyes now eternally open as it stared blankly into nothingness. The flickering firelight illuminated the red muscles streaked with strips of white fat.

Did the beast feel pain? She looked down at the face of the creature. Its throat hung open almost as wide as its mouth. Alek had sliced so deep he'd almost decapitated it.

Her stomach churned as she looked back at the brown fur with small strips of fat still attached. In her mind, she replayed the way the meat peeled away from skin and how Alek hacked and sliced away at the corpse, pulling the flesh away from its body.

She turned her attention back to Alek just as he sliced open the core and dark brown internal organs slithered out. Perhaps it was from exhaustion or maybe it was from watching someone gut a dead animal for the first time, but after seeing that, she felt as if her stomach was turning inside out. Her hand cupped over her mouth. Vomit slid up her throat before sinking back down into her stomach.

"Hey, Alek," Sagan said, eyeing her with a raised brow.

"Yep?"

"Astra and I are going to take a short walk. I'll get to prepping the skin later. We'll be back by the time dinner is finished. She looks like she could use some fresh air."

Sagan walked over to her and stretched out his hand. With hesitation, she accepted. She wasn't sure that she wanted to be alone with him but at the same time, she knew she would have rather had the company if given the option.

* * *

The chilly air felt good as it sucked inside of her inflating lungs. It was getting dark outside and the golden hue that was once over the horizon had now faded to a dim light, becoming nothing more than the remnants of the day's last moments. On the distant horizon, the first of the brilliant stars shined. They looked like tiny diamonds glistening against a darkening background. It was then that she noticed one of the stars was brighter than all the others. It was at least three times the size of the speckles of light surrounding it and flickered in a gorgeous shade of blue. Was this the star that Vojin had told her to follow?

She walked up to the river and sat down on a long flat rock. The cool clear liquid splashed over the gray stones as insects with two legs and long pinchers clung onto the rocks, allowing the water to soak their tiny bodies before flying off into the rolling field.

Astra let out a long exhale and watched a puff of her breath float in front of her face like a misty cloud. The river called to her, so she sat down by the water on a cold flat rock. There was something soothing about the sound of running liquid. She heard the crunch of Sagan's shoes against the ground before something heavy was draped over her shoulders. Her chest pinched and head snapped down. What was this? It was nothing more than a fur.

"Thank you," she whispered, wrapping the fur around herself and hoping he didn't notice how skittish she was.

"Hope I didn't scare you! It's cold out here and it's just going to get colder," Sagan explained before taking a step back. The brown fur weighed heavily over her shoulders but felt comforting. He was right. It was cold, and she knew that it would have been only a matter of moments before she would have found herself shivering. "You can keep it. I used it when I first got here and it kept me warm. If you wrap yourself up really tightly, it feels like someone is hugging you. That helped me when I used to miss my family." The speckles in Sagan's eyes softly glowed as he smiled with dimples forming on his pale cheeks. But behind those black eyes was the faint glimmer of sadness. He turned his head and raised it towards the heavens.

"Used to miss them? Do you not miss them anymore?" She couldn't imagine a moment on this planet where she didn't miss her mother and father. She knew that would never fade.

"I still miss my family. I know I've been gone for a few years but sometimes I find myself wondering if they still miss me. I try to push my homesickness aside so I can be strong for Alek, but it never really leaves," he replied.

"Why are you trying to be strong for Alek? He seems just fine."

"He's not. He acts like he is, but I don't think he ever got over what I did. I don't think he ever forgave me."

"What does he need to forgive you for?"

"For being the reason he is on this planet."

She folded her arms together. "What do you mean?"

"I went through a rough time and Alek knew I was getting into some trouble. So, when his family decided to go to their log cabin for a summer break, he invited me to come.

I went and everything was going great until I decided to take a walk. After I didn't come back for a few hours, Alek told his family that he was going to go out and make sure I was okay. He figured I had gone down the trail to the waterfall. His family didn't think anything of it and let him go. They didn't know I was a drug addict, but Alek knew.

He found me stumbling around the waterfall and mumbling to myself. When he tried to get me to come back with him and lay down for a bit, I refused. I ended up running behind the waterfall and it was there that I saw this rip in the middle of the air."

"A rip? What do you mean?"

"It's hard to explain. Imagine looking at something that looks like a tear into another Universe."

"Oh... creepy. So what happened?"

"I thought I was tripping so I wanted to experience this "new world." Alek saw what I was walking towards and started screaming out at me. He told me to stay away. I wasn't listening and got close to it.

It all happened so fast. He tried to grab me but slipped on a rock and fell into the rip. So, I jumped in after him.

We were knocked out for a while but when we came to, we woke up here."

98

"Why did you even do drugs? I get it, life gets hard, but I don't understand why anyone would want to destroy their life over a moment of bliss."

"It was the only way that I could get a moment of happiness. I felt like I was losing my mind after what had happened to me and I couldn't take my own reality anymore."

"What happened?"

"Though I am normally an open book, that is a chapter of my life I really don't want to get into. Let's just say I failed someone I loved, and I will never forgive myself for it."

She thought back to the death of her mother and felt her heart sink. "I understand." She meant it. She understood what it was like to have a part of her life that she would rather not think about. It was a part of her life that she wished she could take back and undo, but she knew she would never be able to.

CHAPTER 8

Sagan stood up and turned to her. "We've been out here for a while now and I'm pretty sure dinner is ready or close to ready. I don't know about you, but I feel like my stomach is about to eat itself if something doesn't get in there soon."

"Oh sweet God, yes. When was the last time that I even ate?"

"Earlier, you ate a heart."

"For the love of all things holy, please do not remind me of that and since I don't remember doing it, that doesn't count."

"I'm pretty sure it does."

"No."

"Eh, I am going to go with a yes."

"I am going to stick with a solid no."

She pushed herself off the ground and immediately noticed an aroma that tantalized her senses. She inhaled the smoky scent, allowing more of this delicious smell to slip into her nostrils. Her stomach growled. The sensation crawled from one side of her body to the next as it cried out for food, demanding the nourishment it desired. She could almost taste what was cooking over the fire and the images of how the meat was prepared seemed to slip from her mind as she walked towards the cave.

* * *

Elde snorted and nuzzled Sagan as they approached. Alek lifted his gaze from the meat and smiled, motioning for them to come and sit down beside him.

"God, this smells like grilled beef. Remember when we used to eat those burgers at your dad's cookout?"

"Yeah that was good, but do you remember your mom's pandebono? She made the best pandebono with hot chocolate."

"That shit was legendary." Sagan licked his lips. "My mom always knew how to cook."

"How was it out there? Is it a clear night?" Alek asked while pushing another piece of flaking wood into the fire.

"Yeah it is."

"Really? Man, I love clear nights."

Astra's eyes trailed up towards the meat, sizzling over the crackling fire as it hung from a long thin vine. She noticed it was not only strong enough to hold up this heavy animal, but also did not seem affected by the flames, with the exception of the deep shade of ember red that it glowed.

She could see the dangling legs of the animal, roasting over the fire. The flames had already eaten away the eyes of the animal, leaving nothing more than a hollow reminder of the windows to its soul.

Alek stood up and pulled off his dirty shirt, cocking a satisfied smirk as he revealed a thick chest with a small patch of curly dark hair on his sternum. She rolled her eyes as he reached up and removed the meat from the vine while flexing his muscles. He then dropped the meat down upon the mat that was used to drag her as if he was trying to show just how heavy it was.

"Impressive, huh?" His eyes lingered towards his own muscles. "The meat, I mean."

"The meat is the only impressive thing in this room," she retorted. His face dropped. *Good. He needed to tone things down. He was starting to get under her skin.*

Sagan rolled over laughing until tears came out of his eyes. Gasping for a breath of air, he reached out to Alek and said, "That was the first and hardest time you have ever been rejected and I am honored that I could witness that train wreck."

"Whatever, man."

Astra eyed the food as she sat down beside the mat, while Alek cut through the roast with a sharpened grey stone. Juices rolled down the flesh, creating a pool of liquid, which soaked onto the mat.

Her mouth watered while she stared at this food. The last time she had a decent meal was when Vojin had fed her. She remembered how he planted the seed so that a stranger who stumbled across the plant would also have food to eat.

She heard Elde snorting behind her and clawing at the ground. He was so near, she could feel the impact of his heavy feet through the ground. Would Alek pacify this beast with something to eat before he turned on all of them?

"Well, someone is especially hungry today!" Sagan exclaimed while watching Elde throw his head around, flicking the drool in all directions.

Alek laughed as he threw a piece of meat at the creature. The beast swallowed the cooked flesh whole, eagerly licking the residue off of his stiff lips before he rolled over beside Sagan with a grunt. He leaned back, resting his head on the animal's stomach and closed his eyes for a moment.

"How hungry are you? Do you want a big or small piece?" Alek asked her, raising his eyebrow ever so slightly.

"I am starving," she said as she wearily eyed the meat. Her jaw tensed. Yes, she was hungry. But to see a face attached to what she was about to eat was something she wasn't sure she could ever get used to.

Slicing off two large pieces of meat, Alek leaned over the mat and handed it to her. For a moment she stared at the dripping meat before hesitantly sinking her teeth into the flesh. It felt rubbery in her mouth, with an aroma of honey coated beef but had a salty deer-like taste.

Juices seeped out of the sides of her mouth as she swallowed the large chunks of greasy flesh. Astra didn't realize how hungry she was until she swallowed the food, and in that moment there was no stopping her. Like a rabid animal, she only halfway chewed one piece before biting off another, nearly choking on the size but not stopping.

Sagan and Alek stared at her with a look of pure amusement plastered onto their faces. They smirked as they watched her wipe the dripping grease off her chin with the back of her hand.

"Watching you eat is like watching a wildlife documentary on hamsters. I didn't realize that it was physically possible to fit that much food in a human's mouth until this moment," Sagan said, with the corners of his lips curling up.

"It's fascinating, isn't it? Eating with me is as mysterious as a box of unlabelled chocolates. Just wait till you see what I can do with the next meal."

"Well, just don't choke," he chuckled. "Alek's terrible at the Heimlich maneuver and I am clueless myself. So, if you choke, you're on your own."

"Mental note taken. Next time I consider choking, I'll reconsider."

After that conversation she realized it was time to take a break, in order to summon the tiniest bit of her dignity back before continuing her meal. She never normally acted so primitively while consuming food.

"Congratulations. You are the first human in the history of my life that enjoys my cooking. Are you thirsty yet?" Alek proudly smiled as he handed her the empty shell of a large nut filled with warm water.

"It's because her taste buds died out in that heat!" Sagan pitched a small rock at his friend, hitting him in the shoulder. "I remember one year when I was over at Alek's house, he tried cooking for his mom for Mother's Day when he was like—how old were you again?"

Alek groaned as he rocked back, wrapping his arms around his legs. "Oh my God really? We are telling her this story?"

"Yep! We sure are! Alek was ten or eleven—I think. Anyway, this guy right here tries making a box dinner where literally the only thing you had to do is add water and boil. The next thing we know, the entire kitchen was filled with smoke so thick you couldn't even see your hand in front of your face. The pasta was so burned at the bottom of the pan that your mom just threw the whole thing away. What made things worse was that the smoke alarm was blaring on full blast and the fire department was alerted! Two fire trucks came screaming up to the house and the entire neighborhood came outside to see what was going on. His mother was mortified, and I had the honor of watching this disaster unfold."

Alek raised a brow and scoffed. "So maybe I am no five-star chef, but I have survived living on an alien planet with this asshole for years," he responded while taking a large bite of food. "I think that is an accomplishment."

"In other words, Alek was able to survive on the planet because he had a real man around."

Alek threw a small stone back at Sagan, hitting him in the chest. Pointing the tip of his knife towards him. "You know you wouldn't last a day without me."

"Says the one whose ass I had to save, how many times?" Sagan narrowed his eyes before raising three fingers.

"And how many times have I saved your ass?" Alek responded before holding up four fingers.

"Touché, you son of a bitch. You got me there."

"Not to change the subject but I have to admit," Alek turned to her as he spoke, "I'm glad we found you. It's nice to have someone of the opposite sex around. I was starting to feel that there was too much testosterone in here."

Astra's chest pinched. Yes, they did find her. But did they expect her to stay with them as if they were one big happy family? No. She couldn't. She needed to get back to her father. She hoped he wouldn't give up searching for her, because the moment that he gave up, would be the moment that she knew he could snap. He almost killed himself when her mother passed. She knew because she found a rope in the shape of a noose on the floor of his closet. He never went through with it and she often wondered if maybe she was the reason why he kept living.

Even worse, the longer she stayed on this planet the more of a risk she was to the rest of humanity. Sidero wanted to use her for something that could potentially eliminate all of mankind. He saw humans as a disease and told her she was special. Why would he think she was special? There was nothing special about her life. She was nothing more than an 18-year-old girl who grew up in Tennessee.

Either way, she knew that there was a possibility that Prosperine was still looking for her and just as great of a possibility there were others doing the same. Was Vojin dead? There was a good chance that he was since Prosperine was still looking for her. But she couldn't give up. He was her only hope. She decided she would hold onto the faith that he was still alive. She needed protection from these monsters who wanted to commit mass genocide. Finding him was her only option and her only hope. She needed him to still be alive for the sake of her own safety, her father's sanity, and the lives of billions of people back on Earth.

She had to take the risk and search for him. He didn't tell her to wait. He told her to find the brightest star in the sky and follow it. Vojin promised that he would find her. She had to listen. She had to leave. But she also knew she couldn't tell these men the truth about her. She couldn't tell them the intentions of the ones who were searching for her. They couldn't know the danger she was to their friends and families back home.

"I can't stay here. I gotta go. I'm sorry." She pushed herself up. Yes, it was dark outside and yes it was dangerous but at least she would be able to see the brightest star and follow it. Was the risk worth it? Vojin did mention that it was more dangerous at night. But at the same time, she could get a head start if she began right now and she would at least know that she was going in the right direction.

"What do you mean? Are you leaving?" Alek asked.

Her stomach clenched. Should she tell him the truth? Should she tell him that she knew a way back home and the only way to truly find it was to find Vojin first? Astra wasn't sure if she could trust him, so she decided to leave out information and tell him just enough to get him off her back.

"Look, I am thankful you took me in and even more grateful that you saved my life, but my friend is out there, and I need to find him."

105

"I thought you were the only human you knew out here before us." Alek crossed his arms.

"There was a man. I mean he wasn't a human but he could become one on command. He sacrificed himself to keep me safe and he might still be out there."

"So, let me get this right, we save you from a monster who is after you and you want to go right on back to where you were at?"

"I never said I wanted to go back to where I was at. I need to find my friend, which is in a different direction… or at least I think it is."

"You don't even know where you are going?"

"I do know where I am going, or at least I know the general direction that I am going in."

"Why are you going after this person?"

"Because he saved my life. He might not be human, but he's still my people. He's still my friend."

"You wouldn't survive long enough out there to reach him. Do you know how to fight?" Alek goaded.

"No."

"Do you know what you can and cannot eat here?"

"No."

"Do you know any fucking thing about this planet?"

"Well, I know it has bitchy people like you."

"She's got a point there," Sagan agreed.

"Have fun dying out there."

"Well since you are clearly an expert at the ins and outs of this planet, how have you guys made it here so long without getting killed?"

Sagan slowly blinked. The film on his second pair of eyelids made his eyes seem extra shiny each time it remoisturized the eye. "It wasn't easy. We had to figure out the rules of this world and we've almost died many times. Those experiences taught us things we'll never repeat.

How about tomorrow we start teaching you everything you need to know and then you go search for your friend? I know

106

that you've been through a lot, but survival is hard here and the sooner you learn, the better," Sagan said.

"I don't have time to learn those things. My friend is probably hurt and I need to know he is okay."

"How do you plan on finding your friend? This is a big planet and you don't know your way around it." Sagan wondered.

"He told me to follow the brightest star in the sky."

Alek folded his arms. "How will you know what herbs to feed him if he is hurt? Or what steps you need to take to help him if he is bleeding? Are you an alien veterinarian?

She'd heard enough. When the last words left his lips, Astra spun on her heels and stormed outside towards the river. She couldn't stand Alek and as irrational of a choice leaving when it was dark seemed, she needed to at least begin this journey. This would be the only night she would walk in the darkness, she decided. When it became light again, she would take a nap before beginning again. Being careful and alert was key no matter how dark or light it was.

The sound of chirping had died to silence when the last of the sun's rays disappeared behind the horizon, so the only sound she could hear was that of the river, splashing against the rocks. This place was far quieter at night than the canyon she traveled through with Vojin.

She searched the sky. The heavens were lit with stars of all shapes and sizes. There were two moons which stood on each side of the illuminated rings around the planet. The smaller of the moons reminded her of a small Earth, while the larger moon was the color of egg yolk and speckled with spots. Just beyond the distant mountains and across the river, was the largest star in the sky, sparkling brighter than any of the stars that surrounded it.

"That is what I need to follow," she whispered.

"Hey, wait! Don't leave just yet." Sagan jogged towards her.

He looked even more demonic in the moonlight. His skin almost looked sickly and his eyes were like bottomless pits that she felt like she could fall into.

"What is it?"

"Look, I don't know you and you don't know me, but I can't in good conscience just let you leave like this."

"Excuse me?"

"If I thought Alek was in danger, I would go through hell and high water to find him and make sure he was okay. He's family. This friend of yours—what's his name again?"

"Vojin."

"Okay, Vojin, that is your family. And now that you're in my life, I consider you my family, which makes him a part of my family too by default."

"I am not your family though. I don't know you."

"No, you're right. You don't. But there aren't that many of our kind out there. So, any human who lives here I will see as my family."

"Not to state the obvious but you are not human anymore."

Sagan's face sank. "I know I'm not. It doesn't take away from the fact that I still feel like one of you, and I might not know you, but I see you as a part of my life. You don't just turn your back on family."

"What are you getting at?"

"If you are willing to leave tomorrow morning, I will come with you and I will help you to find him. It's pretty dangerous to be here in the open at night and it's even more dangerous to travel alone."

"What are you talking about?" A deep voice snapped from behind Sagan.

Astra looked behind him and saw Alek with his arms wrapped around his chest. He looked bigger in the night. Almost like a monster lurking in the darkness.

"I've decided to go with her."

"What? Why are you risking your life to help her find some creature? You don't even know her."

"We risked our life to find her, before we knew her and I would gladly risk my life to help her find her friend. What is the point in living if you don't have things to live for? I have no intention of hiding in a cave for the rest of my life, knowing that I could have gone out there and helped someone in need. Yes, it's risky but it's worth the risk."

"You're not a missionary nor are you a hero. Your place is here, where it's safe."

"No, I am not a missionary and I'm no hero. I can agree with you on that. But my place isn't hiding in a cave like a coward. It's out there helping Astra find Vojin."

"Vojin?"

"Her friend."

"And what if you die before you reach this "friend" you have never met before?"

"Then I will die knowing that the last thing I did in my life was trying to do something right for once."

Alek stiffened. "Well that's on you. She can sleep on my bed if she decides to stay one more night."

"Well, what's the verdict, Astra?"

She looked up towards the heavens. The star lured her to follow it but she knew that her chances of survival and getting to Vojin would be raised if she had Sagan to protect her.

"I'll stay one more night and leave in the morning."

They turned around and walked towards the cave. In a way, she was relieved to have the added protection, but other fears pounded her mind. Could she trust him? Would he be someone she could rely on for protection? He had kept her safe before and he seemed trustworthy but then again, Vojin did tell her not to trust anyone.

She didn't have a choice. Though Vojin's intentions were good, she had to at least give this stranger somewhat of her trust if she were to have a chance of even finding him.

As soon as they entered the cave, Alek picked up a fur and laid down, facing the wall. It was clear to her that he didn't like the idea of Sagan leaving.

"Are you sure it's okay that I take his bed?" she asked, looking at both of the men. Alek didn't budge.

"Yeah, he will be fine. You're going to sleep over there in what I like to call the private quarters." Sagan pointed to the area behind the rock.

"Where will you sleep?"

"I normally end up using Elde as a spooning buddy. I always wanted a pet. Now I have an alien." Sagan turned his attention back to the fire which was now becoming more of a smouldering remnant of what it once was, with the occasional burst of flame when a piece of wood decided to split from the heat.

"You do realize that you're technically the alien and in his mind, it's you that might be his pet?"

"No, I don't think he sees it that way because we feed him. Name one animal that feeds you?"

"Outdoor cats bring you dead mice and birds."

"Good point, but if I am Elde's pet, he is the lucky one because I am the best damn pet ever."

"How's that?"

"I'm like one of those ugly pets that you can't help but love. You know, the kind that you look at on some janky website advertising "free to a good home," and as soon as you see the photos your stomach twists but heart flutters. Well, on a side note, I am ready to sleep. Tomorrow is going to be a long day for us."

"Thanks for doing this. It means a lot to me."

"It's not a problem. Let's just get your friend and get the hell back here. I know some pretty good ways to help the body heal. So, if he is still alive but hurt, I should be able to help him."

"Thank you."

Astra had no intention of ever coming back to this cave. She couldn't tell him that because she knew she needed him to help her survive. Maybe Vojin would know how to reverse whatever this man had and maybe he would even be willing to show them the way home too.

She walked over to the bed. It was a nice little area that felt like it had privacy because of a rocky cover jutting from the ground. Folded neatly by the wall, was a black and white pelt, thick with dense fur in the form of a pillow. In front of the pillow were several pelts of various furs, all one on top of the other. She felt her lips curl; to sleep on something similar to a bed, even if it was on the floor, seemed like it would feel heavenly.

Her muscles relaxed as she sank into the bedding and shifted her body to the side. The cold night air swept into the cave causing the hairs on her skin to raise, so she buried her body deeper into the sheets. The pelt reached up to her cheeks. It was warm and soft, trapping in her body heat while blocking out the cold.

Small egg shell flowers crawled up a gray vine close to her face. This plant was beautiful, having numerous petals of different sizes that folded and unfolded in the darkness, emanating a soft light. Her fingers delicately grazed along the vine. The plant pulsed on her fingertips like an artery full of blood. With every movement, this beautiful plant spat small particles of a dusty substance out from its center, emanating a sweet floral aroma.

She tried to adjust herself to a more comfortable position, but it seemed like a nearly impossible task. The hard ground made her wish she was lying on a soft memory foam bed. Her heart sank as she thought back to the life she once had. She missed the little things now more than ever, and for some reason, when everything around her became quiet, her mind screamed the loudest.

Astra wished she could hear the songs of evening crickets and smell her mother's warm apple pie baking in the oven. She missed hearing her horse whinny in the field and the familiar sound of the lawnmower as her dad cut the grass. She missed how annoying her aunt Lilly seemed when she came over at the most ridiculous times of the night, just to gossip about the latest town news, and how her mother would sit down with an iced tea and patiently wait until she was done. She missed the little things she never realized she would treasure until they were taken away from her. Now she wished she could relive all of those moments and experience those memories once more.

She closed her heavy eyelids and buried her face into the fur. At least with sleep, she could escape her own reality.

Astra found herself standing on a large white and blue glacier in the middle of an endless ocean of tossing water. Clutched in her hand was her warm heart. Every time this organ twitched, a glob of fresh blood slithered down her forearm and landed in a large puddle of red at her feet. She was stripped of everything she knew—as bare as she was when she first came out of her mother's womb and as alone as she felt inside.

She gazed into the pool of blood as images of her once happy family appeared in the reflection. An icy shiver ran down her spine. They were nothing more than reminders of what she no longer had.

She could feel the ache in her chest as the memory of her father tucking her in at night appeared on the blood. He looked down at his daughter, kissing her forehead and mouthing the words, "I love you." She wished she could hear him say that to her right now.

Tears stung her eyes and rolled down her cheeks. Her fingers grazed across his face on the crimson puddle. As the puddle rippled, the image of her father disappeared and an image of her mother, with her back turned to her, was shown in the reflection. Slowly she turned around with her long brown hair cascading down her shoulders. She looked up at Astra with a look of hurt and betrayal crossing her face. Her large bloodshot eyes sadly gazed into hers as she pointed to her and whispered, "Why?"

An icy chill ran down her body. For a moment, she was frozen in place, the emotional anguish was stiffening. Her mouth opened as if she had something to say, but her words were trapped within her. What would she even say to her mother? It felt like a razor was slicing into her already infected heart, causing unbearable agony to radiate through her soul.

"I… I'm so… sorry," she choked on her own words as a deep sinking feeling built inside of her core, creating a dark pressure within her. Like a balloon with too much air in it, her emotions built so rapidly, she felt like she would explode at any second. Her muscles shook uncontrollably as her mother faded away into the pool of dark blood.

Her heart beat faster in her hand as she reached out her other fingers and gasped for air. Please don't go away. Please don't leave.

She longed so much to jump into the puddle of blood and hold her mother in her arms. "Please… Please forgive me," she pleaded, as the heart she held in her hand bled heavier.

CHAPTER 9

Astra snapped awake to see Elde standing over her body, looking down at her uneasily. His hot breath burst onto her face with short clammy puffs as he gently pressed his wet nose against her cheek and eyed her with his disturbingly strange eyes. For a moment, she didn't move. Was she still having a nightmare or was this monster truly this close to her?

What if he turned on her? Would she have the strength to defend herself? Using what? She thought back to Vojin and remembered what he said about a weak spot. Elde had that weak spot. She noticed his temples were sunken in. It would be an easy target to see but difficult to hit if he attacked her.

"I see you're up finally!" Sagan's voice burst through the silent cave. "Elde, come here before you give the poor woman a heart attack." The beast lifted his head and turned towards Sagan. He slowly made his way over to him. "Let me tell you, Elde has been staring at you for the last half an hour. I don't know why but I think he has a thing for you. You make quite the impression."

"I'll make a mental note of that," she replied, trying to shake the dream from her mind and pretend like everything was okay.

"I've been up for some time, so I was able to grab some stuff for the trip. Do you know how to handle a knife?"

"I have a weapon." She patted her pockets.

They were empty. Where did it go? Where was the dagger Vojin gave her? Her teeth ground onto one another. Where was her only form of protection? She shot up quickly and searched around the cave, feeling like her heart was about to explode.

"Are you ok? You look worried about something."

"I had a knife. Where is my knife?" she snapped, looking under the fur she slept on. "I didn't even realize it was gone until now and I'm worried I lost it when I fell. I know I put it in my pocket."

"Oh… Everything Alek found in your pockets he put in his bag to keep safe. Sorry, we meant to give it back, but we forgot. We just didn't want anything to fall out when you were unconscious, since we had to drag you several miles."

"Where is it?"

"Over there." Sagan pointed with his pursed lips. "There must have been someone looking out for you because not only was it not damaged in the fall but you somehow managed to not cut yourself with the knife. How you pulled that one off is beyond me."

"Luck I guess." She searched the numerous bags lying around the cave. She needed to find that tooth. Where was it? Without it, her chances of survival would decrease significantly. "Which bag did you put it in? I want it back. I feel safer having it on me."

"Take a breath, love. It's in that one." Sagan pointed to a leather bag leaning on the side of the cave.

She walked over to the bag and sat down before lifting open the buff leather flap and searching the inside. There were a few dried herbs, what looked like an unfinished weapon, some rope, and finally, nestled safely at the bottom was her dagger.

Was he right that it wasn't damaged in the fall? She took it out and lifted it. Yes, he was right. Everything seemed to be intact and surprisingly enough, the poison not only had remained in place, but was fresh within the vein. She sighed as she lowered the weapon.

"Did your friend give that to you?" Sagan wondered.

"Yes, he did. He wanted me to be able to protect myself."

"That was nice of him. He sounds like a good friend."

"I am lucky I met him."

"I can teach you how to use it during our down time."

"What downtime?"

Sagan smiled. "At some point we will have to find shelter. We'll train there."

"That sounds good. Thank you."

Astra traveled towards the entrance of the cave and peeked outside. The sun had crawled from its grave and reflected its light on the river. She walked further onto the green grass and watched the wildflowers dance in the wind before she approached the river and stood by the water.

As she stared at the nature, she thought about all the creatures on this planet. Was she really in a world ruled by demons? Was Elde a demon? Even though Vojin had explained that they were not really demons, she couldn't help but wonder if maybe they were. They all looked evil to her. Then again, they seemed to think the same about her species.

She ran her fingers through her tangled hair and tried to get some of the knots out. What would today bring? What dangers were lurking around this planet? At least on Earth she would have been able to have a general idea of the dangers she was facing depending on the region she was in. Her jaw tensed with the thought of traveling into the unknown with a complete stranger, but she knew she had no choice.

"Today, I want to give you some pointers about this place," Sagan said as he approached her from behind. She slid the tooth into her pocket. "That way if we ever get separated, you'll know what you can eat and what the different plants can be used for."

"Yeah, that sounds good. I don't really know much about the plants out here."

"You guys leaving now?" Alek asked from behind her.

"Yeah," Sagan replied, adjusting the brown bag on his shoulder.

Alek walked up to Sagan. He stepped in front of him and for a moment, he didn't move or speak. He just stared at his friend with glassy eyes.

"You need to come back safely and come back as soon as you find her friend. I'll wait for you all here and keep Elde company, but I need you to come back in one piece."

"I will."

For a moment longer Sagan and Alek stared at each other before Alek wrapped his arms around his friend. Small creases formed around his tightly shut eyes and it looked like he was holding back tears. He then turned around and walked back into the cave without another word. Was it too hard for him to say the final words of "goodbye?"

She gave Sagan a moment of silence. This must be hard for him. Her eyes grazed across the tumbling green hills on one side of the river and the flat, rock covered lands on the other side, before ending where the river disappeared into the distant mountains.

"Where are we going?" he finally asked after a long pause.

"That way." She pointed to where she last saw the brightest star in the sky. "The star seems to be just on the other side of the water, so I think I need to follow the river."

"You sure?"

She chewed on the edge of her lip. The last thing Vojin told her was to follow the star and he would find her. Though there was a chance that he died during that fight, something in her gut told her he was still alive. Something was whispering to her soul that he would find her and help her get home. She needed to listen to that whisper, even if it was just empty hope.

"Yeah, I am sure. But we need to cross the river. Is there a safe place to do that?"

"I know just the place. Follow me."

They began their journey through the rolling hills beside the blue river. It was just warm enough that Astra took off her jacket and wrapped it around her waist. For the most part, the skies were clear with the occasional cloud that would pass over the sun.

On occasion they would pass under shady trees that grew from the water's edge. Though the cherry bark was smooth, the trunks of the trees were uneven in texture with holes throughout. Roots wrapped around the stones, drinking from the water that splashed from the river.

117

She breathed in, closed her eyes for a moment and saw her father's face. He looked sad. He always looked sad when she thought of him, now that she was on Pannotia.

After a few hours, they finally stopped at a section of the river that had a bridge made of floating stones. These stones were the color of cooked salmon and were about two feet in diameter. It was hard to tell if they were natural or created by someone else since they were perfectly oval and seemed out of place on the river.

The water, which made the stones bobble ever so slightly, was calmer. Sagan made his way across them. They were only about a foot apart so he didn't need to take large steps. Every step he took, the stone dipped slightly under the water, but remained floating.

"Come on Astra! It's safe, don't worry."

She stepped on the first stone and felt it sink a bit. The water caressed the rubber at the base of her shoe but didn't go beyond that. Now that she was so close to the stone, she noticed that it was covered in small holes of different shapes and sizes. She took a few more steps and looked over at her friend who was already halfway across and waiting for her. Creatures of every shape and size swam beneath her in the deep river. Some were long and scaly while others were short and smooth. Though she couldn't see the bottom of the river, she imagined that it was also teaming with life.

"I've never seen anything like this," she whispered as she knitted her brow and watched an eel-like creature, at least thirty feet in length, slither through the cool liquid. "That thing is crazy big."

"It's harmless. Don't worry."

"I hope you're right," she said under her breath. "How deep is this?"

"God, I would not want to find out through swimming to the bottom."

She ground her teeth while she imagined how awful it would feel to sink to the bottom of the river.

"How dangerous are these waters?"

"Not dangerous at all."

"What about that massive thing that just passed under me?"

"The snake looking thing?"

"Yes."

"Oh, that was just a baby. I know because I've seen them get so big that you don't know where they stop or start. They are harmless. I've even swam with them. All they want to do is eat plants and sleep. You will sometimes see them come out of the water for short periods of time to breed."

She stepped onto another bobbing stone. "I take it you have witnessed this event?"

"Yes. It was like watching a creepy animal documentary that you just want to end. At first, I thought they were fighting, but then I realized those weren't screams of pain."

"I wonder how awkward it is to step out after a good night's sleep and there are two river snakes just doing it right in front of you? Do they stop having sex and move to a more private area or are they like explorative hippies, unafraid to display the goods?"

"Mmmm, think free love," Sagan replied as he turned his head towards her.

"Ah, as expected. Speaking of love, I love bathing and I haven't washed in... let's not mention how long it's been, but I'm sure you can "smellstimate" the time. How do you guys keep clean?"

"Well, for the love of God and all things holy, take a bath tonight. I smellstimate it's time. We take baths in this river and have never had a problem with any of the creatures. They just leave you alone and the more curious ones are curious from afar," he said with a chuckle.

A bath was something she had wanted to take for a long time and the thought of washing the dirt off of her seemed like a reality that was too good to be true. She looked down at the water and was almost tempted to jump in, but as another large creature passed underneath the stones she stepped on, she decided to find another time when the water wasn't so deep.

They finally made it to the other side of the river and stepped onto dry land. It was different, going from rolling hills, to a flat land covered in massive rocks that were oftentimes far taller than she was. Some of the rocks were piled on top of one another forming mounds, while others were scattered across the land. Between the rocks, were small green flowers that blended in almost perfectly with the grass. The flowers had six petals and a dot of yellow in the center which was so small she almost missed it.

Her eyes itched as she passed through the land, and she rubbed her runny nose. She must have had a small allergy to the pollen.

Sagan stopped and put his finger up to his lips before pointing behind her. His eyes were wide and suddenly became tense. The muscles around her neck tightened. She knew without even having to look they were about to become the prey to a predator.

Astra turned around. There it was, a beast the size of an Asian elephant. It blended in almost perfectly with the boulder half its size that it stepped out from behind. The monster had black horns that twisted to the sky, and it stared at the river with its wide-set azure eyes. It didn't see them yet, or at least it didn't appear so. The beast walked over to the river, with muscles bulging under a sable fur. Bending down, its long honeydew tongue scooped the water into its massive mouth. There was no fur on its head that was shaped similar to a mapusaurus and as it opened its mouth, it looked like its jaw was split in half in the center.

"Don't move," Sagan mouthed, with a knife already in his hands.

Although he told her not to move, every morsel inside of her wanted nothing more than to run. The seconds they stared at this beast, waiting for its next move, seemed like hours. A single droplet of sweat trickled down her brow as she touched the side of her pocket, too afraid to reach inside and pull out her weapon.

Astra felt a tickle in her nose. Shit. It must have been the pollen from the flowers. She tried to hold back a sneeze but suddenly felt her head lurch forward and the sound erupted from her lips.

The beast's eyes snapped towards them. It rose on two feet and opened its dragon-like jaw, before it pushed out its shoulder blades until they broke through its skin, becoming spikes. Sharp teeth the size of her forearm glistened in the sun's light as an ear-piercing howl erupted from the beast's muscular throat. Its black claws slammed onto the ground before the monster grabbed onto a nearby boulder half her size and hurled it at them. Astra's heart lurched in her chest as the boulder barely missed her head, coming so close to her she could feel the wind rush by.

"Run!" Sagan yelled and raced up a hill towards a large rock formation just a few hundred feet away. She followed him and pulled the weapon out of her pocket.

"I don't want to die. I don't want to die," she thought to herself as she moved her feet as fast as she could.

It lowered its large head and charged towards them, gaining momentum as it did. As fast as she could, she raced towards the rocks, hoping Sagan knew where he was going.

"Climb! FAST!" he yelled out as he jumped up on the rocks and pulled himself higher and higher. As she approached the rocky formation, she turned around just in time to see the creature only feet away. It was too late. She didn't have time to climb.

She twisted to the side. The beast barely missed her and rammed its head into the cracking rocks. A rain of pebbles bounced off her skin as the monster pulled back and shook its head, howling with rage. She jumped out of the way as a large rock rolled loose and crashed down beside her. The beast bared its teeth, and she could have sworn that for a moment, she had seen it smile.

121

She was trapped. The rocks were too steep for her to climb and the beast was only feet away from her. A loud roar exploded from its mouth. It lifted its fist up to the air, ready to crush her.

Sagan leaped from the ledge, onto the back of the monster and landed between his spikes, ramming his weapon into its flesh. With a growling roar, the demon stumbled back and grabbed at Sagan, barely missing him, once, then twice, but before it grabbed at him a third time its head snapped towards sound of a soul crushing roar.

Out of the river came Elde, his once clear antlers glowing a smoking umber red. He left a trail of boiling water in the churning river behind him, and his lips were raised above his teeth.

"Climb!" The voice of Alek was heard clearly.

She turned her head and saw Alek running from the direction they came from. Onto the ground he threw a large bag that he had been carrying on his back. Attached to the bag was a rolled-up fur and on the sides hung a bundle of dried meat.

Elde bared his razor-sharp teeth as Alek ran up behind him with a knife in each hand. The monster let out another deafening roar and slammed its fists, leaving craters in the ground below it. Sagan grabbed onto the knife, pulled it out of its skin, and again stabbed it into its back. The monster reached behind him, barely missing Sagan. He was just out of reach from its deadly claws.

Elde lowered his head and charged, colliding with the angry beast who snapped its jowls towards him. The beast raised its claws and slashed them across his side. Alek ran up and gouged his knife into the ribcage of the beast. He used it and the help of Sagan's hand to push himself on its back.

"Get Astra to safety!" Alek barked as he pulled the knife out of its side and began hacking away at the back of its thick neck.

Sagan ripped his knife from the creature and leaped off its back just as the beast grabbed a hold of Alek and threw him fifty feet across the land. He rolled to a stop, coming inches away from hitting his head against a large boulder. He looked like a warrior with streaks and droplets of the other creature's blood covering his body.

"CLIMB!" Sagan's scream was drowned out by another roar. He hiked up the rocky formation, this time pointing out another rock that was lower to the ground.

Astra again tried to scramble onto it but found that she didn't have the strength to push herself up. It was then that she felt a pair of strong hands lift her from her hips and she was able to climb onto the safety of the first rock. She looked down. It was Alek. He motioned her to keep moving.

Quickly she followed, climbing as fast as she could. She leapt from rock to rock, higher and higher until she finally made it to the top, only twenty-five feet off the ground.

"We're safe up here. He can't climb," Sagan panted. He smiled at Alek who sat down beside him and wiped the blood from his weapon with a cloth he pulled from his pocket.

She couldn't seem to catch her breath and her hands shook uncontrollably. That was close. Too close. Astra looked down as they ripped at each other with their teeth. She had never seen anything so violent. Both creatures fought without fear or mercy.

Elde once again rammed his sizzling antlers into the beast. The creature ripped open Elde's side with one of its black claws. It then picked him up and threw him into the side of a rock. He shook his head. His skin was split open at the side of his face from the impact he made with the rock. Again, he lifted his lips over his nose, showing his massive teeth dripping with saliva.

Elde charged. They collided. He snapped at the beast, barely missing it once, twice, three and four times, before biting down on its throat and ripping a chunk out. The beast sliced open Elde's chest just as his antlers burned into its side.

Though she wanted to turn away, she could not. Her eyes were locked onto this horrible vision, hoping for the best but afraid for the worst. How would she survive in this world when creatures like this lived here?

Elde peeled back a chunk of the creature's skin, causing a vein to explode onto the green grass as it ripped in half. His chest

123

heaved with every breath as it dripped in blood. She wanted to help him, but she was paralyzed with fear and knew she would do nothing more than get in the way. Turning to her side, she looked at Sagan and Alek who blankly gazed at the battle. They were unaffected by this macabre scene. Had they seen this before?

With a howl, the beast collapsed on the ground. It struggled to get up but fell again. Elde snorted and stomped his feet, looking down at the creature. He shook his head, splattering the grass with droplets of his blood.

Elde wrapped his mouth around the defeated animal's neck who closed its eyes. With a quick thrust, he ripped the throat from this creature's body, consuming the bloodied flesh. As the beast's head fell to the ground, its tongue lolled out of its mouth and its muscles became limp. A puddle of crimson blood formed, slowly creeping its way across the grass.

Elde looked down at its chest. A small area about the size of her fist began to bulge and as it did so, a cracking sound was heard. Broken ribs tore open the flesh, creating a bloodied opening the length of her hand. The bones stuck out of corners of this opening like shards of pine. He narrowed his eyes as a red mass covered in thick purple veins pushed through. The opening stretched wider as this mass bulged from the cut. Finally, what appeared to be an organ the size of a softball fell onto the ground. In an instant, it was consumed.

"How did he do that?" she asked as she cringed at the blood coating his lips. "What did he just eat?"

"A heart," Sagan responded. "He's telekinetic but I've only seen him use it to pull the hearts out of the ones he kills. It's easier if he pulls it through the throat instead of breaking open the ribs but for some reason today, he chose to do it through the chest."

"This entire concept is disgusting," she replied, her upper lip tensing.

"You'll get used to it. At first it is a bit much, but after a while you become numb to it."

"I'm not sure I can become numb to death."

"I didn't think I could either, but now that it has become such a norm in my life, I am shocked at the things that I am used to."

CHAPTER 10

By the time she climbed down, Elde was fully healed and his horns were no longer glowing and hot. Though he was coated in red, she knew that it was only a matter of moments before he would enter the water and wash himself clean.

Elde approached, his sharp teeth once again covered by his lips. A string of bloody drool dripped out of his mouth. He snorted and sniffed any cuts she had. His massive head made its way over every inch of her body before moving to the men and doing the same.

"What's he doing?" She wondered as she watched him lick a deep gash in Sagan's calf. "Oh my God, I didn't even see that! Are you okay?"

"I know it's gross, but look." Sagan twisted his leg. Like a spider weaving his web, his skin weaved together, leaving no evidence of his previous injury.

"Does he have healing spit?" she wondered with a curled lip.

Sagan laughed and threw the brown bag over his shoulder. "No, it's the blood from the animal he ate. Fresh blood here heals. Old blood though, depending on the animal, is dangerous when consumed. The whole thing is kind of weird if you ask me." He turned to his friend. "What are you doing here? I thought you were going to stay back at the cave and wait for us?"

"No. You're my family. I can't just leave you like this. If you are going to make stupid decisions, I am going to be right there with you to get you out of them."

Sagan smiled and wrapped his arms around him. "I knew you'd come around."

Alek looked down at the corpse of the animal. "We can't have what just happened, happen again. At some point we are going to be attacked and we need Astra to be a lot stronger than she is now. Let's gather some herbs and then get that root we had when we got here. She could use that. We need food for tonight and she needs to learn what is edible and what is not, in case we get separated and she ends up on her own."

"What root?" She wondered.

"I'll show you soon and I will explain everything."

Alek and Sagan gathered herbs, fruits, and a variety of nuts for about half an hour. They placed them within the satchels as well as hung them on the outside to dry. Once the bags were full, Sagan pointed in the direction where they needed to head to and they began their journey, this time as a group of four.

The land continued to be rugged for the rest of the day, but the piles of boulders became less in number and more spread apart. Some of the land they walked through was covered in green grass while other areas were covered in red flowers. These flowers reached about the length of her ankle and became so numerous that it was oftentimes hard to see if there was any grass underneath.

The air became more humid the further they walked and left her skin uncomfortably sticky. She could feel sweat had formed between her shoulder blades and wanted nothing more than to dive into the crisp waters of the river. The sun felt hotter here than it did back near the cave. Even though her shoes were typically comfortable to walk in, she had walked for so many miles that she could feel the soreness of blisters which had formed on the back of her ankles. Everyone but Elde seemed exhausted. The animal walked with a bounce in his step and would occasionally nudge them if one of them started to slow down more than the others.

Finally, they came across a rocky structure in the shape of a "U" around twenty feet away from the river. Though it didn't have a roof to protect them from the elements, the shade that crossed over the structure at least provided protection from the sun's harsh rays. The structure was about ten feet high and looked more like the remains of something rather than a natural occurrence.

"We've been walking for most of the day and this is the first place in a while that will give us protection and keep us somewhat hidden. Let's make camp for the night to be safe," Sagan said as he wiped the sweat from his brow and leaned against Elde.

"But there is still light out," she pointed to the sky. Yes, she was exhausted. Yes, rest sounded heavenly. But she needed to get back to her father and she couldn't wait even a minute longer. Astra needed to let him know she was alive. He needed to know before he lost hope. "Shouldn't we go on a bit further? At least until it's dark?"

"Don't be stupid," Alek rolled his eyes. "If we go on until it's dark, it will be too late. There isn't another shelter here for miles."

"I hate to say it, but I am with Alek on this. We have already been attacked once today and I wouldn't have the energy to fight the way I'd need to if we were attacked again."

"How do you even know that there isn't a shelter? There are rocks all over this place! Maybe even something with a roof, like a cave or something."

"There isn't. We know this area and we built this because there wasn't anything around."

She gazed at the rocks casting shadows across the ground. "How did you build this? These rocks are at least a couple hundred pounds a piece."

"Well pretty girl, we are stronger than we look. Especially the creepy man over there." He pointed to Sagan who winked in response.

Alek sat on the ground and motioned his hand for her to sit down. "I'm going to teach you about these plants."

He took off his bag and pulled open the flap of his brown satchel. He then set it down in front of his folded legs. A smell permeated the area with the strong musk of different herbs which seemed only to get stronger as the time trailed on.

Alek first pulled out a freshly cut green plant with small red and yellow buds on it, a brown round root with sharp green thorns covering the base, a veiny root from one of the carnivorous plants with dried blood encrusting the areas where it was cut, and a vibrantly colored nut. Gently he placed each plant by her legs until the bag became empty.

Setting aside the satchel, Alek picked up the first plant and placed it in the palm of her hand. She carefully examined it, along with the others. She wanted to remember every groove, dip and color of each one. Mistaking one plant to be another could lead to unwanted results including sickness, death, or a fate worse than death itself.

She wondered what he wanted her to do with each one. Was he wanting her to study them the way she was, or was he planning on giving her further instructions? As his honey brown eyes met hers, he looked at her in a way that made her squirm. She hated how she felt like a piece of meat without him saying or doing anything. Perhaps she was misreading him. She hoped so.

"What do you see when you look at this?" He questioned, a crease forming between his thick eyebrows as he pointed to the plant. "Thoroughly examine it and tell me every detail. What do you think is edible and what do you think is not?"

"I see…" Squinting, she lifted the plant closer to her face and wiped her runny nose with her free hand. Damn her allergies. "The buds on the plant are twitching when I touch them. I feel like it is still alive because unlike the rest of the thick stem, there is a section in the center that's thin. I know this sounds crazy but I feel something beating, like a heart or something. As far as edible is concerned, I'm honestly not sure what I can eat on this thing. Maybe the flower buds?"

Alek smirked and gave a quick nod. "You're right. It's alive. After you pull it out of the ground, it usually lives for three or four hours. You can find it in shady areas around water sources—like lakes, rivers, and places like that. They usually grow in groups so they are easy to spot.

129

"This plant is sensitive to any touch. You can tell by how the buds move when you barely touch them. I've even heard a few make a weird squeaking noise when I pull them out of the ground. What's even weirder, when they squeak, the plants in the ground, will suck in all of their buds, like they are trying to hide or something. When they do this, it makes it difficult to distinguish this plant from the thicker grass.

"I like to use this plant when I'm dehydrated. You need to take the part of the stem that is the thinnest and push your finger into it. You can tell which part this is by feeling where the pulse is the strongest. Once you have pushed your finger into it, stick the flower buds in your mouth and suck in as hard as you can." Alek handed her the plant. With a mischievous and untrustworthy grin, he snorted, "Have fun sucking."

She ignored his comment and glanced at Sagan to see if he had caught on to the innuendo. He didn't seem to notice and instead looked like he was lost in thought.

Her eyes lingered on the plant that twitched in her palm. It reacted to her every touch, shaking almost as if it was frightened. Was she hurting it? Was it consciously aware of what was about to happen?

"Come on! What's taking you so long?" Alek impatiently waved his hand.

"Chill for a second."

"Why? Are we in California now?"

"What?"

"You sounded like a bro."

"Lord have mercy, am I the only one in this cave who wants to regularly slap Alek?"

"No," Sagan responded with a laugh. "I am right there with you. Why are you hesitant?"

"It seems alive. What if I am hurting an innocent creature? I don't want to be that kind of person."

"Plants don't think," Alek grumbled. "They aren't like us and they don't have a soul. This plant just reacts probably the same way that a Venus fly trap reacts."

"Well even if it did, you wouldn't care. You have no problem killing things to get their meat," she replied, thinking back to the animal he slaughtered the night before. How could anyone look at an animal in the eye and know that they were the result of its suffering and death?

"And you have no problem eating the things I kill. You're going to have to get used to death. Every time you eat meat but then claim that you can't hurt anything, you are doing nothing more than lying to yourself and being a hypocrite."

"How am I being a hypocrite? I've never hurt or killed anything."

Alek snorted. "Oh please, I am sure you have killed bugs in your life or gone fishing, which means you play God, picking and choosing what you see as a valuable life form and what you don't. You may like to pretend like you're a good little country girl who doesn't hurt or kill anything, but you support the death of others every time you eat from their flesh. You might not be doing the killing but every time you went to the market and bought meat, you paid a corporation to kill it for you. Sticking your head in the ground and pretending that meat somehow magically appeared on your burger doesn't change the reality that it once belonged to an animal. You kill what you want to kill and claim it doesn't count because you don't see value in their life.

"Out here, we don't have the luxury of grocery stores where you can turn a blind eye to the harsh reality of the circle of life. You either suck it up and come to terms with the fact that you have to kill to survive, or you're going starve to death. Sagan and I are not going to hold your hand.

"So, what is your choice going to be? Are you going to suck it up and learn how to survive or are you going to continue to sit on your hypocritical moral throne, shaming those who do what they need to do in order to survive?"

She kept her mouth shut. Her cheeks burned as she lowered her head. Why couldn't she just disappear?

131

Sagan placed his hand on her shoulder and looked her deep in the eyes. "Look, I know it's hard to get over the whole death and survival thing but that is how we have made it out here. We can't survive without food, and yes, everything out here seems to have some sort of conscious awareness, even the plants, but we can't think like that. We will eat other things until eventually something eats us. Everything always comes in a full circle."

"I wish things weren't so harsh out here," she quietly said as she hid behind her brown hair.

"One day maybe we will be lucky and somehow find a way back home and if we do, you can live off of chips and pizza. We can go to the grocery store together and buy chicken nuggets and pretend like the chicken laid the nuggets the way she laid eggs. Hell, if you end up deciding you want to go vegan, I will be there right with you eating soy dogs and tofu burgers. You won't ever have to tie a face to what you are eating, but until then, I need you to be a little more open to this. Just do what I do and empty your mind. Pretend like your reality is nothing more than a dream because maybe if you are lucky, one day it will be just a memory of a tough time you survived."

She breathed out a slow sigh and nodded her head. Sliding her finger down the stem, she searched for the thinnest area. As soon as she pushed her finger into it, a hiss poured from the stem causing a stream of blood to trickle out. The plant lurched in her hand.

Hesitantly, she closed her eyes and placed the buds between her lips before she sucked the tasteless juice from it. The plant shook in her mouth until the last drop of liquid slid onto her tongue. Her lips parted. The small withered plant fell out and onto the top part of her hand like a wet noodle. Immediately, the red and yellow buds crumpled up, turning a sickly gray color as the last bit of life left it.

Astra peeled back the skin and gazed down upon the area she'd pushed her finger into. There was a small heart with two of its arteries ripped in half. It was then she noticed between the withered buds lay a cluster of eyes, with their lids now closed. This plant saw its death coming.

Sagan smiled. "There are crazy plants here. I've heard a couple different ones in this place scream, hiss, and make sounds that remind me of crickets. It's a bit much to get used to."

"This wasn't like a Venus fly trap. This thing had a life. It had a freaking heart for god sakes! Why would you lie to me?" She glared at Alek waiting for an answer.

"You'll be fine." Alek grabbed the oval seed and shoved it in her hands. "You need to keep learning."

She ground her teeth but knew he was right. She did need to keep learning or else she wouldn't make it out here.

A putrid rotting scent assaulted her senses. She furrowed her nose and looked down at the oval seed in her hands. It was a heavy seed that was so large it had to be held with two hands. A rainbow of swirling colors floated around on the surface, reflecting the light. She pressed down on the exterior and watched the colors transform, remembering back to the abstract paintings she used to create as a child.

"What's this one good for and why does it smell so horrible?"

"I asked the same thing when I first met you." Alek chuckled at his own joke.

"That wasn't funny."

"It was to me."

"I didn't think it was that funny either," Sagan interjected.

"That isn't my problem. Moving on, we use this for cuts and burns. It works well. I usually find them under trees whose bark looks similar to the colors you see on the seed. They kind of look like rainbow trees with leaves of every color imaginable. They are hard to find because the trees are normally found growing between two boulders. You have to open it by taking the skin and breaking a small section at the top. You can use a knife, a rock, or pretty much anything sharp. The surface is weak. Once you've done that, you need to squeeze the liquid onto your cut or burn and bam, you are good.

"I like this stuff because it will heal it within the day. The downside is it burns like hell's fire when you first put it on. This stuff kind of reminds me of rubbing alcohol or that awful liquid bandage that makes even the smallest cuts feel like canyons of pain."

Alek handed her the next plant with a large grin crossing his face. It was the kind of grin that she wanted to slap right off his cheeks.

She looked down. The rough-textured thorny root was surprisingly heavy in her hand. It had a dripping layer of a slimy-sticky residue over the surface and a strong smell of peppermint that appeared to come from the bottom. The base of the root had a small hole covered in tiny moving antennas. As the slime dripped from her hands, she found herself having the urge to drop this root and take a long scolding hot shower.

"What is this?" She attempted to push her finger into the impenetrable surface. "Oh my God, don't tell me I will have to eat this. I will kill you if you say I'll have to eat this."

"You have a hard time killing a plant. I'm sure that I'm safe," Alek responded.

"Don't test me," she replied and furrowed her nose. "I like the plants. You on the other hand, I am still deciding on."

Alek handed her a sharp rock. His expression suddenly became serious as he barked out orders. "Crack it open just enough to see a slit, but don't open it entirely. Then put the crack up to your mouth. Swallow everything that comes out whole. No chewing."

"What? You're kidding me, right? Do you see what's on this?" Holding up the root, she watched with wide eyes as a glob of slime dripped off the surface and slapped onto the floor. "And you want me to put my mouth on that?"

"Yeah man," Alek bluntly said. "I dare you."

"Are we in middle school now?"

"I double dare you."

"Oh, shit's getting real up in here!" Sagan chimed in from behind them. "Alek just pulled the double dare card! Now you have to. You can't deny a double dare. It goes against the laws of nature."

"No, it does not, and I don't see you sucking up this slime ball," she snapped.

"We've both done it. Now it's your turn," Sagan smiled as he looked at her with his large playful eyes.

She shuddered. "To get the both of you to shut up, I'll do it. But I am not happy putting my mouth on this."

She grabbed a rock and hammered a small crack into the surface. Once the skin of the root was broken, the surface went from opaque and hard to translucent and soft. She looked at the contents inside, unsure how to feel.

Within the root lay a large long bug uncoiling itself. Like a baby bird in an egg, this creature slowly chewed on the clear yolk-like contents it swam in. The bug gazed at her with bulbous eyes full of childlike innocence and licked its plump lips with its pink tongue.

"Swallow it." Alek said flatly.

"You have officially lost your damn mind. It's still alive. That's cruel to do to something that reminds me of a cartoon character. I mean look at those eyes. How can you not love it? On top of that, asking a woman to swallow a bug is not acceptable. You know our reputations. We see bugs, we scream, you take care of it. It's the circle of life."

"In the 1950s swallowing tape worms was a fad. Women would pay to do that crap. As they say, history repeats itself."

"Oh my God, Alek is this a weight loss worm? Because I am going to be pissed if it is."

Alek smirked and raised his eyebrow. "No. You're already a twig that probably will blow away in the next windstorm."

"Was that supposed to be flattering? Because it's not," she replied with narrow eyes.

"You're a cute twig, don't worry." Alek snapped back into the stoic expression he normally held. "Seriously, this is the most important thing you can do to help yourself on this planet. When we first got here, Sagan and I found this thing when we had no

135

food. We were starving and weak. Both of us were so hungry we swallowed it whole, not even thinking about it. Within a few hours we suddenly felt lightheaded and nauseated. It almost made us feel like we had the flu—"

"Yeah it sucked while it happened, but when we woke up, we both realized that we were different, but in a good way," Sagan merrily chimed in.

"What do you mean by that?"

"There is something about this bug which helps increase speed. It gave us abilities we never had before." Alek's face held no expression except for the tenseness he held in his jaw. "I wasn't strong when I came here and overnight I went from not being able to lift over 80 pounds to having no trouble lifting things twice my weight. I know it makes you uncomfortable, but this worm is well worth it. You'll run faster, climb easier, and it really changes you. It helps you get over fear and become more... alien I guess you could say. I wouldn't be telling you to do this if it would put you in any kind of risk."

Sagan walked up from behind her and touched her shoulder, "I'm with Alek on this. This isn't what caused me to have my stunning looks. So, don't worry, that happened a year later. Both of us swallowed this little guy and the worst that happened for me was a small headache and I felt a bit achy. When I woke up the next day, I was fine. Alek was more nauseated than anything and he projectile vomited. It's kind of like the aftermath of ecstasy but without the fun time."

"Really? That detail was necessary?" Alek protested as Elde laid down beside him with a grunt.

"Yes, my grumpy banana," Sagan cooed before turning back to her. "The worm in your hand is a lot bigger than the ones we had, but if anything at all, it's a good thing. I would do it if I was in your position, but honestly it's up to you and what you're comfortable with."

"I am wary about doing this," she said while squinting her eyes. "For so many reasons."

"We understand," Alek replied. "You don't have to do anything you don't want to, but you also don't want to be the weakest link. If you don't do it, you will die. It's not a matter of if, it's a matter of when."

Thoughts spun in her mind as she looked at the tiny creature in her hands, swimming slowly around its home. Should she trust these strangers and take this? She wasn't sure what the long-term effects could be. Yes, short term it helped these men but there was no way of knowing the dangers this could cause. Then again, she knew she couldn't think long term because her odds of even living into her mid adult years were against her. There were too many risks she would take not consuming this creature. An increased amount of speed and strength would help her significantly in surviving on this planet and the last thing she wanted to be was, as Alek had so graciously pointed out, the weakest link.

Hesitantly, she placed the crack up to her lips, feeling the contents slowly flow onto her tongue. The yolk inside of the root filled her mouth with a rancid taste. Her face twisted as she felt the bug slide between her lips and writhe around her tongue before slithering down her throat. Immediately she gagged, feeling the acidic caress of stomach bile slide up and down her throat, scratching the inside with a stinging grit. The feeling of queasiness swept over her as she leaned back against a rock to calm herself down. She knew she'd made the right decision, but what would her symptoms be from doing this?

"See? All that bitching and it wasn't so bad." Alek had a look of satisfaction creeping across his face.

Astra leaned over. She felt the sensation of lightness in her head as nausea settled deep in her core.

"You don't look like you feel well." Sagan's dark brows raised over his black eyes as he patted her on the back.

"No shit. I wonder if this is what it feels like to drink iowaska," she gasped, rubbing her watering eyes.

"Probably, but I wouldn't know. You did well though. Don't worry, it will be okay," he responded in a disturbingly soothing tone.

Her mind spun like a maelstrom. What would happen to her now that she had swallowed this creature? She thought back to its large blinking eyes and wanted to vomit. That creature, that thing, was inside of her now. She wasn't sure if it was all in her head, but she could swear she could feel it moving around her gut.

She touched her throat as another wave of nausea radiated through her body. God, she hated that feeling more than anything else in the world. Her stomach tensed as she fought back more vomit, before swallowing the spit that formed in her mouth.

Alek handed her the next plant, ready to continue as if she was fine, which clearly she wasn't. Astra gazed blankly at the dried root in her hand. No, she couldn't do this. Her need to take a break was far greater than her will to learn at the moment.

"I'm sorry. I need a moment alone."

"Are you okay?" Sagan asked as he reached out his hand. "Do you need someone to accompany you?"

"No. Like I said, I need to be alone."

She quickly scurried out of the camp and made her way towards the river. A cool breeze pulled at her hair, cooling down her palms and forehead. For a moment, she stopped and leaned over, trying to fight the sensation of her stomach convulsing. Though she still felt nauseous, she was relieved to get away from everyone.

The sun mercilessly pounded on her back as Astra searched the water path in front of her. She glanced back towards the camp. Elde peeking his large muscular head from the around the rocks. God he was creepy.

That was all the encouragement she needed to start walking. She wasn't sure where she was going; she only knew she needed to empty her mind, away from everyone. Astra knew she would not be long, but she decided she would make it a point not to come back until she felt somewhat better on all levels.

Walking always had a soothing effect on her. She used to do it barefoot as a child through the smoky mountains. She loved how she could wake up early in the morning and experience the intense fog surrounding her like thick, cold, smoke. She would take these walks before she had to go to school, which was her way of starting the day off on the right foot. By the time she was done, she was wide awake and ready to learn.

Tennessee. Every time she thought of that place, she felt a different emotion. There would be times she would think of a memory and smile, before feeling her heart sink into her chest, while other times she felt her anxiety shoot through the roof. What would happen if her father gave up? She needed to get back to him soon. She needed to get back to him before it was too late.

She stopped by the river and allowed the water to touch the edges of her shoes. Tauntingly, the sun lit the world around her, feeding the overly cheery flowers standing upon the grass as they reached up to drink the golden nectar of the light. The meadow flowers danced in the wind with every breeze as small creatures resembling hummingbirds flew from one bud to the next, drinking from the liquids within. Though she was still surrounded by large stones, the land no longer looked cluttered.

Her eyes lowered to the ground as she thought about all the times when she would play in the creeks that flowed through the Tennessee mountains. Feelings of loneliness and homesickness came in emotional waves, crashing over her. She longed to be in her own bed, engulfed in a good book or eating an ice cream on a hot summer day. The thought of having a sweet tea on her dad's porch while watching her horse galloping though the field seemed like a distant heaven. Just to relive one of these moments, to experience that joy just once more, she would have gladly given her life.

CHAPTER 11

Sweat trickled down the side of her face as she gazed at the water flowing gently towards the distant mountain range. She looked down at her dirty skin and scrunched her nose. A bar of soap would have been exactly what she needed.

Astra walked over to a large stone and sat down on its flat surface. She took off her shoes and socks before dipping her legs into the crisp water. The water provided almost an immediate tension relief to her sore feet and calves.

She slipped off her clothing and placed them on the stone beside her before slipping into the cool water. This was the relief she needed. Her muscles sank deeper into the liquid.

For a few minutes, she remained where she was, trying to calm down her nausea. She needed a distraction from the way her body physically felt, so she decided it was time to wash her clothing.

First, she grabbed her scarf which was stained with blood and dirt. It was a harsh reminder of the fear she felt the moment she first arrived on Pannotia. Cleaning the cloth was almost therapeutic. In a strange way, it made her feel like she was a step closer to getting home. When she finally finished cleaning the dirt off her clothing, she laid each out on the rock to dry in the sunlight before she turned around and swam deeper into the river.

Small river creatures about the size and shape of a legless lizard nibbled at her skin, tickling her with their soft lips. These small creatures were beautiful and vibrantly colored despite their serpent-like appearance. They glided through the water with grace while looking at the world with their yellow-blue eyes.

In the utmost state of relaxation she dipped her head into the water, fully immersing herself and swimming further into the river. In the distance, her ears picked up on burbling sounds and the echoing of two creatures communicating in the deeper areas. The noises they emitted were so strong she could feel the vibrations through her bones.

Astra was in awe at the aquatic heaven she swam through. She was at the edge of an underwater cliff. Bright vibrant-green plants, stretched up towards the sunlight from the cliff bottom below. Each plant had a bright pink bud at the top which moved independently from the current. These flower buds seemingly gulped the water as they excreted puffs of lavender and fuchsia from tubes underneath the petals.

Small fish and river creatures of all shapes and colors, danced between the plants waving in the current. Creatures that reminded her of giant clams with small protruding tentacles, bounced from rock to rock on the cliffs edge. They scooped the algae from the stones onto the top of their shells with their long tongue.

She tilted her head as she observed a large prehistoric-looking fish approaching one of the clams. Slowly the shell opened, revealing a single eye surrounded by teeth. The fish quickly attempted to swim away but the creature within the shell reached out, grabbed the fish, and pulled it into its shell, which snapped shut on its victim. The only remnants left of the fish was a small puff of blood seeping from the predator's mouth.

Her muscles tensed as she saw a long eel-like creature swim towards her. It had thick yellow skin and bulky fins. The river animal moved through the water quickly and rigidly. Astra was unsure whether or not she should swim away or hold still. She reminded herself of what Sagan had said about the river being safe, before remembering he also mentioned that river animals kept their distance. This one most certainly did not seem like it was going to.

Before she could make a rational decision of whether to swim away or hold still, this beast was already on top of her, touching her body with its slimly scales. As the river monster coiled around her torso, she noticed a thin layer of skin covering its bulbous yellow eyes. Could it clearly see her or was she was nothing more than a blurred image?

Astra refused to move. Her heart pounded through her ears as her head tingled. She needed air. Her lungs ached for it. But what would be the consequences of swimming to the surface? Would this river monster attack her? Would it leave her alone?

Feeling a pressure in her head, she realized if she didn't get oxygen, it wouldn't matter what the beast's unpredictable actions would be, she would drown regardless. She needed to get to the surface, but the animal continued to coil around her body.

She had to take the risk now. There was no other choice. She shoved the creature away from her and rushed towards the surface, which felt like an eternity away.

Finally, her face broke through. She gasped for air, gulping as much as she could into her lungs before swimming towards the rocks. Where was the creature? Was it going to leave her alone? She turned her head. The water burst open behind her and the river monster slithered towards her at an accelerating speed.

Astra kicked her legs harder, trying to get away. Her muscles ached with the stress she was putting on them as she thrashed her arms in front of her, pushing herself towards the land as quickly as she could.

The eel followed her closely behind. It opened its mouth and flashed sharp teeth before sinking back below the surface of the water. It was ready for its meal and she was on the menu.

Her lungs burned as they convulsed with every cough. She raced towards the rocks and tasted the cold water as it sloshed into her mouth. The eel burst through the surface, only a few feet away. Teeth bared, it snapped at her legs, trying to catch her flesh, while barely missing.

She felt a tooth rip into her calf. Crimson water churned behind her as blood seeped from her body. The beast opened its mouth to bite down again and as it did, she pulled her leg free and kicked it in its head as hard as she could.

The rocks were only a few feet from where she was. She needed to swim faster and use the few moments the creature was stunned to her advantage.

As soon as she threw her body on the rocks, she swung around to the sight of the beast quickly approaching. It raised its eyes above the surface and locked onto her. For a moment, her chest felt as if the fist of a giant was holding onto it. She didn't want to move. Fear held her as a prisoner. She could feel its anger seep through its soul as it stared at her with the hatred one would have for only its worst enemy. Finally, it turned around and slipped beneath the surface. It had given up, at least for now. Luck was on her side this time but next time that might not be the case.

Astra slipped her clothing back onto her body and touched the knife in her pocket. It brought her a sense of safety knowing that it was there, even if she didn't know how to use it. Her calf throbbed and for some reason her pant leg seemed to stick to her skin. She pushed this sensation aside as another wave of nausea swept over her. Damn that feeling. Damn that worm. She leaned over. Her stomach lurched, pushing vomit out of her burning throat. It tasted like stomach bile and pinched her cheeks.

"I just want to be home. I just want to feel safe again," she said to herself.

Astra never realized how nice it was to just have a simple life, until now. The things she didn't appreciate in her old day-to-day life, she craved to have back and realized she didn't know how lucky she was until she lost it all.

Vojin. He was constantly on her mind. Not just because of his kindness but because he was the key to getting her back home. She missed her father so much her heart ached. She missed his laughter, his jokes, and his quirks. She missed feeling like she had a home and a family.

Did Sagan and Alek miss their family the way she missed hers? They certainly seemed like they had come to terms with their stay here. Did they constantly think about how their loved ones were doing? Did they dream of what it would be like to be reunited with them or had they given up hope? She had a hard time reading Sagan, but Alek seemed like he was content living in a cave for the rest of his days.

Should she tell the men that she knew of a way back? Could she trust them with that information? She certainly didn't trust Alek, there was something about him that seemed off, but Sagan, he seemed like a good person. Was it wrong not to tell him? He was so eager to help her. Would she be able to live with herself knowing that she knew of a way back and knowing that she was just using him to get to where she needed to be? She knew he would have questions when she refused to go back with him. He would be hurt because he risked his life for her and a friend he never met, only for her to abandon him when she got what she needed.

She glanced towards the evening sky. Like a crimson and lavender war, the sun fought to stay in the heavens for as long as possible, even though it knew it would lose the battle to the warrior of the night. Clouds scraped against the atmosphere as the dying sun submitted to the oppression of the darkness.

* * *

"Shit you look pale," Alek said as she approached the camp. He had a handful of flaking wood in his arms. "But don't worry, you're still cute."

"And you still look like a douche," she replied before entering the camp and sitting down by the flickering orange flames.

She looked at Elde lying down on a few of the blankets and leaning against the rocky wall. His white fur seemed to glow in the low light of the fire as he rested his head to take a short nap. He yawned and as he did so, it appeared as though his lips seemed to split in half, revealing a row of enormous teeth.

"Holy shit! What happened to your leg?" Sagan blurted out as he pointed to her sticky pants.

She lifted her pant leg and looked down at her muscle. Though she had ignored the pain as she walked, she had noticed the warm sensation of blood as it coated her skin.

"I was bit by a river monster. Apparently, I am not good at making new friends around these parts."

"I told you not to talk to strangers," Sagan said with a raised brow. "They tend to bite on this planet."

"But he offered me candy."

"Well in that case, I fully understand."

Alek kneeled down on the ground with a nut full of mushed up herbs and pushed it into the cut.

"What is that?" She howled as a radiating pain shot through her leg.

"It's a mixture we make. It helps keep the blood of our kills fresh," Alek said with a serious tone as he placed the nut back into his leather bag. "Though it takes longer to heal, your skin will be good as new in the next few hours."

"Blood from what?"

"The kill I made the other day. I always set aside blood in case of emergencies, but I can't leave it out without preserving it. These plants help that," he nodded. "See? The one you just called a douche isn't so much of a douche after all."

"No, you still wear that label like a badge of honor but you did gain a few points now that you are being nicer."

"How are you feeling?" Sagan wondered.

"Still nauseous but not as bad as it was."

"Are you okay with eating dinner? I would understand if you don't want to, but I think you should at least try. We have a long walk tomorrow and walking on an empty stomach sucks."

"I'll try." She cringed at the thought of eating anything else.

Sagan shuffled through his leather pouch resting against the wall as he gathered herbs and roots which were collected earlier in the day. Once his hands were full of green colorful plants, he walked back over the fire, setting them down in front of the flames. She couldn't tell what he was planning on making, but by the strong smell that permeated from this greenery, she knew it

145

was not something she wanted to eat, despite her stomach's loud demands for sustenance.

"I wanted to give this to you. I made it before I met you, but I feel like you could use it."

Alek walked over, handing her a bag made of fur and stitched together with sinew. Why was he suddenly trying to be nice to her? Was this another way for him to flirt with her? Or perhaps he realized his wrongdoings and wanted to make amends. Then again, maybe he was trying to get her to put down her guard so she would be vulnerable and weak.

Astra touched the square satchel. The thick layer of fur on the outside was soft and the inside was filled with dried herbs and roots of all shapes and colors.

"What's the catch?"

"What do you mean?"

"Since when are you nice?"

"I'm nice!"

"You're confusing, that's what you are."

"It's just in case you ever get lost or randomly hungry during the night. You're too pretty to go hungry," he responded, as lines formed on his forehead. "I made sure all the plants I put in there are the ones that taste the best."

Yep. He was clearly flirting, which was something she wished he would stop.

"I take it these are all poisonous."

"Half of them are poisonous. You get to figure out which ones," he replied with a wink as he got up and walked over to Sagan.

"So, you gave her the purse you made a year ago?" Sagan laughed, "I got to give it to you Alek, you sure know how to make a purse."

"It's a bag. Not a purse. You're the only one who wears purses out here, Sagan," he retorted.

"It just means that I am the only one with a high sense of fashion. I am living proof being in the wilderness on a foreign planet is no excuse not to look a hundred percent," he replied with a confident snap of his fingers before he got back to work.

"So, why the sudden kindness?" she asked. She needed him to admit in front of Sagan that he was flirting so that his friend would at least be aware and hopefully would recognize how uncomfortable it made her feel. She hoped he could help put a stop to it.

Alek sighed. "What, was my first response not good enough for you?"

"No. You want me to be honest, so I expect the same."

"Sagan and I had a talk when you left and I realized he had a point. I've been pretty harsh to you and unwelcoming. I am going to try to make an effort to be nicer, but I do ask that you try to make an effort and trust us a bit more. We don't want to hurt you or wrong you in any way. We are just two guys, stuck in the middle of nowhere, trying to survive."

Vojin was clear, don't trust anyone, even if they looked like her. She wanted to trust them, but she also knew she needed to be careful.

* * *

After dinner, she unwrapped her jacket from her waist and opened it up. She laid down on the grass close to the fire.

"Want a blanket?" Sagan asked as he pulled a fur out of his bag. "I brought an extra one for you."

"I'm okay for tonight. Thank you."

It was too warm to use a fur as a blanket but too cold not to have at least something covering her arms, so her jacket was used in place of a blanket.

She yawned as she closed her eyes and nuzzled her face into the grass. Though a carousel of thoughts threatened to take over her mind, her consciousness ebbed and was slowly pulled into the world of dreams. She embraced this feeling, because the moments she was asleep were the moments she could escape the reality of Pannotia and fall into a place nestled deep in her subconscious.

147

Astra stood in the middle of an endless ocean of steaming blood, touching the gray horizon. This thick sticky liquid coated her ankles with warmth and covered her feet like a crimson blanket. She could feel the bodies of tiny maggots twisting between her toes as the smell of rot flooded her nostrils, nauseating her to the core. Above her head, swollen clouds ached as they longed to release their tears onto the barren ground below. These iron clouds hung ominously low, bearing the memories she tried to forget but could not seem to.

She found herself in her own soul, an endless pit of guilt contained by a barrier of clouds she had formed in order she might forget her past and move on. But forgetting wouldn't happen. Even when she tried, it never took away from the pain which bled her from the inside and rotted the core within.

She looked down at her hands. Crimson liquid dripped from underneath her fingernails, feeding the pool she stood in. She was naked; vulnerable to every emotion she tried to ignore and no matter how hard she tried to cover herself, she was still exposed.

In front of her, her mother appeared, blankly staring through her and into nothingness, as if she was in some sort of deep hypnosis. Black tears stained her cheeks, trickling from her bloodshot eyes, while parts of her body rotted away, revealing her tender insides. Her stomach lurched as she looked at pale maggots squirming beneath her mother's skin.

"Hi," Astra whispered, her eyes absorbing her mom's beautiful face, still expressionless and staring into the void. The longer she looked at her, the more her heart felt as if it was pushing out of her chest and reaching towards her.

With a quivering chin and shaking hands she approached her mother and wrapped her arms around her. Inhaling deeply, she could smell the perfume she used to wear, still lingering upon the tattered clothing she wore on the day she died. She could feel the maggots writhing beneath her fingertips, but she refused to let go. Her mom felt so real, she could no longer tell whether this was a dream or an alternate reality. If this was an alternate reality, she didn't want to leave, because in this reality, she was there with the only one who'd loved her until death.

Astra whispered into her mother's ear, "I love you. I miss you so much it hurts." In the moments she held her mom's unmoving body, she longed for her arms to wrap around her, even for a second. She longed for some form of

148

comfort, but nothing happened and even though her mother was in front of her, she still felt alone.

With hesitation, she took a step back, gazing upon the person she'd forever lost. Her heart felt like a body weighed down by rocks, sinking into the middle of the ocean, while her mind tried to make sense of her internal chaos. But making sense of chaos felt like trying to find order in the midst of stormy seas.

"Astra?" her mom whispered with recognition as her eyes came into focus.

Her heart lurched in her throat. "Yes, it is me!" she anxiously responded, hoping her mother would continue to speak to her. But she said nothing further and once again her eyes lost focus as she stared blankly into the distance.

Astra clutched her aching heart. Why does this have to hurt so much?

Her mother's head snapped to attention and looked deep into her eyes. An expression of anguish crossed her once stoic face. Slowly she parted her lips, allowing a large roach to fall out of her mouth and into the blood, quickly being engulfed by the hungry maggots.

"Astra," she said in a voice that sounded like a sad melody. "You can't keep living like this. It's poisoning your soul."

As the words left her mouth the ground beneath them rumbled and cracked open, swallowing the blood and maggots, revealing the ash covered mud beneath their feet. The cracks surrounding them were endlessly deep, touching the darkness without showing the bottom. In the distance she saw the ground beginning to crumble, falling into the eternal darkness. With another rumble, the crumbling ground crept closer like a predator stalking its prey.

"RUN!" Astra yelled, grabbing her mother's hand to try to help them both get to a safer place. But her mom did not move. Not even an inch.

Looking down with desperation, she saw her mother's feet were bound by what looked like a cluster of interweaving crimson veins. The veins seemed to burst from the ground like roots and her inability to forgive herself was the plant it belonged to.

"Oh no, oh no-no-no!" she pleaded as she tried to rip apart the veins that held her mother captive, but the veins remained unaffected and intact. She knew she had only minutes until this unstable ground would swallow them, but she was the only one free to run.

"Astra, stop," she pleaded as she held out her frail hand to help her daughter raise back to her feet.

149

"No! I can't stop," she gasped. "I WON'T!"

She once again tried to free her from her bounds, but she was not even so much as leaving a scratch upon the surface. She screamed as she continued to claw. She couldn't lose her mom again.

"Stop, Astra. I can't see you live like this anymore." She touched the top of Astra's head. Her mere touch brought a deep wave of anguish and for a moment she couldn't move or even breathe.

She took a deep breath in. The ground rumbled and cracked. It echoed through her ears with a piercing jab.

"No," she said with her voice breaking, hardly able to form the words. "I can't lose you again. I can't do this anymore." Hot tears streamed down her face. "Please don't leave me. Please. Please don't. No." Her arms wrapped around her mother as the crumbling ground crept closer, breaking apart and falling into the darkness. The empty feeling of helplessness enveloped her soul and created an indescribable hollowness within her.

"You will never forget me. But holding on to what you no longer have is only causing you to become blind to what you do have." With a sullen expression, her mother grabbed her, gripping onto Astra's body and pulling her close. "I don't want you to live like that. You know I want only happiness for you. I've only ever wanted that."

"I can't let go. I can't forgive myself for what I did."

"But you can," her mother said, stroking away her tears with her thumb. "I want you to be happy. I want you to find peace.

"Holding onto guilt and pain is only destroying yourself. Blaming yourself for something that wasn't even your fault is inhibiting you from living the life of happiness meant for you to live." She wiped another tear from Astra's cheek and gave a pained smile. "I have been watching you from the heavens and my dear, it crushes me to see the internal destruction you have brought upon yourself from the guilt you refuse to let go of. You hold on to this poison as though it was a punishment you deserve. But you don't. Forgiving yourself isn't being unjust, but the guilt you hold on to is only allowing the pain which should have been released long ago, to continue to live. That, my love, is unjust." The crumbling ground was so close it felt like it would swallow them both at any moment. "I don't want to live through your pain. I want to live through your happiness. When you think of me, I want to see you smile, *not cry. I want you to remember that we had an amazing life together and even though it was cut short, my God, it was heaven.*

"Please let go of this darkness. Look at what it has done to your soul. Please love yourself enough to live a full and happy life that looks forward to the beautiful future you can have and not the past you once had. The past is nothing but a memory and memories are what makes life beautiful, so don't allow them to destroy you."

Astra took a step back and watched more of the ground break away. These were her final moments. Feeling her chest tighten, she fought back the urge to try again to free her mother. Her heart was screaming to her mind 'KEEP TRYING,' but instead, she submitted to her mother's request.

Astra nodded her head. She wiped a tear from her burning eyes and could hardly make out the words, "I love you… so much." The realization that the only way to truly free both of them was to let her go was a burden she needed to accept. Her eyes closed. She took a step back, not wanting to see her mother disappear. It was just too much to bear.

"I love you," she heard her mother whisper one last time before her body fell into darkness.

CHAPTER 12

Astra once again woke up to the familiar feeling of a sinking pit in her core. To have a dream and feel like her mother was once again with her for a moment, only to wake up to the desolate realization she was still dead, felt like a cruel form of punishment. She knew she had to let go, but she wasn't sure how. How could she ever forgive herself?

Her father. What would he think of her if he knew she was hiding the fact that she knew of a way home? She had to get back to him, but he would be ashamed if he knew that she could have helped others get home but chose not to.

A gentle breeze touched her cheeks. They were still damp from the residue of tears lingering upon them. She must have been crying when she was asleep. Shamefully she wiped away the dampness and wanted nothing more than to never feel this sensation again. It only reminded her of the cross that her soul bore.

Alek and Sagan were still in a deep sleep. What did they dream about? Did they dream about their family or a life outside of this place? Did they have nightmares they were forever trapped here? She wished that for a moment she could escape into one of their dreams so she would not have to think about her own.

A strange tingling swept over her mind. She felt different this morning. The colors around her were crisper and she felt like she could smell and hear far better than she ever had before. Was this the result of swallowing the worm? What other side effects did it have?

She looked down at Sagan. He looked even scarier now than before. She could see a faint line of black in each of his veins and how his skin was an unnaturally smooth texture. What darkness lingered in him? Was he secretly evil? Maybe she was being too harsh. Or maybe not. She wasn't sure but she didn't know if she would ever be sure.

Whether or not she could trust Sagan was a thought that she constantly played with. There were times that she felt like he was a good person but other times that felt like maybe he wasn't, since he was friends with someone as awful as Alek. Then again, is Alek a reflection of Sagan? They are two different people but in which ways are they alike?

Solar rays shamelessly slapped away the morning mist as they demanded to shine their light through the land. Tear drops of dew clung onto the grass as the sun made a mockery of its sadness, illuminating its pain like a projector. Lingering over her head were feathered clouds, arrogantly covering the blue sky as if they owned the heavens. The pinch of a cold breeze nipped at her nose as she pulled her jacket over her arms and pushed herself up. When should she wake the others? She knew she needed to talk to them about what she knew.

For a moment, she closed her eyes and once again wondered, would she ever feel happy again? Her thoughts were interrupted by a rustling sound, drawing her attention to Alek who was now waking from his slumber. Damn. Why did he have to wake up first?

He rubbed the sleep from his eyes before he turned to look at Astra. "Well, you are up at an unusual hour," he groggily said with a Mona Lisa smile. "Haven't you ever heard of sleeping in?"

"I think it was from falling asleep so early last night. I have this inner clock that only allows me to sleep eight hours max. The only time I sleep more than that is when I'm sick."

"So, if you ever sleep in, I'll be sure to avoid you since that means you probably have the plague."

"That's a good idea but just to be a bitch, I might cough in your direction."

"I wouldn't put it past you for a second."

153

She lowered her eyes. "I need to talk to you all about something important."

Her mind screamed for her to keep her mouth shut but her soul told her this was needed. She knew she couldn't live with herself knowing she was keeping such a massive secret from them.

"What is it?" Sagan wondered as he sat up. How was he able to wake up so quickly?

She felt her jaw tense. Was she making the right decision? A part of her thought she was, while the other part couldn't help but wonder, what could be the worst that could happen from this?

"Vojin told me something when I was with him."

"Okay, what about it? Was there something we need to know about your attack?"

"No, it has nothing to do with the attack."

"So why are you bringing it up?"

"God, Alek, you are now getting on my nerves. Let the woman speak before you show your true colors."

"Thank you, Sagan."

"Alright, what's the big news?"

"I might know of a way to get home."

"I'm sorry, what? Are you sure?"

"Yes Alek I am sure, but this is why I need to get to Vojin."

Sagan's eyes lit up. He punched the air and with a smile on his face, his words flew from his lips almost faster than he was able to form them. "Are you mother flipping kidding me? I need details right now and please to God, tell me that Vojin is just down the street, because I have been late for Sunday dinner for the last several years and I am ninety percent sure that Alek's momma will have my head for missing her famous Sunday dinner for so long."

"Man, I don't think that is the reason why she would be mad at you, but we really need to keep things serious right now and get more answers."

"I know. I know, but what she doesn't know can't hurt her. We will just say we got lost in the woods and survived eating berries."

"How are you going to explain the hot mess that has become your face?"

"Oh, this beautiful thing? All I need is a pair of contacts and some foundation and I will be as bland as you. Then, once a year at Halloween, I will go as myself and enter into as many competitions as I can. I guarantee you that I will win enough prize money to buy an island and live a life of luxury."

"Okay enough with your jokes. Clearly, we need details on this information," Alek said with a flat face as he turned to Astra. "What does Vojin have to do with getting back home?"

"Vojin told me that there was a door which could help me get back to Earth."

"Where?"

"Apparently it is pretty far from here."

"How far?"

"I don't know Alek, I don't have a map."

"So how do we get to this door if you don't even know where it is at?"

"Which is where Vojin comes in. He told me to find the brightest star in the sky and follow it. If he is still alive, he will find me."

"That doesn't tell me shit," he snapped. "I need more direction than some cryptic poetic words. Did he tell you anything else?"

Why did she even open her mouth? How could she have not seen this coming?

"No. That's all he said."

"So why did he help you? How do you know what he was telling you wasn't a trap?"

"A trap for what?" she asked.

"Well, clearly there were creatures looking for you or we would have never known you existed. So, tell me Astra, why was

155

he helping you? How do you know that door is the way home and not the reason why you are here in the first place?"

She lowered her eyes. She wanted nothing more than to scoop up the words she'd spit out and bury them far away from anyone's memory.

"I don't know," she whispered.

"You don't know what?"

"The answer to your questions."

"And when were you planning on telling us? Were you just planning on using us to get to your friend and then wave goodbye?"

"I-I just… I don't know how to answer this."

Sagan walked up to her and held out his hand. "Come on," he said with a nod.

"Come where?"

"Let's get the hell out of here for a bit. We will chat, just you and me."

"But we need to find Vojin. We don't have time."

"You can spare half an hour. Come on."

"Why the hell am I being excluded from this?" Alek asked with crossed arms.

Sagan turned to him and tilted his head. For a moment he looked more demon than he did human. "Because you've been an ass lately. I get it. You're scared because you don't know if she is a threat or not and you are protective over those you care about, but she isn't our enemy. She's our family and all that we have out here." Sagan turned back to Astra. "Come on, let's get some air and let him have a little breathing room to remember that this isn't how his mom raised him to be. She would be disappointed if she saw how he was speaking to you."

"She would be even more disappointed in you," Alek snapped. "If you didn't feel the need to drug yourself up just to get through your day, we wouldn't even be here in the first place. If she would have known the screw up that you really were, she would have never welcomed you into our house."

Sagan's sinking face was quickly replaced by a curling lip and hard eyes. For a moment he glared at Alek, his jaw tightening so much that the blue veins in his pale face bulged. He cringed as he bit his lip and shook his head. "Go to hell, Alek."

Astra followed Sagan as he stormed away and began to walk alongside the river.

"Are you okay?"

He took a deep breath in and blankly gazed at the river. "Come with me. I want to show you something."

They walked alongside the water in silence until they finally came to a spot in the river with an oval section at the side that shimmered a slight color of lavender. The section seemed a little bit out of place since the main part of the river flowed in one direction yet the water around this oval spot seemed to churn in a circular motion. Sagan reached his fingers beneath the water and lifted a section of the river as if it was nothing more than a bedsheet. The water still looked like it was flowing over his fingertips, yet his skin remained dry. She gazed into the gaping hole and it was then that she saw Sagan had opened up a passage into a chamber. What she had thought was water flowing through a river, turned out to be a hologram hiding a door.

"What is this?"

"This part of the river is an illusion, but this place is safe. It was abandoned long before I got here. I like to call it my man cave."

"Why didn't we stay here last night?"

"Because there is no way in hell I would have found it after dark and to be honest, I forgot it was here. I just remembered this morning. Well, as they say, ladies first."

She chewed on her lip for a moment, gazing down at the rock stairs that led to a small room. She could see all the walls were nothing more than water, somehow forming around a pocket of air. "Is it safe? What if it collapses on us?"

"I've never ran into a problem."

"Okay," she muttered while rubbing the back of her neck. She lowered her head, ducking under his arm before she made her way down half a dozen stairs.

Sagan closed the door, which allowed the light that gleamed down from the water, to illuminate their surroundings.

Creatures of all shapes and sizes made their way through the river. Some looked similar to the fish she was used to seeing, while others displayed long teeth or hooked arms with an oddly shaped body. Though most of these creatures swam in schools, others enjoyed keeping to themselves, but all kept their distance from the chamber.

"Is there anything more you are comfortable telling me with regards to Vojin and that door he spoke of? If not, I understand, and I will respect you and your boundaries."

She looked at the one in front of her. Should she tell him the truth? Should she tell him that she was in danger but not only that, the safety of humanity would be compromised if she fell into the wrong hands? If she didn't, and he wasn't aware of the danger he was putting himself in, was she risking even more? He needed to be on his guard at all times and he didn't have the same urgency she did when it came to finding Vojin.

"Please don't tell Alek anything I am about to tell you."

"I promise I won't."

She felt her fingers shake. Was this the right decision? Vojin told her not to trust anyone but maybe that is because he didn't know Sagan. Would he have trusted him?

Astra explained everything. Though, at first, she wanted to leave some of the information to herself, she found the more she spoke, the more she needed to get everything she kept inside of her, out. Sagan listened intensely to every word that she said. There were moments where he didn't blink and other moments she wondered if he was even breathing, but his eyes consistently remained burrowing into her. Finally, when she'd said all she had to say, she sat in front of Sagan with an open heart, feeling the weight on her shoulders lift but her jaw was clenched as she waited for his reaction.

"Let me get this right, there is a demon named Prosperine who is searching for you and wants to bring you to their leader, Cadoc, because you are considered an antibody to the virus?"

"Yes."

"And humans are the virus?"

"To those that live here, we are not just seen as a virus but as being one of the most evil in existence. Apparently they think I am the key to opening this gate, that will allow an army to kill everyone on Earth."

"Are you the key?"

"I don't know. Vojin didn't tell me if I was or wasn't."

"This is bad. This is real fucking bad." He gripped onto his hair as he bent his head down for a moment. Sagan pushed himself up. With bulging eyes he stared at her, flailing his arms about as if he came to a realization that he could hardly contain. "I know I promised to keep this a secret, but we can't keep this from Alek. He needs to know."

"What? NO!" she howled. "You gave me your word you wouldn't say a thing. Why are you suddenly changing your mind?"

"Because I promised before I realized we have an atomic bomb on our hands and mankind is the destination!"

"What are you talking about?"

"You're the freaking bomb! YOU ARE!"

The blood drained from her face as these words left Sagan's mouth. Her chin quivered. "I am not a fucking atomic bomb and I didn't choose this!"

"Mankind is a virus and you are the antibody. What do antibodies do to viruses?"

"I know this! Why do you think I need to get away from this planet? Why do you think I am trying to get to Vojin! He is the only one who knows how to get me back! He can help. I need him. He is the only one who gives a flying fuck about me and was willing to help me get home!"

Suddenly the air around her felt too thick. She needed to get out of this place. She needed to breathe and even though the walls were not moving, she felt like she was drowning. The longer she remained in this prison, the more trapped she felt.

Astra rushed up the stairs, pushed open the door, and scrambled out. She walked through the field, away from Sagan, away from Alek, away from the reality that was chasing her.

Footsteps pounded the ground behind her. She felt Sagan's fingers wrap around her arm, stopping her in her tracks.

"Let go of me," she hissed.

"Please just listen to me."

"Nothing you have to say to me is something I want to hear."

Sagan looked at her with hair as wild as his eyes. "It might not be something you want to hear but it is something you need to hear."

She crossed her arms and took a step back. "And what exactly are you going to say? What? That I am a liability? That these things that are looking for me probably won't stop until they get what they want? That I have the leader of God-knows-what sending his people to search for me so that I can destroy my..." She touched her chest and curled over. "I can't do this. I can't."

Sagan wrapped his arms tightly around her. "Breathe," he softly said. "Just breathe."

She buried her head into his chest. His heart throbbed under his thick muscles. All sound faded away, until it was just her and the beating of an organ that sustained life. How many billions of hearts would stop if these monsters got a hold of her? How many innocents would be slaughtered because they were viewed as evil? How would they use her? Was it in her blood? Was it her soul? Was it some hidden knowledge she was not aware of?

"Please listen to me. First, Vojin isn't the only one who cares about you, we do too. Which is why we are helping you get to Vojin in the first place. Why would we risk our lives for you if we didn't care? Second, I need to tell Alek because we have to get you back to Earth for the sake of mankind. We have to find that door. If they get a hold of you, everyone we know and love will be slaughtered."

"I don't trust him, and I hardly know either of you."

Sagan's arms fell as he took a step back. "I know. You don't have to trust him but if you could just please trust me on this. I want to help you."

She bit her lip and looked deep into his eyes. Her stomach tensed. He looked evil. How could she believe him? He was about to go back on his word when he promised her that he wouldn't tell Alek. What else was he lying about? "How can you help me?"

"Vojin mentioned the door and he told you to follow the brightest star in the sky. We are already doing that, but now that I know you are still being chased we have to make it a point to do training everyday between our travels. Vojin was right when he said that it is too dangerous. The creatures that live here are vicious and hard to kill even for someone who has training. We both know you don't know how to handle a knife, but it is imperative that you learn." She looked down at the ground and kicked some dirt. "It's fine. You don't need to worry. Both Alek and I will train you, but Alek needs to know what we are up against. When it comes to his family, he would die trying to protect them. So, let's make sure he knows how important it is to keep you safe."

* * *

Elde greeted them with a snort and a growl as they approached camp. Though his face lit up when he saw them, her face sank when she saw his. She wanted nothing more than to avoid this moment in time and wished that she could skip ahead of this part of her life and jump to the part where she was safe at home. But instead, she was forced to wait for the reaction of a man who was seen to fly off the handle with even the smallest of things.

Alek approached Sagan with a hug. He shook his head and looked blankly at the rock wall. "I'm sorry. I shouldn't have said those things."

Sagan shrugged. "Maybe you were right about it. Maybe your mom wouldn't have wanted me around had she known I was a drug addict."

Alek's dark brown eyes lowered. "She knew."

"What? What do you mean she knew?"

"That's why we invited you to the cabin. It wasn't just to get away. We were going to have an intervention and if you were willing, help you to detox. My dad was already prepared to be your physician."

"Why didn't you ever tell me?"

"I was angry. When I woke up here, I blamed you."

"I don't think this was an accident."

"What do you mean?"

"I think it was fate."

"Well fate clearly hates us if this is where it brought us."

Sagan turned to Alek. His black eyes seemed so much darker. "Alek we need to talk. It's serious."

"What's going on? If you are not throwing out jokes, then either someone has died, or you have really bad news."

The walls seemed so much tighter now that the air had become thicker. Her heart beat faster as Sagan seemed to search for the words to say. Why couldn't he just spit it out? Why couldn't he just get it over with?

"I'm going to go," she blurted out.

"Wait, what? Why are you leaving now?"

"I just can't be here for this. It's too much. I'm sorry." She turned around and walked towards the river.

Elde quickly approached her and grunted as he nudged her hand. She ignored him and walked alongside the water, gazing at the clouds that had settled over the distant mountaintops.

There was a nudge on her shoulder before the feeling of a snout creeping up onto her cheek accompanied by a long tongue covered in juices.

162

"Oh God," she gagged, as she wiped off the excessive saliva from her cheek. "That was sweet but so gross at the same time." Elde's lips curled into a smile as he laughed a strange laugh that sounded more like choking. She shook her head. "Since when do you laugh?" As Elde shrugged and licked his lips he looked into her widening eyes. "Wait, you can understand me?" Elde nodded his head and once again smiled. "Oh, I underestimated you. I'm sorry."

He huffed before turning his head back to the camp that was just out of ears reach. She didn't want to imagine what was about to happen.

Alek suddenly stormed out, with red cheeks and a flat expression. He had eyes as cold as ice and the veins on his muscles bulged out further than they normally did.

"You can't be out here alone," he said sharply as he approached her.

"I'm not alone. Elde's here."

"Look, I understand why you were so secretive now. I get it. You were scared and confused. We don't know what these monsters are planning with you, but we can't let them get a hold of you. Are you willing to be trained? Are you willing to learn to fight?"

"Um… yeah. I thought that was already established."

"Good. We need to start tonight but let me make something clear—yes, we need to get you to Vojin, wherever he is, but you will not be unaccompanied ever again. We can't risk you getting caught and we can't risk you being the weakest link. You have to know how to fight back and if you get caught, you sure as hell better kill yourself. Are we clear?"

"Wait, what?" she gasped. "What are you talking about, kill myself?"

"You heard me."

"I have no intention of killing myself and I can't believe you would even expect me to do that."

"Let me clarify. If you get caught and you don't kill yourself, I'll kill you. I am not risking the life of my family and everyone else on Earth over some bitch I hardly know."

Elde's eyes snapped over to Alek. He lifted his lips over his mouth and revealed his sharp teeth, accompanied by a low growl. Elde stepped between Astra and Alek. He shoved his snout against his throat and forced him to step back.

Alek shook his head and pushed a knife up to Elde's throat. "I dare you," he snarled.

Elde pressed his teeth onto Alek's throat. The sharp teeth pinched his skin, drawing blood.

"Elde, stop," she pleaded. She could only imagine the horror that was about to happen.

The beast curled his neck around Astra and glared at Alek. He lowered his lips and nudged her towards the camp and just as he did, Sagan stepped out with his arms crossed.

"What happened?" he asked as she stormed passed him.

She refused to answer. What would she tell him anyway? That his friend was once again a complete asshole to her? That he threatened to kill her if she was caught?

"What the hell happened?" Sagan barked as Alek walked in. "And why are you bleeding?"

"Your dog is the reason why I am bleeding. I did exactly as I told you I would. I let her know that we were going to start training today."

"No man, though I was on board with the training tonight, we need to wait till morning. Let's rest up and do a session early."

"Why?" Alek snapped.

"Because clearly some shit just went down that I am not aware of and it's already been an exhausting day."

CHAPTER 13

Astra's lungs expanded, stretching out the unbearable weight which lingered on her chest. She hardly slept that night and now that it was the early morning, she dreaded what the day would bring.

This is why Vojin told her not to trust anyone. She shouldn't have trusted them. Why couldn't she just disappear? She hated her reality, but what she hated even more was Alek's threats echoing off the corners of her mind.

"Let's start training now before we begin traveling again. You need to know at least the basics of how to defend yourself," Alek said from behind Elde. "Are you ready?"

No, she wasn't ready for it, nor was she ready to be around him. She was in the presence of a ticking time bomb who at any moment might decide to explode. What if he changed his mind? What if he decided to kill her regardless of her possible capture? She was nothing more than a liability not only to their lives but also to the lives of billions of people.

"I'm already on it. I'll do training today," Sagan said with a nod as he pushed a knife into his pocket.

Elde stood up and shook the dirt off his fur, before stepping to the side. She touched her knife in her pocket. Her chest pinched as she walked around Alek who refused to move out of her way. Instead, he stood there, with a sly smirk crawling across his face as his muscles bulged out of his crossed arms.

Her eyes sank into his. There was something so evil about him. Far more than anything she had come across so far on this planet. He was the kind of wicked that was disguised in the flesh of man. He was dressed as a sheep that bit like a wolf and though he was the only other human on this planet, she wished he wasn't. She would have rather been alone for the rest of her life, than to be around someone like him.

"I'll be waiting for you both when you get back. Don't leave anything out of the training," Alek nodded.

She hurried alongside Sagan who seemed all too eager to start this. As they walked through the emerald grass, she wondered where they were going. Her eyes trailed across the rock cluttered land, from the bushes covered in tiny golden flowers to the splashing blue river.

Would he be easy on her today or expect too much? Did he realize how novice she was? She thought back to all the times she tripped over her feet. She could hardly read a book without getting a paper cut and in school, when they taught dance, she always knocked into everyone around her. Would she be a disappointment? Was she even trainable? She needed to learn how to fight, now not only to keep her safe from the demons, but also to keep her safe from the very person she had to face every day.

After walking a short distance from the camp, she watched Sagan bend down and gently touch the ground with his fingertips. He closed his eyes and smiled which sparked a curiosity in her. Why was he touching the ground? She leaned over and pushed her fingers into dirt. She felt the earth pulsate under her fingers like a massive heart beat.

"Why are we touching the ground and what does this have to do with training?" she asked curiously.

"You need to know as much as you can about this planet if you want to survive here. This world is alive. It's like a giant body and everything on it plays a different part."

"Wait… What? What do you mean, it's alive?"

"This world is a living being. Everything alive is connected to it. Do you feel how the ground is pulsing underneath us? It means if we were to dig a hole, there would be roots in the ground. These roots are dry and easy to break which is good because if we are ever in need of fresh water, this is what we need to feel for. The roots in the ground have the same function on this world that our veins have to our body. I learned this the hard way."

"What do you mean by that?" she questioned, lifting her fingers from the ground.

"Well, when Alek and I first got here, we were hiding and watched a small animal digging a hole in the ground. Once it got about a foot deep, it cracked open one of the roots and drank from it. We were thirsty, so as soon as it left, we tried it ourselves.

The area we were in although was green, had no lakes or rivers for us to drink from. Because of this, we were worried the water supply would run out. For months, Alek and I made the hole bigger and bigger. We were trying to make a small pond for us to drink and bathe in.

Every time we would get a decent amount of water in the hole, the sun would dry it up by the next day. So, we would dig the hole a little bigger and break more roots, but the same thing happened. By the next day, the pond would dry up.

What we didn't realize was that draining the land of water was equivalent to draining blood from a body. Except we drained it too quickly. The water didn't have time to regenerate, so it had a domino effect. Slowly everything died around us. The grass turned brown and became brittle, the flowers wilted, and all the leaves fell off the trees.

After a while, there was no water left. Alek and I knew that we had to leave when we watched that tiny animal show up again looking for water. When it found none, it collapsed.

I still remember the way it looked at me. I will never get that expression out of my mind. I think it knew we were the reason there was no water left. The only reason we survived was because we selfishly stored water in nuts and drank from that.

So we left, and we found a place with water above ground. It took a while for us to find it, but we finally did…"

Her eyes crawled over the rock speckled land as his words drowned out in the background. Though she knew she should listen, the thoughts on her mind were deafening. This planet was a massive body and the creatures on this land would attack her how lymphocytes assaulted viruses. If she didn't know how to properly defend herself, she didn't want to imagine the outcome.

"So, how hard is training going to be today? Are you going to start right off beating me up or what?"

"That worm you swallowed is going to help you with your strength and speed. It should also help you learn faster so hopefully I won't be beating you up for too long. By the end of the day, you'll be good enough to fight something larger than you. It's just a matter of remembering what I teach you and not overthinking."

"You're asking me not to overthink. Overthinking is what I'm best at," she replied, not believing a word he said to her. There was no way she could be as good of a fighter as he claimed she would be, especially not after just one day of training.

Sagan cracked a faint smile, "Well in this case try not to. Just trust that your body will remember what it's been taught without having to consciously think about it."

"How long do we have to train? We need to keep looking for Vojin."

"We are going to train you every day. We will try to keep the training to the morning time but if need be, we will do a session at night. After training, we will search till dusk or till we find an adequate shelter."

"Why not regularly at night? Can't you just train me after we have at least made some progress?"

"Because you need to start every day with more knowledge on how to defend yourself. Every minute we are out here and not safe in a shelter, we risk being attacked. Even in a shelter we are at risk but at least we are not in the open. These creatures are fast and strong and if what you are saying is true, they won't stop till they have you."

Sagan pulled out a handmade knife before he pointed to the weapon in her pocket. "Put that somewhere safe… Maybe by a tree while we are fighting. Use this one instead."

"Why?" she asked in a flat tone as she looked at him with narrow eyes.

"That knife looks like it has some sort of liquid in it and I don't want to know what that liquid could do to me," he replied as he raised his eyebrows and winked.

"It would kill you if it even touched your skin."

"Exactly my point. I didn't pencil death in my planner—just saying. Plus, since I'm teaching you how to fight, I don't want to risk kicking you in the wrong place or you falling the wrong way and your own knife cutting you. That doesn't sound like a fun time."

He was right. If he kicked her the wrong way and put pressure on the vein, the poison would likely eat through her clothing before seeping onto her skin and causing an excruciating death. She hesitantly nodded her head and placed her knife by an oddly shaped tree which grew horizontally across the ground with vibrant leaves that curled in at the edges. The roots of the tree were wrapped around a boulder that came up to her knee.

Astra walked back over to Sagan and examined the weapon he had given to her. The knife appeared as though it was made from a black rock. It had a sharp point at the end and an uneven surface with a thick handle wrapped in strips of pale leather. Though she was sure the rock was already in a pointed state when it was found, she could tell it had been sharpened.

"It was the first one I made out here," Sagan nodded, as she ran her finger over the edges.

"How long did it take you to make this?"

"I worked on it over the course of several days." His eyes wandered over the land. "Okay, where should we start?" Sagan paused and chewed on his lip. He seemed deep in thought until his face lit up. "You never want to pick a fight. If you see an animal and it looks aggressive, try to hide first. Only fight when you have no other choice."

"What do you mean by no other choice? If it attacks me?" Astra shifted uncomfortably. She knew she would have to fight a beast and do this possibly one day in the near future, but the thought of the attack still brought chills down her spine.

"Pretty much. These animals get a look in their eyes if they are about to attack you."

"What do you mean by that?"

"Well, some of them look at you the same way I used to look at hamburgers at fast-food joints. If it looks at you that way, you are the hamburger and you should defend your buns."

She chewed on her lip as she listened to a sound that reminded her of an owl quietly hooting. What if he wanted to "train" her so he could kill her? Maybe this was their plan all along and Sagan knew about Alek's threat. What if this "training" was nothing more than an excuse to get her alone?

She glanced back behind herself trying to calm her spinning thoughts. Why was she having this moment of paranoia? Was this instinct or just fear? Once again, her eyes slapped over to Sagan who returned a look of concern.

"What happened?" he wondered. His eyes felt like they were burrowing into her soul.

"What do you mean?" Astra rubbed the back of her neck and suddenly felt exposed. She hated how he looked at her; the way the demon hybrid seemed to not only look at her but through her.

"You were fine one minute, but now you're not. I can read your energy, you know. It's a gift I've had ever since the change."

She knew he could easily snap her neck and hardly break a sweat. What other gifts did he have? Why was he telling her this? Was he trying to let her know that he had the ability to read her thoughts? Her pulse throbbed in her throat as her eyes locked on the demon in front of her. It was as if his gaze was chaining her soul to his. *Why was he doing this? What did he want from her?*

"You're still afraid of me." He looked down at the ground for a moment.

She chewed on her lip. How should she respond? Should she deny it and try to act like everything was okay or should she admit he was right?

"Are you reading my thoughts?" Her face hardened.

"No, but I can read your energy which is similar but different," Sagan responded as he sat down on the ground and threw his knife at her feet. "Come, sit down. I am unarmed now. Let's talk."

She didn't want to talk and being unarmed didn't make him any less dangerous than he already was. The incisors alone in his mouth were the size of a Cane Corso's. She felt as if she was naked in front of him, unable to hide the private emotions she longed to keep to herself.

To make matters worse, she couldn't get Alek's threat out of her mind. His words endlessly echoed, bouncing off the walls of her sanity until pieces of it began to chip away. If Sagan could read energy then that means he could read Alek's energy, in which case he was either choosing to ignore what he saw because he didn't want to believe it, or because he accepted it.

"Have you been reading me this whole time?" She hesitantly sat on the ground several feet away from him and eyed the knife he had tossed.

His face became solemn as he spoke. "Unfortunately, it's something I can't turn off. I have always been taught if there is a problem, the best way to resolve it is to confront it head on. I won't get angry by anything you tell me and I promise that I'll respond honestly to any of your concerns."

She paused. This suddenly became unbelievably awkward. Should she be open about her concerns? He already knew she was afraid of him so what more was there to say? Was admitting he was right showing weakness? Would it help to get it all out in the open? She was not sure which path she should take.

"You scare me but Alek does too," she said, barely able to pull the words out from her lips. "I don't know if I can trust either of you."

"I am a scary looking dude," Sagan sighed. "I know I look like a monster and honestly I don't blame you for not trusting me, but Alek is a good guy. He is harsh, and he tends to say the wrong thing at the wrong time. He is also inappropriately flirtatious with women, which is something he has been since I have known him, but I promise you that he is harmless. I've known him my whole life and I trust him. You have nothing to worry about when it comes to us."

She had admitted only what he already knew but he never mentioned Alek's threat to her. Though she thought she would feel better, she felt worse. Did he know the truth about Alek? He wasn't harmless. His threat felt very real.

"I don't expect you to trust me," Sagan continued. "You don't know me well enough to. I can imagine how scary it is to end up on some alien planet and then find yourself in a group with a grumpy man, a creepy looking guy, and an animal that looks like it could snap at any minute.

"I won't ask you to give me your trust. I will however ask you to give me a chance to earn your trust. I promise you that we are good people. How something appears is not always how it is.

"So, if you are willing, and only if you feel comfortable, I would like to teach you how to defend yourself in case you're attacked. I promise that I won't hurt you on purpose—though you might get a few cuts and bruises from the training. I know my word doesn't mean much right now, but I hope that you will give me a chance to prove this to you."

She nodded her head. Sagan's eyes twinkled as his lips curled into a smile. He stood up and held out a hand, helping her to stand.

"So, what are you going to teach me first?"

Over the next several hours, Sagan patiently took his time showing her different moves and fighting tactics. At first, she felt like a small train wreck, fumbling the knife more than holding it and tripping over her own feet. When she tried to learn how to properly dodge, she would slip and fall onto the ground. By mid-day, she was covered in bruises, not from what he had given her but from her sheer clumsiness.

Could she even do this? Astra knew Sagan had told her she would get better but as she once again fell onto the ground, she found her frustration had grown. Why isn't this damn worm working? She was under the impression it would help her with strength and speed, but she still felt just as slow and clumsy as she had always been.

"Okay, let's try this again but then we need to move forward," Sagan said as his lips curled at the edges. "When you see my arm coming towards you, I want you to duck. I'll go faster this time."

Lifting his arm up, he swung and before she could duck, he stopped only an inch away from contacting her skull. He was so fast she didn't even see his assault come.

"I can't do this!" She picked up a nearby stone and threw it at the tree. It thumped as it bounced off the bark and landed on the twisting roots below it.

"Yes, you can. You are just overthinking. Compared to how you did at the beginning of the day, I have seen significant improvements."

Improvements? What improvements? She couldn't even dodge a basic attack. Yes, she was tripping less over her feet but having the inability to even grasp onto the basics of fighting was only going to lead her straight into the hungry mouth of a predator. She was not only a risk to herself but was a risk to the others and if she could not even do the basics, there was no way she would survive an attack from an enemy.

They made their way back to the camp where Alek was still waiting just a foot away from the enclosure. He had all of their bags in front of him and the furs were wrapped up tightly and tied to the bottom of both his and Sagan's satchel.

"You get that training done?" he asked with folded arms.

"Yeah," Sagan grabbed her bag and handed it to her. He then grabbed his own and slung it over his back. "You ready to leave?"

"Yep. How did she do?"

"She did well. Better than I expected."

"Is that so?" Alek glanced at her out of the side of his eye.

They traveled across the rocky lands, staying just a rocks throw from the river so that they knew they were going in the right general direction. The light was dimmed when a sheet of clouds eventually formed over the blue heavens. The further they walked, the sparser the grass became until they were finally walking on pale dirt speckled with trees and prickly plants that were covered in colourful webs. On the rare occasion, they came across a carnivorous plant and it was almost always preoccupied with a fresh kill. Each kill looked different. Some of them looked like they had fought back when they first were caught. Their skin was slashed open in multiple places, oftentimes revealing bones or raw muscle and sometimes their eyes were gouged out. Other times the animals looked like they gave up as soon as they were caught. The only damage on their skin was caused by thorns, which lifted in and out of the same puncture wounds as if they were milking the creature for its blood. But all of the corpses held the same twisted expression of anguish. It was clear that it was a merciless and excruciating way to die.

They walked alongside the river until the sky began to darken into evening. The sun was still hidden by the clouds so the darkness seemed to come awfully quickly.

"Where are we going to sleep?" She looked for a shelter of some sort but didn't see anything that would even remotely keep them hidden. Whereas before there were massive boulders, now the land was scattered with smaller stones no taller than her hip. Even these stones were few and far between.

Her ears picked up the sound that reminded her of a hooting owl. It seemed like it was coming from a few of the trees that were not too far away from her, but she wasn't sure. She had heard it earlier in the day, but it was so distant that she didn't pay any mind to the noise. Now that it was closer, she felt nervous. However, for some reason she didn't sense that it was a threat.

Sagan plopped down a few feet away by a bulky gray stone just large enough for him to lean his back against. "This is where we are going to sleep for the night. We can't light a fire so bundle up and grab a fur."

174

"Why can't we light a fire? There are trees here and I saw some dry looking bushes by a few of the rocks that we could use for kindling." Astra set down her bag and looked at the blackening sky. She wished the sun would come back out. She hated the thought of being in the darkness without a shelter to hide in.

"Because a fire would draw too much attention in these parts." Sagan handed her a piece of dried fish from his bag. "Eat up. It's gonna be a long night."

After they ate, Alek handed her a brown fur that he had attached to his bag. She laid down on the ground and pulled the fur up to her chin before looking up at the cloud covered sky. The cold pinched at her skin, letting her know that it would be an uncomfortable night. It was colder tonight than it was last night, and her jacket and scarf were just not enough. Luckily the fur trapped in the warmth and as long as she kept under that, she felt warm.

Elde laid down beside Sagan and put his massive head on his lap, while Alek laid down uncomfortably close to Astra and pulled his fur over himself. He was only about a foot away from her. Why did he have to be so close? He could have slept anywhere.

She imagined all the horrible things he could do to her. Was he just waiting for the right moment to kill her or was he at least going to give her the chance to try to get home?

The darkness came fast and soon it was so dark, she could hardly see her hand in front of her face. With the darkness came lower temperatures and she found that even the fur didn't seem to keep her warm enough.

"If you want to stay warm, you can always come closer to me." Alek whispered by her ear.

She pretended like she didn't hear him and rolled her body over to give herself more space. Being cold was better than being close to him.

175

She took out her knife and kept it in her clutched hand. Would she sleep tonight? She wasn't sure. The darkness held too many secrets. But as the night trailed on sleep did eventually come.

* * *

Astra snapped awake to the sensation of a movement by her feet. She looked around but hardly moved her head. It was still dark and the sound of snoring pierced her ears. There it was again. It was the pressure of what felt like a foot or a paw creeping over her body. It moved as slowly as a panther stalking its prey.

Shit. Was she about to be attacked? What or who was creeping over her? Was it Alek? Was he about to kill her? Or was it something else?

Her fingers were still wrapped around her weapon. She slowly pulled her hand out of her blanket as the smell of smoke filled her nostrils. This wasn't Alek.

The beast was now standing over her chest. It was so dark that she could hardly see more than an outline. It weighed about thirty pounds and had pointed ears. This monster stood on all fours and she could have sworn she saw a scorpion-like tail reaching up from behind it. She could feel its needle-like claws sink into her shoulder.

"Found you," a male voice whispered.

She opened her mouth to scream but couldn't utter a sound. Her fingers ran up the handle of her knife. Where was the vein?

Suddenly, the creature snatched her by her scarf and began to run in the other direction, dragging her across the ground by her neck. Astra could feel the course dirt scratching against her clothes and how the cloth tightened around her throat. She couldn't scream even if she wanted to. She couldn't even breathe. Her hands thrashed out and just as she did so, her weapon bit into something soft.

A gut-wrenching scream pierced the air and she slid to a stop. The cloth around her throat loosened and she could hear the sound of a struggle beside her. The bright glow of Elde's horns lit up the land around him as he ran up to her with teeth bared.

Astra dropped the knife and turned around. She looked at her attacker who was now twitching on the ground. His raven eyes rolled to the back of his head as his jackal-like ears twitched. The monster was about the size of a Labrador with a long tail that ended in a hooked point. His body convulsed as his skin bubbled up around a wound at his side. The boils grew larger and spread across his skin. They burst open, letting out what looked like hot steam.

Sagan and Alek ran to her with weapons in hand. They looked down at the dying animal whose eyes swelled out of his head. The beast coughed and as he did, blood sprayed from his thin lips.

It looked like another small version of Sidero but clearly had the traits of Prosperine too. Yes. It was obvious whose child this was.

"Are you okay?" Sagan gasped.

"Yeah I think so."

"What happened?"

"I don't know. It all happened so fast."

Alek picked up Astra's knife. It was covered in blood and still had thick poison dripping off of it.

"Give that to me," she hissed.

He bent down and wiped the blood and poison off on the corpse before handing it back to her. "You might want to wash that off in the river before putting it back in your pocket."

She agreed. "Elde, will you come with me?"

He nodded his head and snorted.

"We'll all come with you to wash your knife," Sagan said. "I am so sorry we didn't see it coming. We should have been closer to you. We should have protected you."

177

She felt the back of her throat tense. What would have happened to her if she hadn't accidentally stabbed the beast? What would have happened if she had dropped the weapon? Would he have taken her to Prosperine or Cadoc?

After washing the weapon in the river, she pushed it back into her pocket and turned towards the men. The first rays of light were just starting to pierce the horizon.

"I don't know about you guys, but I am not going to be able to sleep here after this. Can we just keep walking? I don't want to stay here any longer."

"I don't blame you," Alek nodded. "Let's go grab our stuff and keep going. We'll train you tonight instead of in the morning. I think you have had enough training for the morning."

They continued to walk until the shadows of the trees pointed in the opposite direction that they had in the morning. Everything on her body hurt. She could feel blisters forming on her feet and her legs ached with every movement. The thought of rest sounded heavenly to her but the need to keep searching for Vojin kept her moving.

Every rock, every shadow, and every distant movement snapped her attention. She was torn between feeling afraid that she might be attacked again and hoping the rock, or bush, or shadow that her eye caught, was actually Vojin. The longer they walked, the more trees appeared around them. They finally decided to set up camp by a thick cluster of trees in a small forest. The trees were covered in azure and pumpkin-colored webs of some sort and had roots that seemed to burst out of the ground. Moving around the webs were red bugs about the size of her thumb, weaving their homes through the looping branches. Every few seconds, one of these bugs would clap together their wings. It was then that she realized the strange hooting sounds she kept hearing was because of these creatures. When they did this, a thick web came from their mouth and created a layer of color on the tree.

"I've never seen anything like this before," she said, while touching the soft bark on the trunk.

"They are actually not that common," Sagan replied as he set down his bag and rolled out his fur. "I've only seen a few around but I think they're pretty. I like the sound they make."

"The bugs will not sting or bite me, right?"

A large bug flew from a branch and landed a few feet away from her on the ground.

"Nah, they're harmless," he murmured while fumbling through his leather satchel.

"I am going to go hunt for some food and check out the area to see if there is anything we would need to be weary of," Alek nodded. "You're going to train her tonight, right?"

"Yeah that is the game plan."

Sagan pulled from the side pocket, a thick brown seed that appeared similar to an overgrown acorn. He grabbed his knife and stabbed it deep into the hollow center. As soon as the knife entered the center of the seed, thick liquid drained from the hole and rolled down the side, dripping like thick honey.

"Drink this. It'll make you feel better," he said, while handing her the seed and pulling out another one for himself.

She accepted the seed with a smile hidden beneath her stoic expression and placed it up to her lips. Her throat felt like sand and she longed to coat it with a seal of comfort. The salty and thick liquid seeped slowly into her mouth. It tasted even better than it looked.

"Oh God, you have no idea how much I needed that." She wiped the moisture off her lips with the palm of her hand.

"I know you were discouraged about your fighting skills but honestly you really aren't that bad," Sagan interrupted her thoughts. "You reacted quickly enough to kill the animal who took you last night and during our training session you were gaining in speed."

"I couldn't even duck in time. I know I have a defeatist attitude. It's just hard for me to see that and now I know that learning how to fight isn't just for my own survival, but the fate of billions of people rests on whether or not I can get through that door and safely back to Earth. I don't know if I am the key or not, but I don't want to find out."

"Let me remind you that you had only one training session and since then, you've killed something on your own without any help. That is huge," Sagan replied. "Sometimes it doesn't feel like we are moving forward when we are doing exactly that. You are not that bad. I was pretty impressed with how quickly you were catching on."

"You're just saying that to make me feel better. I would rather you be honest."

"I am being honest. Let's get to training so you can continue to move forward."

"Okay."

Sagan explained to her they would now practice how to use a weapon in the case of an attack. He spent the next hour showing her in slow motion what she needed to do when certain situations arose. At first, when everything was done slowly, the moves were seemingly simple, but she quickly realized even the most basic movements became more complex when speed was applied.

Her jaw tensed and heart pounded each time he swung his arm towards her. What if he accidentally hit her? What if she accidentally stabbed him? Though he was unarmed, she was not, and her stomach lurched at the thought of what could happen in the case of an accident. She didn't enjoy practicing with weapons and wished that she could just go back to being unarmed but she knew if she didn't take the risk, she would not know how to properly use a weapon. She knew her lack of knowledge made her a danger even to herself.

"Why is this so difficult?" She furrowed her brow.

"It'll get easier, trust me," Sagan replied with a twinkle in his eyes.

That night, they slept between the trees of the small forest. Though they once again chose not to build a fire, it felt warmer than it had the night before. The moons, stars, and the rings that looped around the world, lit up the sky. It was a peaceful view to look at through the canopy of the trees, despite the unnerving fact that they were not sure what was around them.

Elde was determined to sleep directly beside Astra and put his head on her stomach. He seemed to have become more protective over her and was beginning to feel like a shadow who was always around.

It was quiet outside with the exception of the occasional hooting sound from different trees. There was no wind, not even a breeze, which was a good thing considering that every noise she heard made her feel panicked. Maybe this was why Elde chose to lay his head on her. Was he trying to bring her comfort and show her he was there to protect her?

CHAPTER 14

She woke up to the sound of a soft whistle dancing through the air. The first rays of misty morning light were beginning to burst through the trees. Astra yawned and inhaled the smell of wild flowers and morning dew, a pleasant, yet unexpected scent.

Her heart lurched at the sight of Alek, standing in front of her with a brown bowl made of clay in one hand and a handful of wildflowers in the other. With a tense jaw she waited for him to speak, not knowing what he wanted, or how long he had been standing in front of her.

Alek handed her a bowl of vegetables and placed the flowers by her feet. "I made you breakfast. We are going to train this morning and then we will continue to look for Vojin."

Slowly, Astra ate the crisp yellow, red, and green vegetables. "Thank you," she said with flat lips as she eyed the flowers on the ground. "How long is this training session going to be? I want to get as much distance in as possible today."

"A few hours. Don't worry, we'll get plenty of distance in, but you need to at least be a bit more prepared if something heads our way. I found a place yesterday while you were training with Sagan."

"Where is this place?"

"Not too far from here."

"You never got me flowers," Sagan gasped as he sat up with a fur wrapped around his body.

"You never deserved them."

"On the contrary, my closeted lover, I always deserve them, and I expect a bit more romance on your part. I feel you need to put a little more effort into our relationship."

Alek rolled his eyes and looked back at her. "Just so you know, I've never touched that man."

"Not in real life, but I am almost positive that you have dreamed about me."

"Sounds more like a nightmare," Alek retorted before motioning for her to come with him.

* * *

Alek scratched the bit of hair on his chin and wiped some sweat off his brow. His lips tightened as he looked intently over the land. "I think you'll really like this place. I know it's a bit of a walk but trust me, you will understand why this place is so…" His voice trailed off as he searched for the right words, "I can't explain it. You'll just have to see for yourself."

"Why couldn't we just train back there?" She pointed behind her. They had walked so far from the camp that it was no longer in sight but at least they were still close to the river. "I don't want to spend my day wandering around."

"Listen cutie, I told you I was training you and I found the perfect spot to do it."

She bit her tongue. Why did he have to speak to her like that? It wasn't flattering or something she wanted. To make matters worse, she wasn't sure what Alek was capable of or what his intentions were. He could easily kill her without any consequences. All he would have to tell Sagan was that they were attacked. He could claim she died in the attack and give himself a few cuts to make it seem like he fought gallantly for her life. Slipping her fingers down her leg, she dipped her hand into her pocket and felt the handle of her weapon. What would she do if he attacked her? Could she kill him, or would he overpower her?

It was sunny outside with only a few clouds littering the sky. The dewy crisp temperature allowed her to keep on her thin scarf and jacket without feeling too warm. This weather reminded her of a cool fall day.

She remembered back to when she would go to the fall festivals with her father and mother. Southerners love their festivals and her family was on board with those, especially the ones in the fall. She never missed a single one. They would even travel a few hours just to catch one of the many the south had to offer. She couldn't wait to get home and go to another one with her father.

The sound of the river was soothing to her sanity. At least she would know her way back if she needed to make a quick escape. Momentarily she paused and craned her neck to see a cluster of twisting trees that stood next to her. Each of the trees looked different from one another. Although they all had prickly black bark, their leaves came in an array of vibrant colors. One tree with blood red leaves stood next to another tree with lavender leaves, while the one next to that had leaves as white as snow.

Walking between the twisting branches, small creatures the size of her palm scurried up and down the bark. These odd animals had hooked wings which were attached to their legs. They used these to glide between the branches when they needed to go a further distance than they cared to walk. A clicking sound that ended in a whistle came out of their small round mouths as they communicated to one another.

"Okay, this is where we will do the first part of your training," Alek said. He pointed to one of the low hanging branches of a nearby tree as he shoved his knife into his pocket.

"What are we doing there?"

"I want you to grab onto that tree and hold yourself up."

"How?"

"Just hold onto it like you are about to do a pull up."

Why did he take her all the way out here to do this? There was nothing special about this area and they could have easily done this closer to camp.

Astra walked over to the branch and grabbed a hold of it. Her muscles shook as she strained to hold herself up.

"Okay, now I want you to swing your legs back and swing them forward," Alek instructed confidently.

She attempted to do as she was told but as she swung forward, her arms slipped from the branch and she tumbled to the ground, landing hard on her buttock. Wincing, she stood up and brushed the dirt from her legs.

"What now?"

"That's going to leave a bruise. Do it again."

For the next hour Alek demanded she continue this same exercise until he finally had new demands. He climbed onto the branch she was under and held out a knife. As he looked down from the tree, she realized that he was trying to peek down her shirt. Alek saw her notice and gave a twinkling smile.

"I want you to grab onto the branch again and catch the knife with your knees when I drop it from above you. When you catch it, I want you to curl your body up and touch your knees to the branch."

With hesitation, Astra agreed. She wanted to cover herself even more, so she repositioned her scarf so that the cloth was covering more than just her throat and she zipped up her jacket up as high as it would go. Damn her shirt for showing more than she was comfortable with.

Reaching up, she gripped onto the branch and adjusted her hands.

"You ready?" he asked.

"Yeah."

At first, she couldn't even catch the weapon but when she finally was able to, her muscles gave out and she dropped to the floor.

Alek shook his head and twisted the side of his mouth. "Well at least you caught it. But don't worry. I can see you're firming up in the right areas. You'll be just fine in no time."

Firming up? Her cheeks grew hot. This wasn't flattery to her, it was embarrassment. Astra wished she could go behind the nearest rock and disappear. She knew she was the weakest link but the last thing she wanted to hear was his thoughts on how her body was firming up, especially after she had caught him looking down her shirt.

Alek tapped the branch he sat upon. "Do it again."

She lifted her jelly arms. They felt like they had weights tied to them, even though there was nothing attached. Lifting herself proved to be more difficult. As her muscles uncontrollably shook from the strain, her fingers suddenly slipped from the branch, and once again she was looking at the cloud speckled heavens with her back on the ground.

"I can't," she said, the words barely leaving her lips.

Alek jumped off the tree and looked at her from above. There was something about the expression he wore that made her skin crawl.

Before she could push herself back up, he had climbed on top of her and pinned her to the ground. Alek nibbled on his lip, looking at her as if she was nothing more than a piece of meat. "You look tense and I have an idea of what could release a bit of stress for both of us."

"Get off of me." Astra struggled to move but she couldn't.

"Come on baby, we are the only two humans on this planet and I'm not a bad guy. I can care for you and I've been told I'm pretty well equipped, if you know what I mean. We could use each other to let off some steam." Alek licked his lips. His eyes trailed down her body, studying every inch of her before he slowly got off her and helped her to stand. "I wasn't trying to shake you up, but don't you want to have a bit of fun? We don't even know if we are going to live to see tomorrow and I think we should make sure that we at least live the best life we can."

"I'm going back to the campsite," she said before spinning on her heels and walking in the opposite direction.

She hurried her pace and walked between the trees. She could feel him right behind her, so she sped up.

Astra felt a firm hand grab her from behind. Alek shoved her up against a tree and unzipped her jacket. She could feel the way the bark scratched against the back of her head. He pushed himself closer to her and his hot breath puffed onto her neck.

"What are you doing?" Her voice cracked as she tried to struggle from his grip but felt his grasp grow firmer.

"We all need something here," he muttered.

Her stomach curled as she felt him push his body up against hers. She could feel something hard pressing against her stomach. She wasn't sure if it was the knife he had tucked into his pocket earlier, or his erect member ready to tear her in half. "You need protection. You need to feel safe and to get back home. I need a reason why I should protect you and not just kill you to make my life easier. You can think of it as a mutual exchange that benefits both parties."

Alek ran his hand up Astra's shirt, and firmly grabbed onto her breast.

"Stop," she said, grabbing at his fingers and pulling his hand off her nipple.

"Why?" He licked her neck. "You taste like honey," he muttered.

Once again, she tried to push him away. "I don't want this."

"Yes, you do," he cooed. "When was the last time you had a man inside of that tight pretty thing? I know you crave it. I saw how you blushed when I was looking at you."

"You misread me. Get off."

Alek grabbed onto her shoulders and dug his nails into her. Her shoulders screamed in pain as her bones struggled not to crack from the pressure he was applying. He took a step back and lifted her high in the air. She struggled to get away but was held captive.

No, this couldn't be happening. Not to her. Not now. A million possibilities of what was about to happen raced through her head. Was he about to rape her? That was clear. By the look in his eyes she could tell that was exactly what he was about to do. How badly was this going to hurt? She hoped it wouldn't be excruciating but knew that it likely would be. Was he planning on killing her when he was done?

187

No, she couldn't let this happen and even if it did, she sure as hell was going to make it as difficult for him as possible. This was not how she was going to end, and she was not about to let him touch her without a fight.

"Stop playing hard to get," he hissed through bared teeth. "Do you want to live? If you do, you need to earn your place around here."

As soon as the words left his lips, she flung her leg forward, ramming her shin as hard as she could into his groin. Alek roared and dropped her as he curled over in pain. She spun on her heels and ran towards the camp as fast as she could. She needed to get to Elde. She needed him to protect her.

Astra ran until her lungs burned. She ran alongside the river, stumbling over rocks as she raced towards the campsite. Looking up into the sunny sky, she remembered Vojin's warning. He told her not to trust anyone. Not even those who looked like her. She now understood why.

She felt trapped and wanted nothing more than to run in a different direction than towards camp. Going back to camp meant going back to Sagan, who was loyal to his friend, and the monster who attacked her would be arriving shortly after she did. What was she going to tell them? Would Sagan even believe that Alek would do such a thing? It was doubtful. Sagan held Alek on a pedestal. No matter how heinous of a man Alek was, Sagan refused to see the truth about his friend. Even if Alek had been a good person on Earth, the good in him died at some point on this planet.

She slowed her pace as she approached the camp, but her heart sank as she saw Alek and Sagan talking. *How did he get there before her?*

She ducked behind a rock only fifteen feet away, so she could listen to what he was saying.

"Where did Astra go?"

"She'll be here in a minute."

"Why would you leave her?" he gasped.

Alek lowered his voice as he leaned towards Sagan. "If I tell you, you have to keep this between us. She's already embarrassed enough about it."

"Of course. Is she okay?"

"Yeah, she's just a bit hurt. Towards the end of our training she came onto me. I'm not talking subtle flirting. She full on tried to jump me. I think I may have led her on with my comments, but you know me, I hit on all women but it doesn't mean I want her that way. I pushed her off and I told her no. I didn't want her. She was pretty angry about it. So, I left to give her a moment to cool down."

"Oh, that poor girl. She was probably just lonely and wanted to feel close to someone. Is that why your energy is so off?"

Alek shrugged, "You know I don't like rejecting people. She's a sweet girl but... I don't know. She just isn't my type. She's kind of bland looking to me."

Sagan groaned. "Hey don't talk shit. I think she is pretty, and I am sure there are many men out there who are into women who would agree with me."

"Not on this planet there aren't."

"Alek, you got to chill with the assholeness. What has gotten into you lately? Please tell me you were at least nice about it. Don't tell me you insulted her like that."

"Are you kidding? I would never insult her. She is a sweet girl. I just told her that I didn't think it was a good idea. I used the whole, "it's not you, it's me" line and from now on, I am just going to have to be more careful with accidently leading her on. I just don't want to give her mixed signals."

The sound of their conversation faded away as her mind went numb. Her legs buckled and she sank to the ground. What was she going to do? Her ears rang. Astra stared blankly at the rock in front of her and wrapped her arms around her legs, slowly taking in a deep breath to calm her nerves. How dare him.

Should she just leave? No. She couldn't. She needed them to keep her safe so that she could find Vojin. Vojin would keep her safe. He would have killed Alek for what he tried to do.

189

She felt her heart leap as a soft nudge caressed her shoulder. It was Elde. He nuzzled her cheek and made a purring sound from his throat.

She had never felt so relieved so see anyone. Astra wrapped her arms around his thick furry neck and buried her face into his fur. She knew she would be safe as long as he was close to her.

"I don't know what to do," she whispered to him. "I don't want to be around Alek but I don't have another choice. Please don't leave me alone with him. Even if we are training, please come with us." Elde squinted his eyes as he looked at her. It was clear that he was wanting her to tell him more. "I don't want to talk about it."

The beast nodded his head. She slowly pushed herself up and leaned against the rock. Should she tell Sagan the truth? No. She couldn't. He would never believe her over his best friend.

Would Alek come after her again? She hoped not, but she had the feeling that he wasn't done with her.

Her fingers ran down her pant leg until she felt the hard handle of the knife in her pocket. If he tried to rape her again, would she have the strength to kill him? Would killing him lead to Sagan killing her? This was a sticky situation that she didn't know how to get out of.

Astra stepped away from the rock and approached the men. Her eyes burned into Alek. God, she wished he was dead. She imagined cutting off his balls and throwing them to Elde to eat.

Damn him. He tried to take away her innocence and she would never be the same. From this day forward she knew she would forever remember the asshole who tried to rape her. Even if he died that very moment, she would never forget his face or how it felt to have a man try to force himself on her. She could almost feel his hot breath on her neck and the way her breast hurt when he grabbed it. Her shoulders were bruised, she could tell by the way they ached and her heart beat so hard that she wondered if it would explode.

To take her knife and burrow it right into him was exactly what she wanted to do. She hated him more than she'd ever hated anyone. She hated every part of him and thought of every possible way that he could die. But she couldn't kill him and that is what angered her the most. This planet was too dangerous for her to make it on her own and she needed the extra protection. But he was also a threat to her safety. So, who was more dangerous, the monsters who were searching for her or the monster who stood in front of her?

"Are you okay?" Sagan greeted her with bags packed and touched her on her shoulder.

She flinched and moved away. "Don't touch me," she hissed. "I'm fine. Let's go."

In silence they walked for the rest of the day. She passed by the area where he had attempted to rape her and as she did, she turned and glared at him. Alek blankly stared back but then cracked a small smile, which made her hate him even more.

There was a tension that lingered in the air, so thick that it was hard to breathe and even being around him made her want to scream. Should she sneak away at night? Maybe if she told Elde, he would leave the group and accompany her. Then again, if he knew what Alek had done, she was sure that he would kill him. Maybe that wouldn't be a bad thing, but it could backfire if Sagan killed her in retaliation.

The further they walked, the more trees they were surrounded by. The trees in this forest looked like they were of different species, but they all were dead, without a single leaf in sight. Some had flaking gray bark and roots that disappeared below the ground, while others were brown with grooves throughout the trunk and the roots were lifted so much that you could peek through the holes.

This section of the forest had no life with the exception of them. No other animals or bugs were seen and even the grass seemed to be weary of sprouting on the crusty black dirt.

The sun had begun to set, casting eerie shadows across the land. It was going to be a clear night and a cold one at that. She wrapped her scarf closer around her neck and watched a puff of air leave her lips.

"We should camp here tonight." Sagan dropped his bag to his side.

"Sounds good," Alek responded as he unwrapped both furs but put them one on top of the other before unpacking strips of dried meat. There was now only one fur left and that fur was attached to Sagan's bag. "You want some Sagan?"

"Sure."

"Astra?"

Her eyes once again burned into him. The sound of her name on his lips repulsed her. She wanted to slap the meat out of his hand. How dare him pretend that everything was okay when it wasn't. How dare him take both of the furs knowing she didn't have anything to cover herself in. He was selfish. He was awful and she knew why he took both furs for himself. Because if she wanted to stay warm tonight, the only way she could was if she lay down with him.

I would rather freeze to death than lay even a foot away from that pig, she thought to herself as she turned and walked a little further from camp.

Elde followed closely behind her and grunted. He nudged her shoulder and looked in the direction of the camp.

"I can't. Not tonight."

He nodded his head and laid down on the ground. Once again, he grunted and pointed his snout to his stomach.

"Am I laying by you tonight?"

He again nodded before looking at Alek. He turned and saw Elde and as soon as their eyes locked, Elde lifted his lips above his teeth. It was almost as if he was challenging him to come closer or perhaps, he was showing her that he would protect her from him.

She sat down and leaned her body against Elde, resting her head on his thick torso. She could hear his heart beating under his thick fur.

Goosebumps covered her arms. She zipped her jacket up to her neck. Why couldn't she just have picked a warmer jacket when she was in New York? A fleece lined coat sounded like heaven.

Elde placed his head over her body. His horns glowed faintly and as soon as they began, a wave of warmth washed over her.

She wished Elde had come with her earlier. He would have killed Alek as soon as he tried to rape her. But she was also sure that Alek wouldn't have made the attempt had Elde been there. No. That man waited until he was alone with her and he waited until she was in a weakened state of exhaustion before he tried.

She looked at Sagan who was about twenty feet from her. He seemed content, sitting on his fur as he munched on a piece of dried meat. She could hear him talking to Alek and laughing as if he didn't have a care in the world.

What angered her the most was that Alek didn't even seem remotely remorseful for what he did. Once he was finished with his dinner, he buried himself between the two furs and fell fast asleep.

Sleep. Tonight she wouldn't get any. Yes, she was safe with Elde but the fact that the man who tried to rape her was only a stone's throw away, made her feel like she was facing hell.

Sagan's face narrowed as he stared at Alek with dark eyes. It was strange how a man who seemed to be so happy only moments before now looked at his friend as if he wanted to beat him. But he had seemingly hidden this expression from his friend while he was still conscious.

Sagan got up and quietly walked towards Astra with a handful of dried meat. Elde lifted his head as he approached and stared at him.

"He's asleep, don't worry. Are you hungry?" he asked while trying to hand her some meat.

She shook her head and pushed the meat away. It would likely be a while before she could even think about food.

"Come with me," he mouthed.

Slowly, she got up and as she did, Elde stood up with her. Snorting, he nodded his head as if he was reassuring her that it was safe. She shook her head and touched his snout.

193

"Please don't leave me alone with Sagan," she whispered in the beast's ear. "I'm scared."

Elde pushed her towards Sagan with his snout, then looked at Alek, raising his lips over his teeth. She knew then that he was going to stay to make sure that Alek wouldn't try to follow them. Elde for some reason trusted Sagan. She wasn't sure why, but she could tell that he did.

Sagan reached his hand out to her. "It's okay. I won't hurt you."

She refused to take his hand and instead walked past him. Her hand slipped into her pocket until she felt the smooth handle of her weapon. Sagan looked down at her pocket and nodded his head as if he was reassuring her that it was okay. She knew he could feel how frightened she was.

They walked for about five minutes, until they were out of ear's reach. The sky was almost completely dark with the exception of the glow from the night-time heavens. There in the sky was the brightest star, shining its rays of hope down onto her. Where is Vojin? She needed him now more than ever. Was he okay?

Sagan leaned up against the trunk of a tree. His lips formed into a hard line as his midnight eyes stared blankly into the distance. Taking in a deep breath, he looked at her as she stood beside him. She flinched as he lifted up his hand, pulled back the collar of her jacket and pulled up her scarf, revealing bruises on each side.

He ground his teeth together and looked her dead in the eye. Her throat tensed. She didn't know what he was about to say but she wasn't sure she wanted to know.

"I need to know what happened. I need to know the truth."

Astra swallowed the lump in her throat. Her cheeks grew hot as she opened her mouth to speak but no words were able to leave her lips.

Sagan's brows furrowed. "I understand this must be scary for you. But I can't help you if I am left in the dark."

Her chin quivered. "Well Alek told you, didn't he?"

"Alek lied."

She lowered her head to her chest. Her teeth ground together as sweat formed on the back of her neck. How was she supposed to respond to that? She wanted to scream out "Yes he lied." She wanted to tell him everything that happened but what would be the consequences of her actions? Why would he side with a woman he barely knew? Why would he believe her over a friend he has known for years and someone he considered to be his brother?

Sagan put his hand on hers causing her heart to lurch. She pulled her hand away, almost expecting him to grip onto it harder, but he didn't. He tucked her hair behind her ear. His eyes stared at her as she looked away. She didn't want to be touched. Not by him. Not by any man.

"I promise you, nothing will happen to you if you just tell me the truth. I will never hurt you. I will never lay a hand on you."

Taking in a deep breath, Astra looked up towards the heavens and watched as a shooting star streaked across the sky. She wished she could sprout wings and fly away and pretend like nothing ever happened. If she kept her mouth shut, she was risking Alek coming after her again without Sagan knowing. If she told Sagan, he might turn on her or he might turn on Alek. She didn't like either because both outcomes could prove to be problematic.

Sagan touched her shoulder. She once again flinched and moved her shoulder away. "I can read you. I can feel your fear. I see the marks on your shoulders and you've hardly said a thing since you came back from training. I already know. I just want to hear it from you."

She ground her jaw. "Nothing happened."

"Bullshit. I don't believe you for a second. What did he do to you? Why are you protecting him?"

Touching her tense throat, she looked up at the night and watched her breath steam out in front of her. Protecting him? No, she would never protect someone so evil. She was protecting herself. "I'm scared," she finally said after a moment of silence.

195

"And you are allowed to be scared. What happened to you was scary and it was wrong."

"He wanted to get me alone and he succeeded. He came onto me and pushed me up against a tree. I didn't want to be with him, so he threatened me. He told me that he needed there to be a mutual exchange if I wanted his protection and if I wanted to give him a reason to let me live. He forced himself on me and touched me in ways I didn't want to be touched. He licked my skin and told me I tasted like honey. I swear I didn't want him. I told him to stop. He didn't. He would have raped me, but I kicked him before he could and ran. I don't even know how he got to the campsite before me."

Sagan sat in deafening silence with his brow furrowed and his fingers resting on his lips. The veins on his neck bulged from his skin, crawling all the way to his forehead.

"I know he is your friend," she continued. "But please believe me. I'm not lying. I swear on my life, I'm not lying."

"I'm going to tell you something about my past and I hope you don't judge me for it."

She turned to Sagan and watched him in silence. Was he a rapist? Had he harmed another woman? She almost didn't want to know but at the same time, she knew she needed to.

"My sister was raped years ago. She was scared to tell anyone because the man who raped her was a well-liked person. She finally opened up to my family and no one believed her, not even me. We didn't think he was capable of doing what she said he did to her."

"What happened? Did someone end up believing her?" She hoped for the best. She needed to hear something encouraging. Did the man end up in jail? Did the family finally believe her and turn their back on this family friend?

Sagan's eyes glazed over as he looked down at the old leather bracelet wrapped around his wrist. "She killed herself." His hands curled up into fists as he momentarily paused to compose himself.

"Who gave you that bracelet?"

"She gave it to me for my birthday. It was the last gift I ever got from her and I haven't taken it off since her funeral. I sometimes wonder, if only I had believed her, would she be alive? I was her older brother. I was supposed to protect her and instead of protecting her, I sided with the rest of my family. I will never let that go. I will never forgive myself for what I did, but I can't change the past." He turned to her. His brows narrowed over his midnight eyes as he ground his teeth together. "I can do something about what happened to you. Come with me."

CHAPTER 15

She felt her heart lurch into her throat. *What was Sagan about to do?* Her imagination pushed an endless reel of possibilities through her mind. She rubbed the back of her neck and hesitantly followed behind him. He walked in silence until they reached the camp. She could feel the rage building up inside of him.

"Look what the cat dragged in," Alek said as he stood up. "I was worried about you both, but your pet wouldn't let me look for you."

She wanted nothing more than to disappear. To be in his presence was suffocating.

Sagan walked up to Alek. His muscles bulged out of his arms. Black veins formed on his skin.

Alek crossed his arms. "What's going on?"

"Shut up," he growled, baring his sharp incisors as his eyes became wilder. It looked like he was about to explode. His chest heaved as he glared at his friend like he wanted to kill him. In the moments that she looked at Sagan, she realized he wasn't there. His mind had travelled to another place and whatever had replaced him was far darker than she ever expected.

"Excuse me? What the hell got into you?"

Sagan shook his head and ground his teeth together. Grabbing Alek by his throat, he rushed his body towards a tree trunk and smashed him up against it before pinning his friend using his forearm. The trunk of the tree groaned from the pressure and began to lift off the dirt. With wild eyes and grinding teeth, Alek slammed his fist into the side of Sagan's face, but his friend didn't move. It was as if he didn't even feel the impact.

Elde walked up beside Astra and nuzzled her. She wrapped her arms around his neck, almost afraid of what she was seeing. What was he about to do to his friend?

Sagan's head twisted to the side as he glared at Alek who was unable to free himself from the alligator grip that held him captive. His voice was chillingly calm. "How does it feel to be pushed against the tree? Do you feel helpless yet?" Reaching down he grabbed Alek between his legs. Sweat formed as Alek choked back a scream. "How about now? How does it feel to be touched by someone you don't want to be touched by?" Slowly a malevolent smile crossed his lips. "You know, I haven't gotten laid in a while, how about I fuck you? I'll fuck you to keep me from killing you." Twisting Alek around, he slammed his friend facedown into the ground and climbed on top of him.

"No, get off me," Alek yelled out.

She stood, paralyzed, as her eyes forced her to witness the violent act in front of her. It was one thing to go through the trauma of almost being raped but to see what she went through from the outside made everything all the more terrifying. What was Sagan about to do to him? What horrible act was she about to witness?

"Please stop," she whispered, her words barely leaving her lips as her eyes burned. "Please don't do this. Don't do this."

Getting close to his ear, he licked the back of Alek's neck and moaned. "You taste like honey."

"Stop! I get the point!" he yelled out, struggling to get away but unable to.

"That's how it feels you piece of shit. That's how you made her feel and she will never get over how you violated her. I don't care how much history we have. I don't care who you are to me. If you ever even look in her direction the wrong way, I will kill you myself. Do you understand me?" Shaking from head to toe, Alek nodded his head. Sagan released him, stood up, and took a step back.

Alek glared at him before he stormed into the woods.

"He'll be back by morning," Sagan said darkly. "But I promise you, he will never lay a hand on you ever again. He needs time to think, and we will give him that time."

"Why did you want to reenact what happened to me? Why would you do that in front of me?" She felt hot tears stinging her eyes as she tried to hide her shaking hands.

"Because diplomacy doesn't always work when it comes to a person who is willing to rape a woman and threaten her life and you needed to see that I have your back. He needed to know what it was like to be you. He needed to know that if he ever hurt you, that the one person he has left in the world who actually gives a damn about him, will kill him. I'm sorry if I scared you, but I needed to make sure that you would remain safe amongst the people who surround you."

"But you almost raped him."

Sagan's head snapped in her direction. "Megan, I would have never raped him. I would have never taken it that far. I was just making a point. But I needed him to know what it felt like to be you. No one is going to hurt you. NO ONE!"

"That's not my name."

Sagan's chest heaved as his wild eyes stared at her. Taking a step back, he shook his head and opened his mouth, snapping himself out of his rage.

"Astra," he whispered.

"Was Megan your sister?" Sagan stumbled back and sank to the ground. She walked up to her friend and sat down beside him. "What happened that caused you to snap like this?"

Sagan looked blankly in front of himself. His lips twitched. "I walked into her bedroom on the night of her thirteenth birthday. It was a few months after she was raped. She was sitting on the bed with her hand under the pillow. I still remember how she looked up at me when I came in. I won't ever forget the expression she wore. It was similar to the one you had when you were telling me what happened." Sagan took in another breath as he looked up. "She said, 'Will you believe me now?' Before she took the gun to the roof of her mouth and pulled the trigger.

"When you told me about what happened to you, all I could think about was her. All I could see was her, looking through your eyes, begging me to keep her safe. When I pushed Alek against the tree, I could still hear the way the gun sounded. I could still see the way her skull blew upon and how her body went limp. I could still hear the way my mom screamed when she came in and saw me holding my sister's corpse. It was like I was reliving her death over again. I couldn't fail you the way I failed her."

For the rest of the night, she didn't leave Sagan's side. She couldn't go to sleep and found herself staring into the woods. When would Alek come back? Would he seek vengeance on them both for what had happened? Her eyes fell upon Elde, sleeping soundly beside her.

She turned to her side and looked at Sagan who was staring blankly at the starry sky. "I can't sleep," she whispered.

"Why not?" He turned towards her and leaned against his arm.

"My mind won't stop and I am scared because I don't know how to defend myself."

"You have me, and you have Elde. Anyone who wants to hurt you is going to have a pretty hard time getting to you in the first place. I have an idea. Let's do a training session."

She gazed at the moonlit woods. "But it's so dark."

"Which is exactly why I want to do training right now. I want you to stop relying on your eyes and start relying on your instincts."

Astra pushed herself up and held out her hand to help Sagan. "Let's do this," he smiled, grabbing onto her hand. He took a step back and pointed to his eyes. "The first thing I want you to know is that if you are being attacked and have the ability to go after your attacker's eyes, do so. You need to hit them where it hurts. We are not going to practice that one because quite frankly, I like seeing and I don't want to be your practice dummy. But I want you to keep that in mind. The things I am going to teach you tonight will be what you need to do if you are attacked. Do you remember the defensive pose I taught you?"

She nodded her head. "Elbows down, fists by my temples. I need to protect my face and ribs because those are two weak areas."

"Good. What about your feet?"

"I need to have them at least shoulder length apart. If I put my legs close together, I can stumble. If they are apart, I will maintain my balance."

"And with your clumsy ass, you need all the balance you can get."

"Amen to that."

Sagan showed Astra different defensive moves in case she was attacked. She noticed that unlike last time, this time he showed her all the weak areas on a human she could go after. By the time the sun broke through the darkness, she felt more confident in her fighting. If she were attacked, at least she had learned a few moves that could potentially keep her safe. He taught her to rely on her other senses if she wasn't able to see. It was then that she noticed when she closed her eyes, every sound around her became so much louder.

Astra breathed in the crisp air as they packed up their bags. She rolled up the heavy furs and tied two of them to the base of Alek's satchel.

"You said he would be back by morning," she said. Sagan pushed his bag on one shoulder and then put Alek's bag on the other.

"I did, but he didn't come back. I'm just going to assume that he went back to the cave. We don't need him anyway. We will do just fine without him."

The feeling of weight lifted from her shoulders brought a wave of relief to her soul. She wouldn't have to face him again. Now she could continue her search to find Vojin knowing that those around her were there to protect her.

Astra's eyes hovered over the river that cut through the forest as the morning light began to reflect colors of fuchsia and lavender from the feathery clouds above. The brightest star in the sky had faded away but she knew that following the river was still the right direction. She loved sunrises and being able to witness something beautiful after something so ugly happened was exactly what she needed.

CHAPTER 16

Every day, they practiced combat moves and training techniques, before they began to once again travel in the direction of the star. There were days she would be told to hang from a tree and practice the same moves that Alek had originally taught her, while other days she would learn different hand to hand combat techniques that allowed her to use different parts of her body to attack, such as her elbow, open palms, and knees. She learned how to choke someone, crushing their Adam's apple in the process, and how when her enemy is on the ground, she could axe stomp them in the face or throat, using her heel to ensure more force. At first, she was slow and clumsy, but the more she practiced the better she became, and at an accelerating speed. It was shocking how quickly she learned. The worm she swallowed truly did help.

Sagan didn't stop at combat training. During workouts, he targeted specific muscles in her mid to lower body to help increase her vertical jump. He taught her how to do a backflip, explaining the technique he used. He taught her how to slide on the ground while pulling out her knife and what to do if she lost or broke her weapon. By the end of the week, she was faster and jumped higher than she could have ever imagined.

"You still have a long way to go," Sagan said as they walked alongside the river. "But I am proud of how far you've come."

They were now in an area that was coated in grass and speckled with beryl colored bushes and viridescent trees. The river was no longer a crystal blue color but had now become more of a rusty shade, moving slowly towards the distant mountains.

This area was teeming with life. There were strange insects with long tongues and eight clear wings that flew between pink puffy flowers. Furry mammals the size of her foot with two heads would often be seen laying in the middle of field, seemingly enjoying the sunlight. Massive featherless birds with clear skin and a wingspan the size of a small plane made their way towards the mountains in flocks of five or more. No animal around them seemed to notice their presence and on the rare occasion that they looked in their direction, they would always notice Elde who walked by Astra's side, and then continue doing whatever they were doing.

Astra stopped in her tracks as she saw a figure moving towards them from a distance. Her skin crawled as she recognized the familiar shape of the man she had hoped she would never see again. Why did he come back? She had hoped he had gone back to the cave or better yet, had been eaten by a hungry predator.

As Alek came closer, Astra noticed how unkept he looked. His dark hair twisted and turned in every direction. His fingernails were caked with dirt as were the lines around his face. He looked as if he'd aged ten years and she wasn't sure it was just because of the facial hair that crawled up the sides of his cheeks and puffed out like a dirty cloud, or that he looked like he hadn't eaten since he left the camp.

"I figured you went back to the cave," Sagan said as he crossed his arms. "You look like shit."

Alek lowered his head, refusing to say a word. Finally, his flaking lips split open.

"Can I speak with Astra alone?"

Sagan's eyes burrowed into Alek. "No."

"I don't feel comfortable being alone with you," she said, touching the weapon in her pocket.

"I don't blame you," Alek's voice trailed off. "I just... I don't even know where to start..."

Sagan tapped his fingers on his thick forearms. "Well I have an idea. How about you say, 'Hey, I'm sorry for treating you like an object created to pleasure me and someone that I can verbally and sexually assault.'"

205

"I am so ashamed. I feel horrible for what I did."

"You should."

"Nothing will ever make up for what I did, and I don't expect you to ever forgive me. I don't know what happened to me. I've lost myself being here. I've lost a piece of who I was and though I thought the only threat were the monsters outside, I didn't realize that I was becoming one of them."

Astra glared at Alek. "No, you are worse. The ones who have attacked us have done so because they think we are the evil ones. I don't blame them, when people like you exist."

"She has a point. So how do we know that you are safe to be around her? How do I know that if you come back here, you won't do something worse to her?"

"You don't know. But I do. I swear on my family's life that I will never do that again. I want to go home too. I need to go home. This place is changing me into someone I don't want to be. I hate myself for what I did, and my family would be ashamed of me." Alek turned to Astra. His muscles sank on his face. He was only able to look at her momentarily before staring back at the ground. "You were innocent in all of this and I just took advantage of you. I wronged you to a depth that is inexcusable."

"What you did was unforgivable."

"I know. I can't undo it. I wish I could, but I can't."

"You are not welcome here, if Astra says that you are not. We will leave you behind on this planet to rot if she gives the word. I know we have history, but you are not the man I used to know. The man I knew back on Earth respected women. The man I knew never even raised his voice to a woman because his mom taught him better than that and if this is the man you have decided to become, the world would be better without you." Sagan turned to Astra and put his hand on her shoulder. "What are your thoughts?"

She looked towards her assaulter. She hated him. She hated every part of him and Sagan was right, and in her mind, the world would be a better place without him in it. His eyes still stared at the ground as his shoulders sank even further.

Alek shook his head and turned around. It was clear to her that not even Alek felt like he deserved to come back.

No matter how much she hated him and how much she wanted him to die, she couldn't be the reason that he wasn't able to get back to his family. He was an awful human being for what he did, and she would never forgive him for his wrongdoings, but she decided that she would give this bastard one more chance to redeem himself.

"You look hungry and we have dried meat." She touched her hollow chest. She almost hated herself for doing this. "This doesn't mean I forgive you. I will never forgive you for what you did to me, but I will at least give you one more chance to help me find Vojin. If you even so dare look at me wrong, Elde will be the one to take care of you and I promise you that he won't make your death quick."

Elde nodded his head and stepped towards Alek. The beast's lips curled into a smile, showing the edges of his razorblade teeth.

* * *

It had been a few days since Alek had returned and he seemed more like a shadow than a person in the group. Even though he was distant, she couldn't stand being around him and hoped the day would come soon when she finally was able to find Vojin. He would know what to do. Perhaps he could find a separate way home for that man so that she wouldn't have to see him everyday. She felt like she was living in a nightmare even looking at his face. Why did she show him mercy? Why couldn't she just tell him to go die somewhere?

It just wasn't in her to be that kind of a person. She promised to give him one more chance and so far, he had proven that he was taking that chance seriously.

Astra trained with Sagan every day, strengthening her muscles and learning new techniques, while Alek prepared food and made stronger weapons. He didn't talk much anymore and seemed to be more of a loner, ostracizing himself, which was something she was thankful for. Even when they began their trek each day, he would normally stay several feet behind.

They were finally getting closer to the dark mountains. They seemed so much bigger now than they did before. The sides were steep with ridged edges that looked like it had been carved out by giants. There was no way they could climb over the mountains without ropes and proper gear. She knew they would have to find paths between them and hoped she wouldn't lose sight of the star.

The land she stood on was mostly flat with the occasional tree or bush. It was strange to see such an even terrain contrasting against a line of mountains. They probably had a day or two before they reached them and by the looks of it, when they did arrive, it wasn't going to be an easy trek.

Today they had decided to spar in the evening instead of in the beginning of the day. Sagan had remembered a rocky enclosure only a half a day's walk away and he wanted to get to it before nightfall so they would have a safe place to rest for the night.

They finally found this illusive enclosure he spoke of. It looked almost like a primitive home, made of gray sparkling stones and a very large stone over the top of it, which created a solid roof. It was the height of a two-story house but three times as deep as a typical home. It had a tall, doorless entryway barely wide enough to fit a human and no windows. Because of this, a very begrudged Elde had to stay outside while the rest went inside to check it out.

The inside was empty but cluttered with stones that were about the size of a football. Small glowing flowers grew between the cracks of the rocks, creating a beautiful pattern throughout the shelter and illuminating the home. Their six curled petals softly glowed a ghostly white, illuminating the area with dim light. It was colder in this enclosure than it was outside and outside it was already as cold as winter felt down in Tennessee.

"I'll gather some wood," Alek grunted before walking out of the home.

"Let's go spar for a bit," Sagan said as he dropped his satchel on the ground and walked outside.

They warmed up for about half an hour before beginning to spar. In the far distance, an army of onyx clouds puffed out their chests as they marched across the sky, draining the color from anything their shadow crossed. Nature itself grew silent as it waited for the growl of thunder that would be sure to be heard once the clouds closed in.

Astra had become numb to her bruises and aching muscles. A cut on her arm felt more like a minor inconvenience. Though she realized she was far from being as ready as she hoped she would be, she knew she was at least more ready for this world than she was when she first arrived. She hoped that if a predator were to come, that she could hold her own.

"You ready to fight?" Sagan asked, raising his fists and punching the air.

"I dunno," she replied with her head held high. "Are you ready to lose?"

Balling up her fists, she nodded her head and assumed her fighting stance. Though it was cold outside, she had to remove her jacket after her warm up because she was becoming too warm. A small droplet of salty sweat rolled down her cheek as she waited for Sagan's first move.

She glanced at the clouds that appeared to be closing in behind the mountains. Would it rain soon? She wasn't sure if the storm was approaching them, but she could tell that it was building, and it had a strange shade of lavender to the edges of the clouds. It reminded her of the way the sky looked when she first got to Pannotia.

Sagan swayed from side to side before thrusting his balled-up fist towards her face. He chose to do a bold and direct approach to his attack which she had anticipated. It was his style. She ducked, feeling the breeze of his arm over the hairs on her head.

Swinging her fist towards his midsection, he lifted his large muscular leg and easily blocked her from impact by kicking his leg into her diaphragm and throwing her in the opposite direction.

Astra lunged towards him, not allowing herself to be slowed, despite her lungs aching within her chest. She twisted, barely missing his punch before slamming into the side of his head with her knuckles. She rolled back before once again lunging towards Sagan to get in another hit. He saw her move coming and blocked her fist, easily moving away from her assault.

He left his side open. Bad decision. With a quick twist of her body, she swung her knee as hard as she could, slamming it into the side of his ribs and knocking the wind from his lungs. He bent over as he lifted his hand.

She stopped. He heaved for a breath of air. Yes, she felt ready to take on this world. Raising up, Sagan placed his hands on the back of his head and breathed in deeply through his nose.

"You've gotten good," he said to her between breaths. "Far better than even I realized. You want to move onto a knife attack?"

"Are you sure you want to lose again?" she sneered playfully.

"Be careful, you might just be the one to taste sweet defeat," he responded with a chuckle.

Sagan smiled and removed two knives from his brown satchel and tossed one to Astra. He then flipped his weapon in the air, swung around, and caught it by the handle.

"Show off."

She lunged towards Sagan with a knife in hand and advanced her attack which she quickly realized was the wrong move to make. He leaped over her head, twisted around, and smashed his foot into her back. She slammed into the sharp bark of a nearby tree, instantly shaving cuts into her left cheek. Her face felt hot as she swung around and pulled a piece of wood out of her skin. Warm blood crawled down her neck, soaking her shirt with a shade of bright crimson. Blinking away the blur from her eyes, she closed her mouth and felt air rush out from a hole that was torn into her cheek. Though she wanted to stop, she knew she needed to train her body to keep going, despite injury. Had he been a threat, she needed to know no matter what, she could still fight him without backing down.

"Are you ok?" Sagan asked between heaving breaths. "You're hurt!"

"Not as hurt as you will be!" She pushed aside the throbbing pain that radiated down her jaw, and got into a defensive stance. Though her head felt light and nausea curled through her, she couldn't allow this to slow her down. If she were attacked, her attacker would not show mercy if she was hurt. They would use it to their advantage.

Sagan's eyes grew wide. "Um… are you sure you want to continue? We can go back and put something on your cheek. It looks kind of bad."

"No! I'm fine." She tensed her jaw, feeling the air once again rush through her cheek. Her head spun as she glared at Sagan. She needed to keep going. She had to prove to herself she wasn't the weakest link and would not be a burden.

She lunged towards him but suddenly bent back. Sagan's sharp knife barely missed her throat. She crouched her body low, twisting her leg around before she knocked his feet from underneath him. He slammed onto the ground and burst out laughing as she quickly climbed on top of him with her knife pressed against his esophagus.

"I beat you," she gasped, not even believing herself. "I beat you."

This was the moment she needed. Though it was a quickly ending fight, she needed to know she had the strength within her to keep going. Sagan was right when he said to empty her mind and allow instincts to take over. As long as she didn't overthink during an attack, there was a possibility she might survive on this planet long enough to get home.

When Astra stood, her legs shook. Slowly she raised her hand to her cheek and felt her fingertips caress the shredded skin. Her slightly blurry vision fixated on the blades of grass she stood upon as she felt the warm feather of blood crawl down the side of her neck.

Elde walked up to her and sniffed the gash. He turned his head and sunk his teeth into his side until blood stained his white fur. Looking up at her, he snorted.

She felt the blood rush from her face as she stared at Elde. Was he serious? No. He couldn't be.

Closing her eyes tightly, she gasped and curled over as a radiating pain swept through her. Her cheek was so hot, it felt like it was touching the flames of hell.

"You have to consume some of the blood," Alek said as he walked up behind her and examined her wound. "It's too deep to just heal on the surface."

She took a step back and shook her head. Even being a few feet from him still made her stomach twist.

"Isn't there another way?" The unbearable pain radiated up to her skull. Even opening her mouth was becoming a challenge.

"Not in this case," Sagan agreed. "I can see your teeth."

She hesitantly reached towards Elde and dipped her fingers into his fresh blood. Slowly she placed her fingers up to her mouth and pushed them inside of her jaw. Though she couldn't taste the difference between his blood and hers, just the knowledge this was in her mouth made her stomach churn.

Astra felt the back of her throat quiver. Never in her life did she imagine she would do something as repulsive as this. She didn't want to think about what she was doing, but within seconds she felt a cooling sensation sweep over her wound as her flesh weaved back together. This uncomfortable sensation left as quickly as it had begun and within a moment, she was touching a fully healed cheek still wet with her own blood.

"Much better," Sagan smiled as he examined her cheek. "Bet that tasted delicious."

"Tasted better than your defeat," she retorted.

* * *

The light of the flames danced off Alek's face as his gaze burned into the fire. With a furrowed brow he sighed. His eyes lifted as he looked towards the darkness outside.

It was late at night. They had already eaten and laid out their furs to sleep on. Astra chose a spot by the wall as far away as possible from Alek. He seemed to notice and made it a point to stay on the other side of the shelter, closer to the exit.

Even with the fire, Astra could still feel the draft of icy air seeping through the cracks of the wall. She zipped up her jacket and pulled at her scarf.

A weighted silence lingered in the air while they all blankly stared in different directions. For the rest of the night, the sizzling and snapping flames were the only sounds heard through the enclosure. Finally, the men quietly went to sleep, leaving her to be the only one awake.

Her thoughts lingered on her father. She missed him so much it hurt, and the feeling of homesickness never faded, no matter how much time she spent on this planet. Her eyes burned as she stared at the flames eating away at the wood.

As time went on, the fire didn't seem to provide the kind of warmth that it once had. She bundled up in the fur and wondered why the temperature was dropping so rapidly.

Astra filled her lungs with sweet, icy oxygen and closed her eyes. She wanted this day to be over so they could once again begin their journey towards finding Vojin. Though she still held onto hope, the thought of the attack between Prosperine and him constantly prodded her. What if Prosperine had killed him? What if he was her only chance back and he was gone? What would she do?

CHAPTER 17

"WAKE UP NOW!"

Astra's eyes snapped open to the sound of Alek's voice filled with desperation. Immediately she felt a bitter cold that painfully seeped into her bones, momentarily holding her captive as her eyes fell upon the frosty remains of the flowers that had grown between the cracks of the walls. They no longer glowed now that the cold had burned them. She opened her mouth and watched a ghostly puff of air crawl out of her lips before she looked around herself in disbelief. When did this happen?

Outside of the entrance, all she could see was a thick blanket of white pouring on the ground as if God himself was turning over a bucket of this icy hell. The blizzard slapped away all evidence of flora, arrogantly coating the ground around it as if what it had to show was somehow better.

Her jaw tensed as she watched ice rapidly close their only way out. Their time was limited before mother nature herself decided their verdict would be immurement.

Alek and Sagan grabbed their bags and blankets and motioned for her to do the same.

"WHAT ARE YOU WAITING FOR? LETS GO!" Sagan cried out as both of the men rushed outside.

"Get out of there!" Alek yelled as he rushed back into the shelter and grabbed her bag for her before leaping over the mound of ice that was quickly forming. "COME ON!"

"I'm hurrying!" She turned and grabbed her blanket, wrapping it around herself.

"If you don't get out now, you're going to be trapped!"

Her gaze averted to the entrance. It was now halfway blocked off by the moving, contouring ice. She watched in horror as the ice reached out and covered the fire pit full of ashes. Astra ran towards the entrance of the shelter. The ice had already formed too high for her to be able to get out without some sort of help. The men yelled as they attempted to chip away at the ice with their weapons.

She threw her blanket through the fast closing entrance and shoved the handle of her weapon into her pocket. Jumping onto the slippery rocks she tried to grip onto the fast-moving frozen mound. Her feet slipped out from underneath her and she felt her face slam onto the bitter cold surface. Her heart pounded as she continued the struggle to get out. She knew her life depended on whether or not she could get through to the other side.

Her shoulders sank as her heart stood frozen within her. The surface was too slippery. She needed to make it coarse and had only minutes to do so before her fate would be sealed.

"Grab my hand!" Alek yelled from outside the shelter, barely able to reach over the surface of the entrance. There was no way she could grab it.

"Come on! You got this!" Sagan yelled as both of the men slammed their weapons into the ice.

"SHIT! My knife broke!" Alek yelled as he pounded the ice with his fists, breaking open the skin on his knuckles.

"Stop!" she yelled from inside the shelter, seeing the ice on the other side turn red. "I have an idea!"

"I shouldn't have left her in there!" Sagan yelled in frustration as he punched the ice, leaving a small crack. "We can't let her die like this. We need to go find Elde. He will know what to do."

She turned around and saw a large rock the size of a football, only feet from where she was standing. Snatching the stone from ground, she watched as the icy substance crawled over where the rock once was. With screaming muscles, she raised the rock above her head and used all of her force to slam it into the moving surface in front of her, before she pulled the rock away. Though it created a hole just big enough to fit her foot in, within a second it was already closed.

215

Astra screamed as she raised the rock above her head again and slammed the stone into the ice, leaving it there as a step. She pushed her foot onto the rock, making sure it was sturdy enough. To her relief, it was. The ice had now consumed much of the shelter. There were several inches of ice on the ground, leaving no stone untouched. The ice crawled up the wall and there was only a few feet left of the opening that they had once been able to walk through.

She leaped onto the stone and with one swift movement, she threw herself through the quickly closing entrance. Her jaw tensed as she felt the ice quickly begin to close in on her body. Was she too late? Would this crush her in its icy grip? She could feel the pressure on her skin as she gripped onto the ice on the other side. Finally, with one firm push, she tumbled out.

Her eyes trailed across the thick white blanket choking the land. She was alone and the only sign of life was her own heart forcing blood through her shivering body. A stinging wind grabbed her hair and slapped it against her face. Where did Sagan and Alek go? They were just here a moment ago but now there was not even a trace of them left. Not even their footprints were found in the snow. It was as if they had never existed. How did they disappear like this?

What was once the river had now become nothing more than a frozen grave, cluttered with the corpses of small river monsters; their bodies submerged halfway in ice and coated in a layer of snow. The look of sheer horror and fear was still etched on their lifeless corpses. Their expression burned a hole in her mind.

She turned from the wind, further examining the land around her in hopes she might find evidence that would point to where the men had gone. The home she found shelter in, had now become nothing more than a mound of ice suffocating all plant life near it.

Astra explored the edge of the land, trying to find the men who had seemingly disappeared into thin air. She didn't think they would abandon her, but she remembered Sagan telling Alek they needed to find Elde. Clearly, they had no faith that she could get out.

She stopped in her tracks as she noticed two shapes in the distance. Was that them? Her heart fluttered as she made out the white dusted hair of Sagan beside his friend. They both stood with their back facing her, beside a large, snow covered boulder.

"Sagan! Alek!" she cried out as she made her way through the snow. The men didn't react. They didn't move and instead they stood as if they were made of stone. Had they frozen to death? Could they not hear her? She approached them till she was only about thirty feet away.

Suddenly her heart lurched in her throat. Stepping out into view, a large black demon glared at the men. Astra recognized this demon and jumped behind an ice-covered tree as soon as she did. Prosperine. No. Not this. Not now.

She felt far from ready to face this beast. Learning to fight was something that she had just begun. Though she knew what she was about to do, every inch of her wanted to run as far and fast as she could.

Her knife was still nestled in her pocket. She pulled it out and looked down at the tooth. How would this end? Would this end with her body buried in crimson colored snow? Would she watch her own breath slow to a stop?

Her heart pounded with such vigor, it felt like a drum strummed its beat behind her eyes. She peeked from behind the tree before she raced to the next one, now only fifteen feet away from them. She wasn't sure how Prosperine didn't notice her, but she was at least closer to the men. The deep pressure of gut-wrenching horror exploded in her core as the demon bobbed her head back and forth between Sagan and Alek. Prosperine wasn't looking for them. She was looking for her.

With six spider-like arms coming out of her black skeleton body, the beast towered over them. A long scorpion tail with a sharp dagger attached to the base acted as a third leg, allowing for better balance. Ash-colored foam dripped from her mouth, containing several rows of jagged blood-stained teeth. She had clearly just fed herself and her eyes clearly showed what her next intended meal would be.

Prosperine twisted her head to the side and cracked the bones within her long thin neck, causing thick gray spikes to burst through her leathery skin. The demon's thin lips curled into a smile so malevolent that even Lucifer himself would cringe.

"Hello boys," Prosperine cooed as she slowly blinked her vertical eyelids over her white, soulless eyes. "Where is Astra? I know you are hiding her."

"We don't know anyone by that name," Alek snarled. He gripped onto his broken knife, which was now nothing more than a serrated tip.

The demon giggled. "I don't want to kill her. I just want to have a little bit of fun before I take her to where she belongs. Where is she?"

"Who are you talking about?" Sagan asked.

"Astra, you stupid hybrid. I don't have time for games. You tell me where she is at, and I will leave you alone."

"It's just us here," Alek replied with a stiff face.

"You are a terrible liar and I don't have time for those. So how about this, I kill one of you and see if the other talks. If he doesn't, I'll kill the next one too. So, who wants to die first?" she asked tauntingly. The men stood in silence, refusing to talk.

Astra pinched herself. This couldn't be real. This had to be a nightmare she needed to wake up from.

Prosperine raised her lips above her teeth and squinted her eyes as she examined Sagan, only inches from his face. She inhaled through her slitted nostrils while a clump of her saliva fell from her mouth and burned a hole into the snow.

Astra could feel Prosperine's disdain for their kind seeping from every pore. The demon's misanthropic feelings were obvious by her facial expression alone while the energy from her hate felt as if it was choking her.

"You look like you'd taste delicious," Prosperine said with a voice that was tauntingly perky. She raised her head to the sky before she wrapped her fingers around Sagan, lifting him high into the air and pinning him against the rock.

"DON'T HURT HIM!" Alek howled. He lunged towards Prosperine with his knife in hand.

Just as the demon twisted her neck around, Alek leaped and flung his arm into the air, instantly slashing open the beast's face with the edge of the broken knife. She roared in rage and dropped Sagan in the snow before slamming Alek's head against the rock with such force that his skull caved in.

Now that Sagan was free from her grip, he lunged towards the beast with his knife in hand as he screamed with a kind of agony and rage that broke Astra's heart. The demon dodged his assaults as blood dripped from her leathery face. It seemed almost too easy for her to avoid his blows now that she knew they were coming.

Astra's mind spun out of control. She stared at Alek's body crumpled in the blood-stained snow. His chest wasn't moving and the skin around his skull had split open wide enough for her to see his brain peeking through the hole that had formed. He was dead. Prosperine had killed him within an instant.

She turned her attention back towards Sagan and flinched each time the beast lunged at him. He seemed to know what he was doing as he glided through the snow, blocking and dodging the demon's assaults. Both of them fought viciously, with the determination that this fight would be till death.

Sagan leaped into the air and spun effortlessly over the demon. He landed onto her back and ripped a chunk of flesh out with his teeth. Blood dripped from his jaw as he slammed his knife into the open wound.

Prosperine screamed as she grabbed Sagan and threw him onto the ground. As he slid across the snow, he pulled out a second weapon from his belt, skidded to a stop, glanced over to his friend's corpse and charged at the beast in front of him.

With a twist of her body, the demon slammed her tail into his arms, immediately disarming him before grabbing Sagan by his shoulders and digging her claws into his flesh. He struggled to get away.

"Where is she?" Prosperine roared as she raised him to her face.

"I would rather die than tell you!"

"Where is she?" Prosperine shook Sagan like a rag doll.

"Do it! Just kill me!" Sagan howled before spitting on the demon's face.

"Tick, tock, tick, tock… your time's up." The demon cackled as she raised Sagan to her massive jaw.

"NOOOOOOOOO!!!!!!" Astra screamed at the top of her lungs, finally finding her voice as the muscles in her legs tensed up. She stepped out from behind the tree. "DON'T TOUCH HIM!"

"Astra!" The demon perked up as she quickly slithered towards her, still holding Sagan captive.

"Astra, run! JUST GO!" Sagan screamed as he struggled in the demon's arms. "RUN NOW!"

Prosperine approached her. In the moments that she spoke, Sagan continued to beg his friend to run.

"I have been searching for you. What a perfect time for you to show up! I have a surprise! I know how much you loved to watch magic shows as a kid. Let me show you a trick! You see him now, right?" Smiling, she jolted her head towards Sagan, dislodged her flat jaw and jammed him into her throat before she swallowed him whole, filling her belly with his body. "Now you don't."

A rage boiled inside of her. Sagan was innocent in all of this and Prosperine just swallowed him. The bulge in the demon's stomach moved. Was he still alive in there? She needed to get him out. She needed to help him.

"You're dead," she said to Prosperine in a voice as dark as death.

At full speed she lunged at the demon with her weapon in hand. No longer did she fear death or pain but instead the deep primal urge to watch the demon's blood seep onto the snowy ground was far greater than any urge she ever felt before. Astra didn't just want to see this beast die, she needed it. She longed to feel her awful heart stop beating beneath her fingertips. She embraced this feeling and allowed it to become the innermost part of herself; her essence.

She jumped as high as she could and dodged the beast's first blow. The demon raised her tail. She landed on the beast's body and swung her knife towards her neck but as her arm flung towards the beast's flesh, one of the long gray spikes that protruded from her neck dislodged and like a bullet, burst through Astra's forearm. She slipped off of Prosperine's body and fell back onto the ground.

Images of death clouded her mind as she took out her rage on this beast. She rolled under the bulging stomach just as the demon's tail came crashing down mere inches from her face.

Astra flipped her knife up from her wrist and felt the pressure of the skin against her weapon before it gave way and sliced through. Shit. It wasn't deep enough, and she forgot to use the poison.

The demon reached down and grabbed her leg. She threw her high into the air before slamming her against the boulder and onto the ground like a limp rag doll.

A high pitched shrill screamed through her temples and a blinding pain shot through her cracked ribs with every breath she took. Astra felt the animal crawling over her. The demon picked her up and lifted her to eye level. She grinned at her prize.

"You should have just come with me in the first place. Now because of you, two of my children and my husband are dead. I hated your species before, but I never thought my hate would become so personal. Don't worry. I won't kill you. I need you alive. But that doesn't mean I can't torture you a bit."

Astra came back to her senses as she once again looked at the beast through eyes of hatred. No. Today was not the day she wanted to let evil win.

"Why do you hate mankind so much?" She coughed, grinding her teeth together as she wrapped her fingers around her weapon.

"Your species is a virus, destroying everything you touch, with no regard to the innocent lives around you that you affect. You don't see it because you are blind. I can no longer stand by and watch mankind continue to live in unremorseful evil. Humans deserve the gift that we will give them. Destruction."

She looked down at Prosperine's chest. There was a small section that looked like it was moving in a slow and steady fashion. "And this is my gift to you," she said, dropping the knife before catching the handle in midair with her feet. She swung her legs out and flung her body forward, ramming the weapon into the demon's beating heart.

The beast dropped her and stumbled back. Astra's mind burned with satisfaction. All pain in her body became nothing more than a nagging thought as the demon collapsed onto the powdery snow. She jumped on the beast and tore the knife from her heart, before slicing it down the monster's stomach. A gargling sound came from the demon's lips as her organs poured out into the steaming snow in front of her.

"Not all of us are evil," she said with a heaving chest. "You will not destroy my species."

"No," Prosperine whispered as a smile crossed her lips. "But you will."

The demon's heart slowed to a stop just as she grabbed onto the beast's brown veiny stomach, ripping it open with her bare hands. Immediately, sour smelling fluid, pieces of partially digested animal and Sagan's limp body spilled onto the ground.

His icy black eyes stared into nothingness. It looked like his soul had already left his body. She grabbed Sagan by his face, quietly begging to the heavens there was some chance he could still be alive.

Astra wiped the fluids from his skin and gently tapped his cheeks with her fingertips, begging him to wake up; but she received no reaction, not even a flicker of life. She placed her quivering fingers over his mouth and felt her stomach sink. His lungs were no longer inflating to receive the precious oxygen that would sustain his life.

No. This couldn't be his time. There had to be something she could do to bring him back. She rapidly pushed down on his chest before breathing inside of his mouth two deep breaths. Though she was trying to remain calm and in control, she felt as though her sanity was slipping away from her. She wanted to collapse in the snow and scream at the top of her lungs until her voice became nothing more than a memory. Her heart heaved with the kind of anguish that could only be felt by the souls that were eternally dammed.

Her attention snapped to the horizon. The edges of her jaw tensed as her eyes absorbed the hour glass shape of a wingless angel, wearing a dress made of diamonds and embroidered with gold.

Astra lowered her eyes to her friend whose lips were the color of a bruise. Her fingers shook as she felt for a pulse but found his heart had given up hope.

"No, NO! Please don't leave me," she pleaded while gripping onto the collar of his shirt

Though she tried to hold on to hope, her chest ached with the realization that her hope was in vain. He had not survived but she couldn't accept he was dead.

She screamed as she pressed down on his chest, trying to beat his heart for him. Her soul was as cold as the snow surrounding her. Why did he have to go like this? What was she going to do without him?

"Stop," the woman whispered from behind Astra as she gently placed her fingers upon her shoulder. "He's gone but I might be able to bring him back."

She looked up at the woman with bright red hair who appeared more like a mirage, fading and coming back with the wind's breath. Was she an illusion or was she really there? Astra wasn't sure, she wanted to trust whoever was in front of her, but desperation clawed away at her soul. She didn't care how Sagan would be brought back, just that he was brought back. She couldn't do this journey without him. If he died, a part of her would also die.

The woman gently pressed her mouth onto his lips and exhaled a warm lavender cloud. The cloud lingered within his mouth like a cup, as tendrils of smoke curled around his lips and caressed his cheeks.

"Isla, daughter of Ifrinn," she muttered as she pushed her fingers onto his chest. "Please come."

For a moment, nothing happened until suddenly the ground around them rumbled. She smiled as she stood and within a moment, the ground split open just a few feet in front of her. A woman who looked like she was in her late twenties pulled herself from the ground and stood. She was naked, wearing nothing more than a golden necklace around her neck and a black snake draped across her shoulders. She had raven black hair that flowed behind her like smoke and eyes the color of blood. Her skin was so pale it looked like death itself embraced her.

"Zephyra, my friend. What is it that you need?" the woman asked.

"Isla, can you ask Ifrinn if he will bring this man back?"

"If I am to do that, I must read his soul heart first."

Isla looked down at the corpse of Sagan. She pushed her fingers into his chest and pulled out an orb that was as clear as murky water. Isla searched the orb as if she was reading something, before her eyes met Astra's.

For a moment, her heart felt like it stopped beating. As Isla stared into her eyes, she felt as if her soul was splitting open. For a moment, she couldn't move or breathe and her mind begged this woman to please look away.

"You can trust this man," Isla said, breaking the gaze with a smile crossing her lips. Turning to Zephyra, she nodded her head and pushed the orb back into Sagan's chest. "I will see if my father agrees." Isla smiled and turned back to Astra, "I will see you soon," she said before she disappeared into the closing ground, leaving no trace she was ever there.

"Who was that?" she asked as she turned to Zephyra.

Zephyra pointed down to the corpse of her friend. "That was the daughter of the god of the underworld. I did what I could. She might be able to bring him back from the dead but it's now up to her father to decide if he is worthy of that."

Astra's fingers clung to her shirt, as the lingering tension felt as if it was crushing her heart. *Please come back.*

The seconds her eyes were glued to him felt like an eternity of time. She couldn't breathe. Even the smallest breath was waiting for the moment he took his first.

Sagan gasped for a breath of air, sucking in the lavender smoke that still lingered over his nose. He rapidly blinked his raven eyes.

"You're alive!" she cried out as she wrapped her arms around Sagan.

Though she normally was not one to want to embrace anyone, she found she didn't want to let him go. In the moments she saw him take his first breath, all the suffering she had ever lived through seemed to temporarily vanish. Her painful memories became still in her mind, allowing fleeting happiness to wash over her. In a daze, he slowly wrapped his arms around his friend.

She looked up and over to Zephyra.

"Who are you?" Her eyes searched the woman the same way her mind was trying to search her memories for a clue.

"An old friend," the woman replied cryptically causing Astra to collapse into a state of confusion.

Suddenly, Zephyra faded away like morning fog as Elde approached, wearily making his way through the snow. Elde was covered in scarlet blood, but not of his own. It was then clear to her that he had been fighting another beast.

Elde dropped a warm heart onto the ground in front of her. His fiery eyes gazed down at her as he gave her a nudge with his snout.

She gasped, feeling a radiating wave of pain wash through her chest. Her adrenalin was fading which brought the unfortunate reminder that her body was not impervious to discomfort.

Astra picked up the warm heart and placed it to her lips. Her teeth broke through the soft, jelly-like organ as she pushed this tender muscle from one side of her mouth to the other. It had a strong metallic taste to it but smoothly slipped down her throat as she swallowed before dropping the rest of the heart.

Immediately her cracked ribs healed. She took in a deep breath. Thank God it no longer hurt to breathe.

She examined the land in front of her. The blood splatters on the snow and ice made it look like a macabre painting. It was then that she saw another figure moving towards her from across the river. Who was this? She squinted, barely making out the bulky creature. Her heart felt like it stopped. It was heading right for them.

The sound of a growl diverted her attention for a moment. It was Elde. His eyes were fixated on the figure approaching and his horns glowed a deep shade of red. He lifted his lips over his bloodied teeth and clawed at the ground, ready to fight again.

She gripped onto her weapon. To expect the unexpected was a fate she had to accept. Astra wasn't ready to fight again but knew she had no choice when it came to her enemies.

The snow was slowing down to a stop and the only sound that could be heard was the breath that left their lips. An icy wind pulled her hair off her face and forcefully rearranged the snow around her.

As the figure moved closer, her heart leapt to her chest. Was this true? Was she really seeing this? Vojin was still alive and he had finally found her.

Acknowledgements

First and foremost, I want to thank Yazmin. Thank you for your patience and for sitting by my side on the countless nights I buried myself in writing. Thank you for encouraging me and your honesty when it comes to my work. Thank you for being so supportive and always believing in me, even during the times that I struggled to believe in myself. You push me to be the best version of myself.

To my parents, I am grateful that you taught me to never give up and fight for my dreams. You lead by example and not just by words and because of that, I never gave up. I am the woman that I am today, thanks to you both.

About the Author

Angelika Koch lives in Connecticut with her English mastiff and her Persian cat. She spends her free time traveling around the world and taking photos.

Instagram: @thetravelingfantasywriter

www.AuthorAngelikaKoch.com

Made in the USA
Middletown, DE
24 January 2020